Praise for Adam Baron

'Fresh, honest, very funny, startlingly relevant. His is the male perspective on the modern female coven, its repressed ambivalence, its ambiguous sexuality, its deadly territories of parenting, school gate and domesticity; that he renders that perspective artistically, personally and politically with such wit and intellectual grace makes his novel a rare and complex commentary on contemporary middle class values. The great male American novelists have written passionately about domesticity, parenthood, marriage; there has been no English equivalent, just a hangdog pseudo-comic "dad" literature as disposable as it is dishonest. Adam's book recalls Updike in his *Rabbit* years: sensual, involved, poetic, incorrect, and enthralling in its honesty.'
Rachel Cusk

'Elegant, moving, intelligent and timely. A book by a man who understands women better than they understand themselves.'
Fay Weldon

'Baron is a writer to watch.' *Sunday Telegraph*

BLACKHEATH
ADAM BARON

myriad

First published in 2016 by

Myriad Editions
59 Lansdowne Place
Brighton BN3 1FL

www.myriadeditions.com

1 3 5 7 9 10 8 6 4 2

A CIP catalogue record for this book
is available from the British Library

ISBN (pbk): 978-1-908434-90-6
ISBN (ebk): 978-1-908434-91-3

Designed and typeset in Sabon LT
by WatchWord Editorial Services, London

Printed by CPI Group (UK) Ltd
Croydon CR0 4YY

For F.V.F.

1

SHE FEELS NOTHING. There is an absence where love should be. A long, flat greyness. Another absence: guilt. For this is her daughter she is looking at. This pale, thin girl shovelling Cheerios, gabbing on about Mrs Friel and after-school club. Violin. Yet she feels no guilt at all for this lack of love, feels nothing in fact except relief. She stares as the girl finishes the startled little shapes and begins to spoon milk.

— Come on, she says. Someone says. Her. We'll be late.

— It's not even eight. We've got, like, an hour.

She doesn't reply. Just gazes at the slim, naked-looking spoon her daughter leaves on the side of the bowl until the girl is standing there with her coat on.

— *Mum*! You're not even dressed. What's the matter with you?

In the enclosed, high-walled playground she looks around as though she's never been there before. The children whirl like windblown litter. The adults cling in twos and threes, knots she's been tangled in so often but shivers at today. Why? She frowns, watching as children touch base, remind, cajole, ask permission, while her daughter is lost amid the mêlée. She doesn't care about this. She just wants to leave and she starts to do that but the crowd's too thick, a last flood pouring through the playground gate as if getting to school is not something they do five days out of seven. She could push through but another thing stops her, the past like a raised sheet of glass. Reception. The very small ones, whom she hardly notices any more. They look like wind-up toys and their parents too are different. More focused, their energy heading down as they apply kisses like hats or scarves, faces riven with smiles, voices cut with chipper bonhomie. Did she feel like this with Niamh? Or, before, with Michael? That a piece of her flesh was about to be dragged off into some giant mincer? She turns, disconcerted, wanting now to see her own daughter and look inside for some echo. But the girl, in deep with the most tedious of her friends, is just hair, hands, too many limbs. Someone else's child. The relief she feels now is total and she tries to leave again, though again she doesn't make it.

She's pushed back by a man. Another Reception father, late, blowing his cheeks out as he presses his child into the joggling line. And something happens, something light and startling... happens before she has even taken him in properly. She does that as the feeling grows, takes shape, firms itself inside her until she cannot pretend it is anything other than what it is.

She wants to fuck him.

It's a simple thought. Clear and shiny, almost making her laugh. This man, two seconds old, she wants to fuck him or, more accurately, let him fuck her. He's not tall – her height, though he's handsome. Blond, cross-looking, leaping blue eyes and three-day stubble she can feel on the insides of her thighs. She stares at him, not worried he'll see because he's homed in on his kid, kneeling, making the boy laugh. When he stands she finds herself moving, doing so without thinking, which is so odd because she's a person who, she knows, thinks far too much. She cuts through the Year One line as if it isn't there.

— His bag, she says.

A moment. Face turning. He looks at her. Some grey in the stubble. Lips plump, a little like a woman's. Saved by a jaw that's firm and tight.

— I'm sorry?

— His bag. You're holding it.

And he is. The green school bag he's obviously carried there is still slung over his shoulder.

— Thanks. He laughs.

— My husband still does that. He gets home and I have to send him back if it's book-change day.

— Thanks, the man repeats, and hands it down. Then the bell goes and the mess begins to straighten.

— What's your name? she asks, pulling the man's eyes back from his son. He's reluctant, not wanting to miss a second of his boy. But he's too polite not to turn to her.

— I'm James. Jim.

Her first disappointment. A dull name. Jim at uni, so swept by love of her he could barely move, three thrusts and come filling up her navel. But she smiles.

— Hello, James. Amelia. He's new?

— Dom? This term. He tries to turn and look at the boy again but she fixes him, cool and casual, pretending not to notice his discomfort. Second intake. He was born in April...

— Michael was the same.

— Your son? He smiles now, relaxing. What year's...?

— Now? He left – at real school now, as he calls it.

— So...?

— What am I doing here? She laughs. My daughter. She...

But for a second she cannot remember what year her daughter is in. Or, in fact, her name. She begins to stutter, about to make something up when the lines begin to move, as though a Dyson has started up. Reception is first and he does it, so un-English, just rips his eyes away from her. He shouts and waves until the line is out of sight, shifts to let another late child in, after which another woman takes him. Rachel Green, parent rep, hands waving like tethered birds as she talks to him about something they have clearly spoken of before. School clothes. PE kit. All of which spikes a sudden jealousy that swarms over her like a virus. It grips her belly with nausea, so lurching she can't stop herself.

— I've got some, she says.

Their shoulders are turned from her. They're in their own talk-configuration which they have to realign. It's awkward but Rachel beams even brighter.

— Amelia! Niamh okay?

Niamh.

— Fine. Judith alright?

— Great, Rachel says, about to expand. Before she can, however, Amelia snaps her head back to James.

— Old school clothes. If you're looking. Quite a lot. Michael's old stuff.

— Oh.

— If you'd like it?

— If I'd...?

— Like it? Been meaning to bring it in for ages. Lots of sizes.

— Right. I mean yes. I'll buy it from you, naturally.

— Nonsense. You may not even want it. Boys. They go through stuff. But some of it'll be okay.

— Then thanks.

She smiles and nods but doesn't go on. She wants Rachel Green away. She turns right back to her and grins into her over-made-up face until, awkward, she moves off to her dumpy daughter. When Amelia turns back to the man he looks uncertain. She ignores this and asks if he's busy. Busy now. It startles him until she calms him with one of Rachel's smiles, so full of wholesome mumminess he's put right back at ease.

— Unless you're running off to work. We're just across the Heath. You could come and get them.

— I'm working at home today. Great, he says.

And they leave. She flashes another bright smile and receives one in return. As they exit the playground a voice calls out *Mum!* but she doesn't look back.

Instead she leads the man up the Vale towards the flat expanse of grass that is Blackheath, where her children have had playtimes and sports days, Saturday football or cricket for as long as she can remember. Her house is on the far edge and she heads towards the windows, black as skull sockets, still chatting about clothes, the expense of them, what a waste it would be to buy them new. Again he protests that he wants to pay but again she tells him no, that a lot were given by other parents; that's the way it works. She also insists that if there are any he feels are too worn he needn't take them. All the while she is filled with astonishment at what she is doing, bringing this man back to her home. To fuck him. Astonishment too to hear the words coming out of her mouth, this talk of Heath trainers for summer and windcheaters with the logo on. For there are no clothes. She took them to the summer fair last year, something she is sure Rachel Green remembered.

— Coffee? she asks.

He's standing in her kitchen. This man. James. He's looking around and the first thing she can tell is that his house is not as big as hers. Something in the way he checks it out, not with overt jealousy, just the way he seems to notice and assess it. Unless he's an estate agent. But he's not, and it's not the work-at-home comment that tells her. She couldn't want to fuck an estate agent. After fifteen years of not wanting to fuck anyone but her husband. She wouldn't have found herself wanting this with such certainty, before she'd even seen him properly.

— So what do you do... James?

— I'm an academic.

She looks for irony. Finds none.

— Right. What in?

— English.

— A professor?

— One day. Doctor.

— Doctor Jim. Like a picture book.

— Ha. Not sure three-year-olds would be interested in a character who spends half his life in the British Library.

He has spoken. Opened a small flap of himself, like the ones Michael and Niamh used to piggle open with tiny fingers. The picture beneath is one she likes. Funny, self-deprecating. Confident though, getting over her big house. She sticks a bullet in the Nespresso machine but instantly regrets it. Just as she knew he was not an estate agent, she knows he's not a Nespresso man. He's got one of those cinch-waisted stovetop things with burn marks up the side. She knows this like she knows her own name.

— They're upstairs, she says, brightly.

Not her room. Can't be. Not hers and Richard's. She's been taken out of her life, something that happened before she set eyes on this man. In the night perhaps, her moorings cut by some demon? She doesn't know, just woke up like this as if from a dream. Or into one. She'll think about it later, do the wondering, though she knows it's a fact, a done thing she can't deny. Not this nor any of the emotions ganging up to get inside her. But she hasn't drifted away completely. Not in their bed, her novel spined, Richard's pyjamas stuffed beneath the pillow. The spare room will be fine, though the mattress is springy. Will he mind, when he's going over it in his head as she knows men do, replaying her tits, her arse? Will it occur to him that, as well as her two-kid belly, the bed could have been a touch firmer?

— A spare room, he says. What I'd give. Though my in-laws would be in it all the time.

— Tell me. Not that I don't like them. Sometimes wish we'd never told them about it, though. Pretended it's a cupboard.

— A loft conversion, he says, somewhat randomly. But we're in a conservation area.

She begins to rummage in the built-in wardrobes.

After a decent interval on all fours, pushing boxes around, taking things out, putting them back, she emerges. Stands and winces.

— I'm really sorry.

— For…?

And she nearly comes out with this phrase: I haven't shaved my armpits. She nearly says that right out, just throws it into the air, which would be it, wouldn't it? Bridges burned. He's looking at her quizzically and she nearly does it, but instead she explains that she thought the clothes would be there.

— Richard.

— I thought you said Michael.

— My husband. He was clearing out. I just remembered. He could have put them in the garage. He probably has but where they'll be...? I could call and ask him but he has meetings in the mornings and never answers his phone so...

— It doesn't matter. Another time. Just let me know.

And then they're just standing there. Two people in a room. Looking at each other. The bed to the left of them, so wide and still and empty. So indecent as beds always seem to her, glimpsed through the doors of other people's houses. Does he know? Has he guessed? Less than a second has gone by but she thinks he must have. He's still got his coat on. Only then does she realise that. A Barbour, but one of the trendy ones in black. Keep it on, she thinks. *While you fuck me.*

His phone rings.

It is, of course, his wife. He pulls the phone out and she feels her lips part, aware that this is when she'll find out if he knows what this is. What's happening here. He smiles and turns a little in on himself. The smile grows as he chats with a casual openness that tells her that he does not know, that he has no idea, that the sign *please fuck me* that's pinned to her forehead is invisible to him. She watches as he answers questions about a doctor's appointment, then a nursery, recognising the name. Which tells her where he lives. She pictures the woman on the other end and can only know for certain one thing: she's younger. Nothing else.

— Getting clothes for Dom. She's... the needle jumps and she knows he's forgotten her name... a woman from St Saviour's, only she can't find them. Really kind. I have but she won't take anything. I'll tell her. Bye.

And he hangs up. She smiles and walks past him, back down the stairs, feeling his eyes on her back as she follows, knowing, actually, that she's almost certainly imagining that. He's probably looking at the landing space. She fires up the Nespresso machine and they drink the coffee, on which he makes no comment, though he does talk about his wife and his children, his house and his work, doing so because she asks him detailed questions. Not that she cares about or even listens to the answers. She just wants him to be there. Not leave, though he does that eventually, extricating himself from her like a silent but very determined escapologist. She closes the door behind him and then runs upstairs to the spare room window, wondering if she was right. And she was. That nursery is in Greenwich and he said he walked there in the morning. She watches him stride that way across the grass until the distance scrubs him out.

Downstairs again she picks up his coffee mug. Stares at the place his lips have touched. She shakes her head and then notices her daughter's bowl which, for some reason, is still on the table. She cleared the rest away that morning but not that. The spoon is still there, bowed upward, a few drops of yellowing milk collected in it. She leaves it, goes over to the sink. She washes his mug up and then dries it, before putting it away in the cupboard.

She's back. Time has passed, though not a day. A day is something you can expand into, a space in which to set out. Not the shrivelled zone between nine and three-thirty, the room with no windows, the ceiling always moving down to crush her. She walks into the playground, early for the first time in years. Self-conscious as she heads to one of the chess tables near the back wall, as if everyone who sees her will know what she is doing there.

Which one will be his? Earlier, she paid no attention to the kid. Will she be able to guess? When Mrs Mason leads Reception out she looks at the first and the boy would fit. She begins to think she's right but then comes one so blond, with such utter blue eyes, that there can't be any mistake. She blinks, unable to pull her gaze from him, just as she wasn't able earlier, with his father. The demeanour is similar: a little set apart, a little too serious for that age. Or any. She pushes herself up and moves forward, wanting a clearer glimpse, to see the moment they reconnect. But a greater surprise is waiting for her. The space fills and she edges through, relief and recognition lighting the faces of the children whose parents are already there. She turns, looking for him, amazed when the blond boy laughs and launches himself from the wall into the arms of a woman. Nanny? Not if he's an academic and anyway the glee is far too great, wrenching open even this considered child. So this is her. The phone person. It has to be, though her hair is wrong. Dark, nearly black. When did you ever see a blond man like that with a woman with curly black hair? She wears glasses too, something so wrong she wants to pull them off. Pretty? No. Beautiful. A late beauty, finding her in her twenties, perhaps even later. Something secretive about her. Withheld. And no yummy mummy here, the scuffed poacher's bag over the shoulder and the general rush speaking unequivocally of work. A teacher? No. But what? She turns and moves closer, honing in on the mac. It's Jaeger – classic, expensive – and she's thrown by this, made horribly insecure until *ting*: charity shop. The high street clothes beneath tell her this and, rather than soothing her, it actually makes her feel worse. No one she knows buys clothes from charity shops any more. Most of them probably never did. For some reason the Nespresso machine pops into her mind and she wants to break it into a thousand pieces, crush it until it's unrecognisable. As for the mac, she wants to touch it, ask its price, if she can try it on.

— Wait. The word juts out of her lips.

She is the woman who met her husband. This information makes the woman nod, but there is more in there than recognition. Amelia is not what she was expecting, that being someone, she is sure, like Rachel Green. Sturdy. Sex all finished with, packed away in the loft. She is still polite however and very thankful, which Amelia bats back.

— Nothing to thank me for yet. Though I did find them.

— Great. If you bring them in, we –

— So if you'd like. I mean. Unless you're busy. We only live across the Heath, she adds.

The woman nods. Blushes. Amelia is leading them out of the playground against a thin rush of late women, mock or real guilt etched into their determined faces, when she hears that sound again.

Mum!

— Forget my head. I really would.

The four of them walk across the Heath, their shadows dragging them towards the waiting house.

2

WHEN JAMES GETS the call he knows what it is. Even before he sees *Treetops* flashing. The name just confirms it and he swears, gutted by a deep, drawing helplessness as his finger hovers over the red button. But he can't do it. And he knows it. Instead he hits green and a sigh drops through him like an airliner.

Not a good day so far. Ida up twice in the night, the morning an overslept frenzy, a rabid hunt for socks, pants, clean trousers, ICT club money, then Dom's phonics book, a last-minute find under the changing mat in the bathroom. *The fucking changing mat.* Alice helps him but she needs to shower so he doesn't notice when Ida takes her clothes off. All of them, as he's coating Dom, undoing the work of twenty minutes. He jams them back on in two, which she resists with silent determination and surprising strength, and then concedes wellies even though they're Dom's and way too big, her last lot thrown off the back of the Thames Clipper. Outside she wants to walk, slapping down the street like a clown, but it's way too late for that. As he forces her, screaming, into the buggy, he feels like a prison guard in the execution room. With someone innocent. The opinion is shared by at least three passers-by, the daggers continuing all the way to Treetops with the howling, which he's no time to calm. Nor has he time to wipe the parallel caterpillars of snot as they crawl into her mouth and which, in other children, leave him utterly disgusted.

The howling rises inside the nursery as he removes her coat, silently imploring one of the carers to take her from him. One does respond but it takes two to prise her off, grabbing as she does at his hands, his shirt, his ears and nose, eventually his hair, a clump of which he's forced to leave behind. She makes a final lunge for him as he backs out and he wants to return, settle her, wants this desperately, but Dom's going on about being late, serious, cautious Dom terrified of that, so he abandons her and flees, feeling ragged and tattered, bits falling off as her screams grab after him. They echo in his ribcage all the way to the Heath, only scrubbed out then by Dom. Who needs to crap. Now. Despite earlier implacable denials he really does and so they do it right there, in the stretching open, other parents filing past with eyes set firmly forward. The only thing to wipe him with is James's handkerchief, which he leaves atop the result like a pall covering a tiny corpse.

Walking back is better. As he leaves the woman's house, his lungs drag in air. He moves fast across the empty Heath, then faster, the feet of a man reconnecting with the world. His body begins to reshape. It's no longer hunched over the buggy he's left at Treetops, nor lopsided to hold Dom's hand. He rolls his shoulders the way the osteopath told him and straightens his back, beginning to feel that yes, actually, he can do this. Morph back to his pre-self. And psychologically too, the shapes that have loomed huge since six a.m. begin to withdraw, others flowering from beneath: his job, his work, the emails he must deal with. And finally, from beneath that, the very centre of his professional intention, the mind of the American poet he's been getting to grips with, the great mind he's trying to unfurl in his latest book. By the time he gets home he feels as if he's almost inside it, that its thoughts are melding with his own, driving him into the future.

But he's been burgled.

For a split second James genuinely believes this. He tidied up last night. Now he just stares, barely an inch of floor space visible. He knew they'd been playing, but still. A long wooden train track runs down the narrow hall, complete with Lego tunnels and stations. He finds more Lego in the living room, cast like ancient, quaked stones. There's a marble run too, a future city this until his footsteps on the floorboards send it crashing. Plastic food. Five different dolls. None, of course, with any clothes on. No sofa any more but instead a TGV loaded with a duvet, a Trunki, three old backpacks and a wooden cooker for the dining car. He spins round, almost unable to breathe, shaking his head to see that in less than an hour no area of their downstairs space has been left untouched.

And it's not just the children.

Hurricane Alice has been through here. In the kitchen he finds marmalade. Tea caddy. Milk. Butter dish. All with their lids off. A single bowl – his and the kids' are in the dishwasher – sits on the table, mortared by Weetabix, one of the white columns on its side spewing crumbs on to the table. Bread is concertinaed from the bag, half a drying pear on the chopping board. All that is missing is Miss Havisham sitting on one of the Tripp-Trapps. And back in the hallway it is worse. A scarf trails down the stairs as though Isadora Duncan has whipped upstairs for a piss. Two ankle boots lie on the floor like guillotined heads and three of Alice's coats are slumped beneath the rack, all with their hang-ties broken. Something shameful revealed here, and not just about this woman. Two weeks is all they last, the little loops that hold women's coats up. The contempt of their manufacturers is clear and in that moment he shares it. Does Alice think of him in Jigsaw? Picking up her fucking coats, trying to slouch them back on the hook, a task that is almost impossible? Of course she doesn't, just as she fails to think of him in the morning, rushing out into her day. For does she not know that he has to do this? Make the place straight so he can work? Yes, because he's told her, and it's not the lost time that really knifes him but the simple, humiliating fact of having to tidy up after her. As if there isn't quite enough of that shit in his world.

Hatred like a blade. Sharp and glimmering. And delightful, for it tells him what to do. Later. Five minutes before she's home with the kids. He'll get it out again. Marmalade, butter, everything. Even the Weetabix crumbs. She can fucking well clear up after herself. He'll grab his running shoes, wait till he hears them outside and then head into the park.

He kicks things into corners, piles brightly coloured plastic into boxes, heedless of shape or match or function. He pulls up track and unloads the high-speed train, desperately trying to wrench his mind back to the New York School. Then gets twenty minutes' reading done before Treetops calls and tells him about the chicken pox.

He's there in ten. But she isn't ill. Not his little Ida. He knows this as soon as he sees her, wrapped in the arms of the work experience girl. Her latest sucker. Nor has she presented any symptoms, he discovers, other than tears in large volumes, no doubt prompted by the sight of other parents coming to rescue their genuinely ill offspring. For a second he thinks about turning round and leaving her but he knows what he'll get if he does. He has no choice but to put her coat on – she's no problem with this now, by the way – and leave with her, his Little Wonder decent enough not to show actual glee until they're outside, whereupon she cannot hide it any more. Part of him admires this ability to manipulate her external world but it has totally fucked his day.

— Shall we go shopping, then? he asks, knowing that if he restocks the kitchen he'll feel, at least, as though he got something done.

— Playgroup.

— You can go in the trolley.

— Playgroup, she says again.

He should welcome this. Not the best result but by no means the worst because if she'd said *park* he'd have had to take her to the playground. And play with her. Constantly, just him and her, his mind not allowed to sidetrack for more than a second. Even pushing her on the swing he is told to sing to her, tickle her, tell her a story, push her higher, lower, and in the sandpit he is her toy, since he never remembers to bring one to trick her mind away with. Playgroup offers, in theory at least, the chance of release, the possibility of downloading her into the matrix of other children. It is, however, a peculiar sort of hell for him, and the first circle of this is the women.

He knew them once, the brilliant girls at uni, so much better prepared for the waiting world than he was, lithe and lean, jagging into life like reef sharks into a bait ball. They were dazzle, push, moments of pure future: until the Happy Day. And now they are bovine. Regardless of shape or size. Something has happened to them beyond the obvious and certainly beyond the necessary. Some trip-switch has blown, their insides as pappy as their poorly contained exteriors. Being with them, sitting on the floor – for some reason always the floor – talking, cutting paper-chains, is like eating barely tastable fudge. The music is a symbol of this for what would be wrong, while the kids are all playing, with Springsteen? A bit of Radio 3? But even when none of the kids is listening a jaunty litany of jingly shit dribbles from the stereo. The women don't notice for they are endlessly chewing over the minutiae of their rescinded selves, as if the true welfare of a small human being could in any way be affected by a choice between Aptimel and Cow & Gate. The whole world is in crisis, but if he brings up the latest Greek bailout they will look at him as if he is insane.

Their attitude towards him is also problematic. They treat him as one of them. This – out of his own insecurity, he will admit – is another reason why he avoids the place if possible, for their inclusivity riles him. He is male. He also has, in his field, a pretty good job. Recently promoted to Principal Lecturer, he earns more than most people would imagine an academic does. Were his position to be advertised, several hundred people would apply, preparing lengthy presentations for an interview they'd punch the sky on getting. The structure of his working life, however, means that he can look after his daughter one day a week, something made easier now as he's on a six-month sabbatical. It's something he feels an intense need to reiterate to these living Henry Moores but they take no notice, unable or unwilling to entertain the concept that men and women can actually shuffle the home and work decks together. Instead they remain within their unshakeable assumption that he is that most loathed and pathetic of creatures.

A House Daddy.

There is one of these – wrong word – men when he gets to St Luke's, the big Methodist chapel in which playgroup takes place. James sees him heading up the wide staircase as he manoeuvres the Maclaren through a snarl of buggies in the hallway so intense it looks like a fog incident on the M4. He recognises this one, though they are all essentially the same: over-nice, chummy failures who would have fallen right off the back of life were it not for a high-earning wife. How they live with themselves – wandering around in the clothing that is bought for them, drinking pints they didn't earn – he has no idea, though most have a look in their eye that tells him they've shrunk down to inhabit the small space inside them that can cope with this. They're like hard-up earls living in the servants' wing, and what the go-getting gals they're hitched up to get from their arrangement he cannot comprehend. What he does know is that he must at all costs avoid them, which he does when Ida scampers up the stairs into the Big Room. He splashes his pound into the Tupperware and makes for the windowsill.

He loves to watch her. No denying that, and doing so begins to compensate for his day's loss, though this compensation in itself is problematic. Nevertheless he cannot be anything other than thrilled by the direct independence of spirit that sends her charging towards the plastic slide where an older boy, possibly three, is having doubts about the steps. After waiting for what seems to Ida like a decent interval – two seconds – she yanks him back down to the floor with a thump and makes a rapid ascent herself. The boy's mother looks around for someone to enter this situation but he slips her gaze. He turns away further when Ida charges round to the steps again, thinking he's actually doing the boy a favour. He's going to have to fight for a job one day, show he's got what it takes. This second battering he's taking from Ida is of great future service to him, though his mother does not seem to agree and James can shirk it no longer. He goes over, pointedly not chastising Ida, just taking her hand and leading her over to the Wendy House. She contemplates this for a second: the entrance, the windows, the other children playing merrily inside. Then she enters it with the enthusiasm of a SWAT team.

James turns again, about to move back to his perch. But a woman he actually likes – or would if he ever found her in a context in which to like her – calls out to him. He finds himself drawn down into the floored sisterhood, an undulating circle that shuffles to accommodate him, surrounding him with acres of hummocky breast. His gaze rebounds like a pinball and he counts four nipples, one just inches from his left knee. Though it's no longer in use, its owner seems to have forgotten about it and it just sits there, a tear of milk clinging on. His eyes can't seem to pretend it isn't there and he is fired by the urge to drag it into his own mouth, get it as far down his throat as it will go. Tip its owner backwards and tup her furiously, milk spraying up to the ceiling. Instead he just blinks as the Daddy appears, homing in on him, his earnest, goateed face nodding as he sits and begins to speak.

For a second James smiles, desperately wanting the guy to have seen his thoughts. Say shit man I feel it too. Don't you just want to fuck some of these squashy babes sometimes? He hasn't though and James is depressingly certain that he is about to talk about football. Attempt a re-up on his low stash of manhood. He sighs. He knows little about the game and cares less. He'd actually rather join the discussion on potty-training to his left, though in the event he is saved from doing either.

— Hey, guys, the woman says, not waiting to be asked, but entering the circle and making it her own.

It is her. Thomasina Davis. The Queen of Royal Hill (Alice's tag). The woman the others defer to for her total acceptance of, and dedication to, her role. She is MUMMY. Organiser of NCT clothing sales and certificated multi-member babysitting groups. She wears motherhood like a commando, a belt clipped full of Velcro wipe packs, drink bottles and raisin-box holders. She astonishes by losing her baby-weight in days and affects a martyrish, unconcerned personal style, the tear in the knee of her sweatpants making her look, from across a room, as though she lives on an estate. She is actually the wife of a money ghoul, one of the cheek-nicked zombies James sees at Greenwich station when he's going in for a nine o'clock lecture. She, for James, is the worst. Her Dulux niceness makes his flesh crawl, sure, as he is, that every sentence she ever utters is in some way self-serving, if only you had the time to figure out how. She's launching in now, multitasking that with fishing out a biscuit full of organic sugar for her kid, beginning to talk about Alice as she raises her elbows to pull her exquisitely cut golden hair into a ponytail. About how lucky Alice is. Able to work because she's got James who can chip in with the childcare. James smiles at the conceit, the implicit self-deception. For Alice is not lucky. What she is is brilliant, driven, which is why she can work and work well in a job that compels her. Unlike this woman who, just like the House Daddy, has found herself to be not, essentially, up to it. An actress, he believes she's told him in the past, though he suspects that actually means high-end-waitress-stroke-panto-extra, and anyway she's long since cut for the safe haven her physiology was always going to offer. James thinks of the men she probably dated in her twenties, the proto-Jeremy Ironses, the RSC Edmunds and National Mercutios, all without a penny to their names. Is it Nige she's married to now? Colin? Whatever he's called, he's a six-foot barrel of pure tedium who looks as though he might be her accountant, but who has in fact given her a four-bedroom house in the Ashburnham Triangle and two kids, every second of whose lives she plans with sweet, ruthless efficiency. The perfect mother whom her teenage children will have dreams about beheading.

— My God! He laughs.

It's Ida. She's at the painting table. Quite, quite naked. The circle turns to watch as she pats neat and very colourful handprints all over her chest and tummy. And then, very carefully, over the clothes of the child next to her.

Alice doesn't ring until seven-fifteen. He's had his running kit on for two hours. He should be Googling divorce lawyers but he's not because he doesn't mind, not in the least, and nor has he re-trashed the kitchen. Something has changed in him. His daughter has melted his soul, dragged him so totally into her world that he's developed Stockholm Syndrome. They've spent the day feeding ducks, riding scooters, getting told off in the Maritime Museum. Two whole hours in the sandpit. Now they're on the sofa with a bottle and Maisie, who has visited her local library to find a sparkly book about fish twenty-three times in a row.

— I hate you, is what he says.

— But in a nice way?

— True. Still hate you.

— Don't blame me. *Please*. I'm...

— Sorry? Apologies for Alice are self-pulled teeth so he decides to help her out. You know you shouldn't leave the place like that and never will again. You have plans for my godlike phallus that will make up for any suffering you have caused me.

— Got it. And as for being late, you'll understand because you met her.

— I did. And I have a question.

The big, charmless house looms into view, the smooth granite kitchen with its appliance museum.

— This church school lark. How the hell are we ever going to deal with the niceness?

3

SHE'S BREATHING. Doing it consciously, in, out, trying to take control of at least one element of her life while thoughts run amok inside her as if she's some gatecrashed party. Earlier she felt as though she was being swept away but she didn't mind that. Now she's scared, utterly bewildered by the state she is in. Three more breaths, each like a lifted weight, and she walks over to the sofa.

— Niamh, darling, turn that off. Tell me about your day. How did violin go?

And the girl does it without complaint. Sensing something. Zaps Tracy Beaker and starts talking about Grade Six.

They just followed her. How easy is this, she thought, turning off the alarm. She asked them to come and they came. Like lambs. There's a power here that she's never considered before. You ask someone to come home with you and they do, unwilling or unable to say no. She got an insight into child-killers and estate agent rapists. Asked if Alice would like tea but the woman said no, coffee if she had it.

— Sorry, machine's on the blink.

— Tea, then, that's fine. Thank you.

Odd that she asked for something that wasn't offered her. Was that rude? Gauche? Knowing she was just finding reasons to belittle the woman, Amelia told herself off. It's refreshing, she thought. Polly Bridge always makes instant and I drink it. Why the hell do I do that?

The woman removed her mac and hung it on the back of a barstool.

Niamh was a delight. Amelia has to admit this. She took charge of the boy, of Dominic as his mother called him, asking him what he'd like to do, if he wanted a biscuit and milk which is what she has when she gets home, though not chocolate ones because it's not the weekend. He followed her but was not submissive, engaging her with direct seriousness on the subject of biscuits, the occasions such as birthdays or bank holidays when chocolate ones can be eaten on a weekday. She realised that he was bright and exceptionally so, a future head boy, she thinks now. She'll have to tell Mrs Frith, though Mrs Frith has an eye to all these things. She wonders if Niamh will be head girl next year, which has been spoken about, and at the mere thought it's there again, the horror of her, made suddenly worse because of the other knowledge that she can now see sitting just beneath it like the answer to a question that took ages to arrive. It's been weeks. Months even. Building. Snapping at her daughter. Criticising her. More and more irritated by her very presence, like watching her in the Nativity, that stupid poem, embarrassed by her prissy, do-good forthrightness, wishing she'd just *shut up*. The feeling growing until it became too strong to deny, a transformation she was aware of but refused to believe in until it left her here. Wherever *here* is. There is a metallic bitterness in her mouth and she pours herself a tumbler of water.

She's older than Alice. Six years? Seven? Not a lot really but she feels like a different generation, that she has travelled over hills this woman has not and they are hills she'll never revisit. She feels like this about James too, though they are exactly the same age. She knows this because of Google, and the Monday Mail email from school. Only three Jameses in the parent list and she knows the other two. James Peterson. She found him on the UCL website, his CV announcing that he was born in seventy-five. Yet he's like his wife, a young parent, feeling it all rushing through him. Trying to catch up with it all rather then watching it trailing away.

They drank tea. Alice engaged with Niamh, who began to show off, though not much. Dom asked to play on the iPad he spotted but Alice diverted this, asking Niamh if they had any felt tips. The two children then sat together at the kitchen table as if they were still in class. Amelia wanted to tell them to argue, rebel, demand the fucking iPad, more biscuits, and chocolate ones too. They have so much faith in us, she thought, as they sat there quietly. So much faith to do just what we tell them. They don't know us. What would it be like for them if they knew us? Is that why she's never felt quite comfortable with the other parents at St Saviour's, has never really shown herself? Is she worried that, somehow, it would all trickle back here?

The clothes were in a Laithwaites box. They're on some plan, a case every three months, tasting notes neither of them look at. When she got back from Lewisham she took them all out of the packaging and scrunched them, dragged them around on the floor. She didn't have time to sew labels so she wrote 'Michael Leigh' in marker pen in the back of the white polo shirts and on the trouser labels. Was it obvious? She thought yes but calmed herself with the knowledge that neither James nor Alice, nor anyone, knows what has happened to her. What is obvious to her would seem incredible to anyone else. That she would do what she has… it would make them think she was insane.

— I threw the grotty stuff away. Didn't want you taking it to be polite. But go through them. Don't take them all if you don't want. Most will be too big but he'll grow, won't he?

— Yes, Alice said, confirming the charity shop guess by her keen, appraising scrutiny. She went through the things quickly, putting them in piles with expert fingers, after which she once again offered money. Again Amelia told her no and she finally gave up trying, asking for a plastic bag though it took two to contain them all. They then stood, for what was there to keep her now? Amelia hunted for some other offer to make, a net to wrap around her. Then she hunted for the reason she wanted to do this: with James the reason was obvious but she had no desire to fuck his wife. Not that she'd ever had a desire to do this with a woman but today nothing would surprise her. So what was it? Michael. The arrival of her son – she didn't want to face that on her own but she didn't know why. And then she did know and it horrified her. She was dreading the feelings she might have for him. Or not have.

Her firstborn. They lie if they say this doesn't matter. A little boy squirming on her chest all red and blue and so completely furious with her for what she's done to him. Every moment of her life with him has been an effort to make up for that blame-cry, including this last year's negotiation of his grunts and blunt dismissals, as if he's taken that project on the Australopithecus too seriously. And now? In spite of the fact that he seems to have become a monster, the idea of a dead grey flower in her heart in place of that vice grip was enough to make her tremble, in a way it didn't with Niamh. She couldn't be alone when he came through the door. She looked at Alice and saw that she was losing her, knowing she wouldn't wriggle politely like her husband but just announce that she had to leave.

— Mummy, I need the loo, said Dominic.

A break. Something to crack the moment, pregnant with imminent departure. She'd take the boy. Show him where the bathroom was and in the meantime think of a plan. An invite to supper? Not the adults, just the child, which wouldn't sound clingy? *I have some lasagne for Niamh and Michael, so if...?* She could present it as an upstairs thought, a change of location idea, tossed out lightly like a petrol-station frisbee.

— This way, Dom, she said.

Did they go on their own at four? She thought so but she honestly couldn't remember. Children were about the now; they were like a drug in that regard. She was about to ask but something told her not to. When he scampered up the stairs behind her she didn't just point out the door to him but pushed it open, watched him trot in, no shame nor any desire for privacy in this moment. She watched as he lifted his green St Saviour's jumper, keeping it in place with his chin. He pulled his trousers and pants down and she gazed at him, at his lithe, perfect bottom, his pale gushing spout. *His* son. The product of him, ineffably beautiful, more so than her own children ever were, and not just his product either but *hers* too, the thought burning her with jealousy as a mid-market scent intruded and a hand rested on the door jamb.

— You alright, love?

— Yes, Mummy. Don't worry, go back downstairs.

— Okay, then. Make sure you wash your hands.

— I always wash my hands.

— I know.

Alice's face, smiling into her own, suddenly grotesque like a carousel pony's. She turned from it, shaking herself out on to the landing as she led them downstairs.

Throughout the lasagne she stayed quiet, cold, withdrawn, wishing to hell she hadn't asked them. Why did she? she wondered, as she washed up, loaded the dishwasher, emptied the washing machine, poured extra milk, put things in the diary from Niamh's school bag, fished out thirty quid for Olga whose day it was tomorrow, stowed shoes, set up the music stand, took two phone messages for Richard, tipped custard powder into a pan? And why did the stupid woman agree? She wanted them gone. Wanted to scrub the house after they had gone, for it was a filthy thing now, made filthy by them. No, by her being there with them, so garishly innocent in their familial new-ness, the pair of them only just hatched. She wanted to take the surface cleaner and spray it over herself, scour her skin with wire wool, plunge the toilet brush down her throat until she gagged. The image of them, the happy mother and the little boy calling back over his shoulder to talk to her, would not leave her neon mind.

— Niamh, she says when, finally, she has managed to get them out of there. Tell me about your violin.

A painful crunch of tyres from outside. Doors. *Bleep.* Two male voices, split by an octave, heading towards the house.

4

SHE JUST CAN'T WAIT to see him. The mere idea cracks a smile across her face as she lopes down Hyde Vale with Dom, her cold, bare feet slapping hard on the pavement. Normally it's the kids who in absence make her want to rush into the immediate future. Speed it up somehow. But not today. Poor James. Desperate to get on, his longed-for sabbatical such golden space, only to find the house the way it was. Treetops calling. Sucked into the mum-fug she still has to endure herself one day a week. She often thinks of him when she's inside it, wondering how he negotiates it all. Why does it have to be like that? Not the kids' fault. No, she tells herself, as she shakes a small stone off her naked left sole, it's Greenwich. Money has swept in like a slow tide, smoothing everything out to an emptiness.

The image pleases her, momentarily takes her thoughts away from him. When he opens the door however her desire returns, is so complete she wants to lock the kids in the kitchen and drag him upstairs. What she does do is cop a quick, barely hidden feel through his running shorts, the repercussions of which are visible for a good twenty minutes. When will the kids notice this kind of thing? Fortunately it's gone by the time the three of them are in the bath together, the sight of which, from the loo seat, is almost too much to bear. As Ida secretly fills a plastic jug from the cold tap and tips it over James's head from behind she knows that she's done it, that she has absolutely everything she ever wanted in life. And not just in this half either because something happened today. Something wonderful and extraordinary though which, for just a short while longer, she needs to keep to herself.

James gets out last, a thousand rivers tumbling down his hard, hairy body. Ida insists that Mummy dry him too, an idea he agrees with, holding his arms right up in the air the way Dom does, squirming when she tries to do his hair. Amid the laughter it comes back again, of course, and she hides it, quickly, behind the towel.

— Pyjamas, she says. The lot of you.

Over supper they control themselves. Part of the game they play. To enact civilised ritual while the bungee cords tighten. She loves this feeling, loves having dinner with him generally, loves it so much in fact that if she's ever asked that dinner question at parties she always says him. There is always something to unpick, lay out between them, use their twin minds like chopsticks to put into place. Today there is the added element of that promise she made plus his blue-striped pyjamas which are given an erotic charge by the fact that she's still dressed. It sends her back to the first time, that flat of his in Brighton. In that tiny bathroom, adding lipstick then blotting it off again with loo paper, hoping to hell that finally this serious, blue-eyed man might be about to kiss her. Then coming out to find him naked. Not cooking, as she'd left him. Starkers. Standing by the window, three o'clock in the afternoon, staring at her.

When she can take it no longer she pretends to drop a piece of penne. Sees that he buys it. She ducks down beneath the table to retrieve it and emerges in his lap, smiling up at him, her tongue reaching into his fly. He laughs mid-mouthful and she pushes herself up, tries to snog him while he's still chewing, almost making him choke with laughter as he pushes her away and swallows. She undoes two buttons from his top, slides both hands into the hard warmth of him, biting his bottom lip now, *al dente*, perfect. He sighs and sits up straighter, his forehead pressing hard on hers as his thumbs run down over her cheekbones. His cupped hands lift her chin, eyelashes flicking her lips before he feathers her throat with kisses that leap beneath her skin to rush and fizz and then explode inside.

What happens then is not of their doing. Their bodies re-emerge from the subterranean caverns they have retreated to, retaking ownership of them and their thought-out world. Chairs are tipped, clothing removed as if burning. Walls and cupboards seem to step aside for them so that they are now on the kitchen floor, against the hall wall, now on the rug in the living room, sensations refusing to respect the boundaries of their skin, instead running back and forth between them. She grabs his face, frustrated that by kissing its broad lips she will not be able to see it. She does kiss him but wrenches herself free immediately, staring into dancing eyes, then his clavicle and chest, and that cock again. They wrestle, fighting but in perfect agreement, her wrists above her head and his teeth on her jugular, her breastbone and then, very slowly, her left nipple. A metal rose seems to bloom in its centre, cutting through the skin, followed by another in her right and then the fight shifts once more, their habitual struggle commencing for the most coveted role: pleasure-giver. He wins. Three fingers and his tongue inside her then his mouth on her belly and then her chest again, arms beginning to hitch her legs up when she rolls out and pulls him to his feet. They pound the stairs like Indiana Jones and she pushes him on to the bed, getting him inside her in two, hard thrusts. He claws at her as if resisting, bucking and shifting, his chest rising until he is sitting up, and she is sitting on him. And this, she knows, is the configuration they will be in when time ends. This fuck picture will spin out into the endless blackness for creatures in other times and dimensions to find and wonder at forever.

A moment of clarity. His fingers open her arse cheeks, his thumb feathering, very lightly, her anus. He wants this. He's never said anything. He's drawn there, though, she knows. Never had anal sex. Never wanted to not even with him and won't ever. But this she likes. Never told him. Never knew. Eleven years to get here, doors of desire opening, just opening at the sight of the two of them moving towards them. She reaches around behind her and presses her palm against this thumb. She pushes it inside her, all the way to the knuckle, and because of the danger of it or the giving him this or the feeling she doesn't know but she comes again, which she normally wouldn't, and he comes too with such violence that she knows it's not semen rushing into her. He is being turned inside out, every single piece of him flowing through his cock and into her as she is turned inside out and flowing back into him.

— I hadn't even finished my pasta. You know how much I love an arrabbiata.

— Yeah, but I thought you were looking fat. Had to act.

— Well, you shouldn't have, especially as that was really crap. I want a divorce.

— Sure. I'm sleeping with your father anyway. Seriously though, I don't want to wear my wedding ring any more.

— What?

— There's a little bit of me that can't feel when I touch you.

She smiles and he smiles back and it isn't long before they're making love once more. It's calmer this time, bodiless, so sweet and simple that it nearly sweeps her away again, as he is being swept. She knows it won't though because it is back inside her mind: this other joy. The call before she left the office, her last student packing up to go. The call she'd secretly been hoping for, been awaiting long months, as if for the boiler repair man, in a small, windowless room inside herself. Certain it had to come but admitting that to no one. Because something had changed this time. Not a small poet any more – minor. Not with this book. And three judges have agreed, which is why she's made the shortlist of the Carson Prize. As James makes love to her she hears the voice of the reserved old lady who called her, and feels again the fist-like pride that is her pride, and not James's. Sees the ceremony she'll take him to but be at on her own. In the life that is hers and not his. Time again, aching for it to speed up, but not towards him. Or anything in this house. As her husband continues to make love to her she waits for it, impatient as she blinks into the darkness.

5

A THEATRE DIRECTOR.

When Alice tells him this James shakes his head. Amazed, and not for the first time that morning. She has already told him the other news, laid it out in front of him quietly, blushing, unable to look at him, staring at her Weetabix instead. He whooped, lifting her by the waist, a huge box of joy bursting open inside him. The clever undergrad he sat with in the EngAm Common Room, who shook like crêpe paper at the open mic. The girl he used to go walking with on Firle Beacon, so willowy he'd worry that the wind would blow her off. He has a sense of where life has taken the two of them and is stunned by it.

Not total joy. For even as he spun her he could feel the guilt. It came from being surprised, which he certainly is that this huge, external honour might be conferred on her. Not that he doesn't love her work. But isn't it just about her? A prize would mean the work is separate. Not just the brilliant communication of her particular connection, no longer something he can be intimate with, he the unique reader for he can see where each individual word has come from. He got a sudden glimpse: a PhD student studying her. Picking up things he himself has missed.

And what if she actually wins? He wants her to but at the same time it would make her less human. He imagines her going on, winning more, burrowing her way to the centre of the British cultural élite. How can you be married to someone who lives there? Or be the child of one? She'll be a great writer, like his American who, thankfully, is well and truly dead. The idea horrifies him but what is worse is the fact that he simply didn't see it, not just now when she clearly had something wonderful to say, nor, worst of all, when he read the poems. For this last collection is – and he would only admit this if someone were pulling toenails from his children's feet – his least favourite of her books.

— A what? he asks, twenty minutes later, when toast is being spread. Or thrown. When they are normal again. I assumed he must do something money-ish.

— Me too. But Amelia told me. Said he's doing Godot now. Old Vic.

— Blimey. Though I suppose that's part of it, the middle-class thing. Fifty quid a ticket, glass of fizz at the interval. No reason to expect a director of that stuff not to want what the people who see his shows have.

— Still hard to see it, though. Amelia, she was so...

— Normal?

— I don't know. Not that, quite. Great clothes, though. Need to wash them. I'll do it; you take the kids, though, if *la* nursery telephones, *c'est moi qui vais y aller, d'accord*? Though...

— What?

— Do me a big favour?

— Did you one last night.

— Two, but it was the other way round. Got dog shit on my shoes. Last night. They're in a plastic bag outside the back door. Dominic, please. You laughed yesterday too. It's not a nice thing to tread in dog poo. Stop it.

— Wait, James says, glancing over at his giggling son, milk dripping from his wobbling spoon. Where?

— On the Heath. Too dark to see it. People are so…

— *Where?*

— In the middle. On the way back. A massive pile just lying there.

— Oh, God, James says, cracking up too now, Dom practically falling off his chair.

He still finds this funny later, when he gets back from dropping Dom. Ida is easy this time, running into nursery with hardly a backward glance. The reason – a fluke discovery – is not the sudden discovery of a deep well of inner security that means she is now happy being left. It is toast. He gets her there fifteen minutes before time to give himself space to calm her in, not simply throw her to the beast and disappear. What this means, though, is that breakfast is still being served to the children whose parents need to bring them really early. Ida sees a big stack of toast and three jam pots, towards which she charges as if she appeared in her mother's womb of her own volition. Has no father. It guts him for a second but what the fuck, he's cracked it. He strolls up to the Heath, laughing with Dom, and they search for it. And it's still there, Alice's Converse print right in the middle. It makes them howl with laughter all over again even though, when they explained it to her, she only pretended to find it funny.

It's Thursday so he takes Dom straight to church. St Saviour's, on the Heath, right by Blackheath Village. The school has an assembly there once a week, one today in the morning. He used to see the kids years ago when he was running, or pushing Dom in the buggy. He'd see them rummaging outside the place or else streaming across the grass from every direction as they're doing now, calling out, joining up, parents waving or joining too. A mass coming-together such as he'd never have believed possible in a city, a village thing that took him all the way back up the A1. Seeing this convocation made him want his kids to come to this school so very much that he was embarrassed, staying nonchalant even to Alice until the letter came. And she admitted it too. *So he goes to Carlton Hill, he'll be fine there*... fuck that. When they got Dom into St Saviour's, and he knew that he'd be one of those kids tearing across that big green space, James had wanted to sacrifice a goat in honour of the council leader and send him its heart through the post. Space in which to move, for their small bodies to expand into, and grow.

Dom flies off at the sight of Milo. James frowns, aware of another incremental movement his son is making away from him. For Milo is a bit, well, dim. In the lowest reading sub-group, big open grin on his face. What he is actually is just a normal little boy. No person yet, just a collection of five-year-old characteristics, not helped, James thinks, by the fact that every toy he has ever seen him clutching is the imaginatively neutral commercial endgame of some huge global franchise. There are other kids in the class – Luke with the freckle mask, very bright, Jack with the football, future school captain – but Dom cuts through them. Friendly enough but it's Milo he's drawn to and James is disappointed, unable to work it out. Is it a relief from his own furious little mind? Or just some chemical thing: facial make-up, smell? The fact that he returns whatever it is Dom feels? The two of them dance around each other like bees and then chase through the crowd in a way James still cannot feel comfortable with, needing to know exactly where his little boy is.

Amelia is standing with two other women – both casually immaculate – over by the church door. They're chatting in that easy way that speaks of childcare swaps and sleepovers, quiz nights in the school hall. He himself, a newbie, feels awkward about this, having yet to connect with any other parents, largely because he and Alice haven't quite been able to bring themselves to launch into this. The round of other kids back to tea or – and the phrase nearly chokes him – play dates. Even Milo hasn't been to their house, owing largely to the fact that he lives somewhere incomprehensible like Hither Green or Beckenham. James feels himself to be on the cusp of this conjoining and is curious, knowing that it would probably be good for his son and, eventually, his daughter. But what would he and Alice have to give up by embracing what he sees in front of him? He doesn't know but he's sure it's something, and if they do dive in they might never be able to find their way out again.

Should he go and speak to her? Rude not to in the light of what she's given them. Clothes, supper, general kindness. He's shy, though, especially as she has her back to him and he'd have to interrupt her and her friends. She probably doesn't even know what it means to them that she's saved them fifty quid or so; in the way of some wealthy people she's probably forgotten her generosity immediately. He decides not to go but then notices Dom, rushing up to a girl who must be the woman's daughter. It's not physical similarity but the way she pulls her hand, Amelia turning with an easy smile. This widens when she sees Dom and she bends, running a hand over his head as he's seen many women do whose kids are older, who will never again have such a small, beaming child in front of them. James watches with a pride he can't explain as Dom starts to tell her something. She listens with great attention before straightening, casting her eyes around. James starts to raise his hand until he sees that it is only fake interest on her face. Put there for Dom's benefit. When she doesn't see him she gives up easily and just smiles at Dom again, before turning back to her friends. He feels relief because he didn't really want to walk over there but he's also miffed to have seen this. He has the sense that in a few days' time they could pass in the street without her even noticing him.

Walking home is different today. No rush or clamour to flee, an easy re-shrugging-on of self. He strolls across the Heath and enters Greenwich Park. A crescent of new-laid bedding plants beams beside the cricket pitch, the energy almost impossible to focus on. It puts him in mind of last night and the wonder of it spreads through him. Ten years soon. He hasn't so much as kissed another human being in more than eleven. They should be bored with each other, or at least have some distant, softened sense of being used to themselves. But that woman last night had a body he'd never seen before, a cunt he'd never tasted. A freckle behind her ear he'd never noticed yet he must have. He was probably obsessed with it five years ago before moving on to a nipple or her belly button, the back of a knee. There is for some reason a constant deferment of their passion, an inability – despite repeated efforts – to get to grips with it. They chase it around their bodies like some escaped animal and have never, once, caught up with it.

And that other thing. Now he blushes, this forty-one-year-old man, blushes to his roots to think of it. Naughty girl. He smiles and an old lady smiles back, no idea why this idiotic grin is pasted across his face. He laughs and walks through the rose garden, staring out across the stark, agonised stems.

Clever wifey, he texts her, before cutting out on to Crooms Hill.

But here his mood changes. Something's gnawing at him. Not Alice or the kids, not even the fact that – because of his day with Ida – he's going to have to spend the morning clawing back to the point in his text that he'd got to two days before. Not even, when he thinks about it, the fact that, of course, Alice knew about her prize before the world spun out on them last night. He knows she was there inside it just as he was. He doesn't resent her need to hold on to the news until it felt right to let it go. What is she, a Labrador? Must she set sticks down at his feet? And, actually, had she told him earlier, it could have short-circuited the amazing thing that happened between them.

It's the theatre director. Why the hell this faceless man should affect him he's no idea and he shrugs him off as he jogs down the overgrown steps leading from the hill to Hyde Vale. In Diamond Terrace, though, it's back, which he can't understand because he loves this place. A gravelled cut through between Hyde Vale and Point Hill, it's where he would live if he had the roll. His Greenwich dream house is here, selected after years of culling from the surrounding streets. There are finer properties, one on Maze Hill for instance with a balcony and door looking right on to the park. This in fact was his initial choice but that was before he began to dislike East Greenwich, the litter-blown maw of Trafalgar Road already speaking the language of Charlton and beyond. The White House he has just passed took its place but it, actually, is too open and exposed, announcing success too overtly. Too many people would know he lived there. He has a need to conceal himself within the city, a corner house on Hyde Vale then holding pole position, the finest in a fine row but still just one of many. But then he found Diamond Terrace and the new house.

Frank Lloyd Wright could have built this. Or some Scandi (he's not big on architects). Sixties? Wide, sloping garden. Neat, neutral brick and flat, geometric roofs, huge windows, open-plan everything by the look of it. He just knows there were planning objections way back when, that the crusty, check-shirted bastards in the Georgian houses on either side oozed bile when this was erected. In the past it has pained him to the core not to own this house, most especially when, for the briefest period, a *For Sale* sign appeared outside, calling him a wanker as he walked by. He was able to ride the pain though because he knew something absolute: he chose his life. No one made him do an MA. Forced him on to a PhD. At any time he could have chucked it, done a law conversion, MBA perhaps. They would not have guaranteed him this or any other notable dwelling but the chance would have been there. But it's his life and he could not have chosen any other – something Alice has, in his weaker moments, reminded him. The fact that we live in a shoebox – and let's not forget that it's a pretty shoebox one minute from Greenwich station – means we're successful. It shows we stuck it out, are doing what we want. And houses, Jesus, is that the absolute end? Is floor space what we're put on earth to desire? And don't forget, my love, you get to sleep with me.

That Alice would not have married a stockbroker is actually his most effective solace. Today, though, it's different. And he nails what's gypping him. That house he went to yesterday. Amelia's house. It's not some pea-souled Goldman Sachs monkey in it – the paltry Faustian pay-off for a life handed over – but a theatre director. Someone who wanted to be that, must have known his odds on the financial big time were slim. But he got it, which means he got it all, every last sweet bit of it, and this particular success bites James hard because he'll never have it. How can he? He stares at the hip, large house in front of him and is bucked by a simple truth: if he did own it, Alice would still want to fuck him. But he won't. Not ever.

It's just a game he plays.

He makes the call at lunch. Doesn't know why. Just makes the call. Chris Carty picks up and James is pleased, though surprised that someone he used to know still works there. So much has happened to him, it's hard to believe anything in his former life has stayed the same.

Chris hears James out and doesn't argue, or even question it. He just says sure, mate, why not, I'll have a ring round. When he calls back it's as though six years have flattened up into a moment. There's been a cancellation. Stomach bug. Chris tells him when to be there, and what he'll be paid, and there's another surprise because it's hardly any more than six years ago.

He's early. Emerges from Leicester Square tube at six-thirty, a little disorientated. He's a country mouse now. He shakes himself together and cuts into the square itself; the venue is off to the left. He approaches it slowly, wanting to check out the vibe, look at the posters, see if his bones still respond. If the reason he was drawn to this odd thing is still buried inside him or if, conversely, all he can taste is the reason why he jacked it in. As he stares at the big rubber lips, however, neither feeling strikes him and nor is he in any way afraid, which was not the case before. Ever. He shakes his head at this, and the fact that it took him four long years to get to the Comedy Store. He only ever played it twice. And now, because he called his old agent at the last moment, at exactly the right time, he's slid right back in there.

He takes a bench. He's printed his old material off and is about to go through it, but the first arrivals catch his eye. After-work crowd, there for the Happy Hour, men mostly, who will later be the slurring, glass-eyed morons he used to hate so much. Looking at them now, he realises that he still does but for a different reason. No reason. Just hates them. They're like a different species and he frowns, wondering if he really is going to go inside that building to try to make them laugh. It seems an impossible task and he wonders what he was thinking, and is about to head straight back down into the tube station. But he stops when he sees a girl come out, and it's not just her tight black Store tee that catches his eye. She's changing the photographs, removing one of a bearded guy he vaguely recognises. Replacing it with one he certainly does. Him. *His* face. Did they still have it? Or did Carty bike it over? He doesn't know but he stares, blinking, the face smiling out at him just as alien as the people filing past. It makes him gasp inside, as if he's shifted back in time, and it also makes him stay: what the fuck does it matter if he only lasts five minutes before these Next-suited IT spanners decide he should leave the stage? How can that, in any way, affect him? Tomorrow he'll be back at the dining room table. It's not his life any more. As he dumps the notes in a bin, and heads off to tell the girl who he is, it feels as if he's at his own funeral.

He goes for pizza. He used to hang out backstage, drink in the atmosphere, try to get a sense of the audience from their response to the other comics. He used to think this helped him. With about an hour of material up his sleeve he used to think that by being fluid like that he could ensure the best result. Now he doesn't care, and as he munches his doughy Four Seasons he's hardly even aware of the time. He even finds some to chat to an American family, who are amazed when he tells them what he's doing.

— Tonight? the dad says.

— In about twenty minutes.

— Good luck! they all say to him.

The first guy is shite. He gets laughs but he's like one of those London walk guides, taking a string of people to a series of dead though oft-visited places. He goes to the exact middle of everything and there's no surprise or zip, no danger, even though his left arm is covered in tats and he's got a bolt in each eyebrow. It's a depressing sight, both the pap coming out of him and the way the audience munches it up. Depressing too because it's James up there. He was better, more subtle; he'd come at a thing with more guile. But he was the same, just a man with words coming out of him, someone a little cleverer than the people listening. Anyone could do this, he thinks, as his name is called.

So what the hell am I going to do?

He still has no idea about this when he walks on. He genuinely doesn't. In the past he'd perhaps have referred to the comic before him, maybe picked up on something he'd said very briefly, both to honour him, which makes him seem like a nice guy, but also to kill that time, make the audience transition to himself. Now he just stares after him, his hand visoring his eyes as he shakes his head.

— That was funny. I know it was. But can somebody please just tell me what the fuck that guy was talking about?

It's a big laugh. He doesn't know why. He shakes his head, holding a palm up, saying he means no disrespect to his very talented colleague. But he's got kids now. *Night*clubs?

Cocaine? Reading the *newspaper* on a Sunday morning? Not a bleeding clue, mate. We have a Tory government? Why did nobody say anything about this at the Nearly New sale last week?

It's his energy that gets the bite. He understands that very quickly. He sees, for a second, the face of the last guy in the wings, sees laughter on it but a little sickness because there's something bigger in the room now. He turns back to the audience and starts to speak, but stops immediately, reaching for his phone. And all he does is call home and, on speaker, wish his kids goodnight. He's not faking it. There is a silence you could sculpt, which he does with one hand as Dom tells him that he can't find Tomsk. He tells Dom where Tomsk might be and stays on the line, fingers crossed high, a massive cheer from the audience when the Night Watch Womble is located in the coal scuttle. Then it's Ida's turn. She doesn't want to say goodnight but to tell him something.

— What is it, darling?

— Mummy trod in Dom-Dom's poo, she says, giggling.

It's never been like this for him. He asks Ida to sing him a song and she comes up with her own rendition of 'Twinkle Twinkle Little Wheels on the Bus of York'. He'd go on forever but Alice comes on and tells him, and everyone, that it's time for sleepy-byes now. As one the entire audience kisses his children goodnight and they're not a different species now but people he loves, who are, in that moment, jammed into his little house, perched on the armrests and the sofa cushions. He goes on to tell them about Alice, explaining the Dom-shit incident, which she really is alone in not seeing the humour in now. He tells them how she leaves the house in the morning and that her visa application for New Orleans has been refused three times. He explains his plan to tidy up but then put all her crap out again, how he photographed the Weetabix crumbs so he could get them all exactly how they were. So she wouldn't know. Then he goes on, unable to stop himself, telling them how he didn't do that but did have to explain to his almost five-year-old son that a piece of Brio track had got wedged down his running shorts. How, later, the kids *finally* spark out, exhaustion rushing in to fill the gap they'd left behind, he and his wife made love.

They're not laughing now. Just glued to him, every single person, fixed as he tells them how roses flowered from his wife's nipples, how he felt her soft breath in the darkest and most fragile corners of his self. They are his, caught in a vibrating stillness, faces gurned with joy and love and tenderness when he pauses, leaves a beat, genuinely seeing it and feeling it so they do to. It is pure and beautiful, a woman in the front row with her hand up to her mouth. After which he says,

— And then I shoved my thumb up her arse.

They die. Roll. More so when he stares at the mobile in his hand, mock-terrified that the line is still open. He runs on, telling them how Ida insists on taking her clothes off in the rain and putting her swimming goggles on. How she chases after Dom at bathtime with a single-minded desire to grab his todger that not even Jordan could match. Told the postman, smiling, to fuck right off. He carries them because he is being carried and when he ties it up they stand, roaring, taking pictures of him while he blushes and exits into the dressing room, where the previous guy looks sickened, though he's nodding, and the semi-famous headline act looks very annoyed indeed.

He knows he has to leave. He wants to hang around, meet the audience in the bar, make them laugh again. But he can't do this, it will just make the come-down longer and more depressing, especially from where he got to. The sooner he lets it go the better, for after all it was just a toe back in, this. He splashes his face in the tiny, stained sink as the storm in his chest dies down.

— Hi, the man says, behind him. James, isn't it?

James turns. He backs up a little, though only in his mind. He's wary, dismissive, instantly on guard: he knows this guy. Not his name. He doesn't even know his face, though that doesn't matter. That suit. There's a shop for them. They only let you in if you can prove you are, unequivocally, a cunt.

He's TV.

James pads his face with a hand towel and tosses it aside. He says yes, and the man nods.

— I remember you.

Lying shitbag.

— Right.

— You were never that good.

Or maybe not.

— No.

— And you looked wrong. Not edgy enough for a young comic. Now you are, though.

— Oh?

— For a dad. You look edgy now.

— An edgy dad.

— Which could go, you know? Really. I was here to see Micky. Guy before you. What did you think?

He doesn't even look round.

— Shit.

— Yeah. Only knew that when I saw you, though. He probably did too, and if I were him I'd give up. But here, he says, holding it out like a Fabergé egg. My card.

James sighs. About to explain. Shake his head at the absolute, sent-in-clowns irony. But he takes the card, does so automatically because he's frowning, trying to hide it, trying to understand what is happening. Two more people have squeezed into the dressing room. The first is big, a powerful-looking guy. Liam Neeson, if Liam Neeson were a real person. But it's the other who sends his eyelids to the ceiling. Because it's weird, so very weird actually that it can't really be weird but just a random, chance thing, like an aircraft wheel smashing through the roof of your house.

— That, Amelia says, was awesome.

6

IT'S EASIER ON her own. Not always but often enough to make it worth thinking about. No one to blame or measure herself against, to feel they've got the easier role. No getting Aveeno cream on a screaming Ida and yelling at Dom not to bail the bath out on to the floor while James is downstairs with David Archer chopping onions. The kids can't play parent tennis either, which means she can focus and take her time and, yes, air-punch, be as messy as she likes. She can indulge them more, their secret, and there's another element. In some small but very important way these two creatures aren't hers and James's. They are hers. She, the primary human. Being alone with them gives her the chance to take this hidden emotion out of the tiny gold box she keeps it in. As she does so she realises that some part of her has always envied single mothers. Not the harrowed, abandoned ones but those who've taken the sperm and run.

She can be one for a night.

Sticks on a DVD. Not to brush them off or contain them but simply to give the thing they've asked for. Wants, with no preconditions, to do this. Mummy, can we watch something? Yes, love, you can. She's not even being strategic. She could use the time to knock down chores, sort washing or sew in name-tags, clear out the art cupboard or order new socks for Dominic; the things she thinks James doesn't realise anyone actually does. But all she does is bang a spud in the oven and get Ida's milk before sitting with them, laughing with Dom when Orinoco gets caught in the umbrella. They close in, Dom's arm curled around her knee, Ida worrying the pulse point on her wrist as she sucks, something Dom used to do and which she sometimes feels during the day, at work. When James calls to say goodnight it feels like an intrusion and it takes a while to realise that he's actually on stage. The idea puts her on the back foot but Dom and Ida behave so perfectly that she dismisses the concerns she has. She's proud of them, and when James hangs up she does then feel a little lost. He's netting things to tell her, while she'll just have this to recount. It's still wonderful but not different and she almost hopes they'll fight or that Dom will reveal some slight school trauma that she can pass on. But they are good as gold. Ida falls asleep in her arms when she's reading *The BFG* to Dom. Dom then actually asks if he can go to bed. She puts them both in and, when they are asleep, is visited by a slow, meandering wistfulness. Is it getting too easy? In spite of the jobs queuing up like passenger jets, are they emerging, as people say you do, into a more manageable region? Into, God help them, a routine? She tidies up, and by the time her potato is done the place looks as if normal people live there.

I want another baby, she thinks, staring into the hall mirror.

What she'd actually like right now is James. The sex has always been great. It has moved in cycles, however, shifting to new places every now and then, something which, before last night, hadn't happened for a while. It did though and she feels like a Victorian newlywed with this great new toy she wants to try out. She doesn't necessarily need or even want it to be so all-encompassing but she does want to know what it's going to be like now. She's nervous, and knows she will be when they do next make love, almost as much as when that unexpectedly naked man smiled at her.

— They're all dead.

— Who? Trying to keep her eyes on his face. Thinking *arrogant twat* before immediately correcting herself. He's just showing himself to me.

— All the other men in the world. I killed them this afternoon. Okay?

She nodded, did so before she knew what she was really saying. Agreeing to. Then he walked towards her, bent down, and carefully slid off her shoes.

She takes the potato out and sets it on the kitchen table, steam fleeing the centre when she cuts it open. She devils it with a fork and sets a corner of butter on the ploughed interior, mesmerised by the way it seems unconcerned, but then shifts and slides until it has given itself up completely. Was that what we should do, confronted by the heat of life?

Pesto next, which James made a few nights back with Dom, before she pushes a small block of cheddar through the grater. She finds herself immensely satisfied by these small movements and decides to eat at the table, not in front of *Masterchef* as she'd planned. She pours herself a glass of wine, another thing she might not normally do alone, and sips it, waiting for the potato to cool. Then she thinks of James, who has probably finished by now, wondering if it went well. By the sound of it, it probably did. She pushes aside her jealousy, or whatever it is, and is pleased, though she doesn't know what he's doing. Why, when his old agent phoned, he didn't say no, I'm finished with that. Money?

A laugh? Because he finds it hard to refuse? Or was there some deeper pull, the thought of which troubles her, though so what if he starts again? She loved going to watch him, especially to cabaret nights, infinitely more classy than the testosterone-soaked comedy clubs. She loved going up to Edinburgh too, though that's it, isn't it? It won't be the same. She'll be stuck at home, except for the odd night when they'll be racing back for the babysitter. Not a comedian's bird, an access-all-areas chick to be envied – a comedian's wife. To be pitied. It seems churlish, this panic, but she can't deny it and suddenly the night she's having isn't half so attractive. She decides to watch *Masterchef* after all.

There is a rap on the door so loud it can only be one person. She sets her plate on the sofa, and pauses the iPlayer, listening to make sure that neither of the children have woken. She goes to the door, miming self-strangulation, but doesn't open it. She needs to compose herself first. She's helped in this by the sign above the door, put there by James for her benefit.

DO NOT ASK NEIL FROM NEXT DOOR WHAT THE FUCK HE WANTS NOW.

OR JUST STAND THERE WITH YOUR ARMS FOLDED SAYING NOTHING BUT THINKING THAT.

OR, AT ANY TIME, CALL HIM A WANKER.

— Yes? she says. Brightly.

They live on Straightsmouth. It's a long street behind Greenwich station. At the far end the trains make it noisy but it's alright where they are, though the houses are smaller. Pretty, though: old workers' cottages with original floorboards and fireplaces. When they first saw it they – James doing a puking gesture – *fell in love with the place*, even though it only had two bedrooms and no landing, a kitchen they could only just squeeze a table into. It wasn't in Lewisham though or Charlton or even leafy but deadly dull Maze Hill. The location was just so handy, physically and psychologically, and the garden was oddly big. The place was wrong in so many ways but just so right and even two kids haven't changed that. The reverse, because they never have to worry about Dom and Ida. They can always hear what they're up to. At night it feels as though they are all so together, half of the family not parcelled off in different corners of a very big house like some of their friends' kids, wired up to baby monitors like heart patients. She knows this will change, begin to annoy her when they are older, but she won't think about that. Even at school she tries not to notice the bigger kids and never wants to talk to their parents. It's her own time she's living in and she doesn't want to see beyond it.

There is one downside to their urban gingerbread house however and he is standing in front of her. Had they known about Neil From Next Door they would have demanded at least ten grand off the asking price. James is convinced they only got the house because other possible buyers visited a website called willmyneighbourturnouttobeacuntofthefirst water.com. They didn't and so have to endure his endless sniping about weekend paddling pool decibels, or parking in His Space. A Stasi-like rapping on their door caused by an inadvertent encroachment on to his side of the trellis with binding wire. It's something James is better at dealing with because of his general love of the absurd, and the peculiarly male attribute of recognising that something is supremely irritating while not actually being irritated by it. She is, and not just because of his incursions into their life, she will admit.

He has a TV so big it lights up the whole street through his window, would work well showing *Jaws* in Greenwich Park. Every item of his clothing is slashed with some sports brand name and his skin is of a pallor that suggests an exclusive diet of saturated fat, predigested in Tesco factories and splurged into white plastic trays marked 'Value'. Not that these distress her *per se*, nor the fact that they share no semiotic commercial connection, not one thing in his entire house, down to the brand of his toothpaste, that she would buy. She's sure of this though of course she's never been inside, the idea of which makes her feel unwell.

All of these things would, in other people, actually fill Alice with envy. There is a tubby family down the street whose kids trundle to the park on battery-powered tricycles while the adults waddle contentedly behind. The KFC buckets she sees in their recycling sacks on Sunday evenings give them something she'll never have, and it isn't just heart disease.

It is Neil himself. The fact of him. That she's never seen him cleaning the windows or struggling up the street with Co-op bags, never once glanced over the garden fence to see him pegging out washing. Those tasks are left to his shorn, clockwork wife, in spite of the fact that she works all hours scrubbing floors while some notional, box-tick malady leaves Neil on the sick. He's just another Man, lord of all he surveys, staring at Alice in bemusement every time he sees her leaving the kids with James as she rushes off to work.

And he *looks* at her. James plays this game.

— So if I was transmogrified into him. If, like, you knew it was me really, underneath, but I was in his body. Would you love me?

— No.

— But I'd be me.

— Then I can't love you. It's your body.

— So what if he was transmogrified into my body? Would you kiss him?

— Disgusting. I'd know it was him.

— But what if he was subtle – what if you didn't know? *Cam on Alice darlin, howsabout a little hanky-panky then? Get you a kebab afta?*

— Package, Neil says, turning away from the door.

She nods. Not as bad as all that. Can't think what she's waiting for, though. Books probably for James, though Neil returns empty-handed.

— Can't shift it on me own.

— What?

— Too big. Give us a hand, then.

He turns again and she hisses to herself. There's nothing for it so she puts the latch on and follows him to his door. She takes in the ancient burgundy shag pile and blue flock walls, knowing that if anyone did buy this house they wouldn't just do the usual middle-class strip-out but perform an exorcism. The horror is not in the decor though, but the huge, rectangular cardboard box that is almost entirely blocking his hallway.

Neil is behind it, shunting it forward until it bumps against the step. Without thinking she helps it over, stunned by the weight, letting it go again as he pushes it out on to the narrow pavement, the peak of his baseball cap tonguing around the side. She wants to stop him, say no, what the hell are you doing? But he's got it out and is turning it like an ocean liner towards her house. She intervenes to stop it tipping sideways into the road and there it is, leaning against their window. And it is massive.

— Wait. When did this come? I mean, what the hell is this?

— No idea have I Alice? Ours not to reason why, hey? You could say thanks for having the thing stuffing up my hall for half the day.

— Yes. Sorry. Tha... But, it's for us?

— Name on the side, Neil tells her.

And it is. James's name. Sent from a company called Park-Gear. She's still baffled though, and when Neil starts to swivel it towards the door she tells him no. Theirs is the end-of-terrace house and they've got a door from the side street going straight into the garden. From where they are, pushing it through the hall and out the back door would actually be quicker, but while she still breathes Neil From Next Door is not going to cross that threshold. She guides while he pushes, round the corner to the brown wooden door, which she goes through the house to unbolt. Unbolt. Unbolt. Unbolt. Unbolt. Unbolt. Unbolt. Unbolt. They get the huge thing into the garden and lean it against the back of the house, Neil squinting at the label.

— Trampoline? Summink like that?

— I don't know, she says again, before showing him out, shepherding him towards the garden gate when he heads towards the back door. Then she stares at the giant package, racking her brains, knowing that she puts her mind on autopilot sometimes, confident that if something is really important and not just general life process James will make her hear it. Nothing pops out. But she can't be angry because there is every chance he has told her about this. A trampoline? Why not? She's curious now rather than outraged, but is faced with a moral dilemma.

She has never once opened an item of his mail. If he ever forgets to shut his Gmail down she keeps her eyes from the messages. And this is addressed to him. Something this size cannot but impact on her life but no, she can't do it. She shrugs, re-Fort Knoxes the garden door and heads back inside towards the frenzied death rattle of their ancient washing machine.

Irritation: the shirts Amelia Leigh gave them have run. Ink from the names. She can't have ever washed them on hot. Alice swears, shoves the whole lot back with some bleach. When she straightens she laughs because yes, now she has two things to talk to James about later. Not that she can, however, at least not that night.

He doesn't get in until four a.m.

Will it be different? This question is in the centre of her mind the next morning as she runs through Deptford and Rotherhithe, and then along the Southbank, her backpack banging into her shoulders. She needs to buy a better one, made specifically for jogging, though she probably won't. She makes do, does Alice, happy to put up with small irritations, which makes her feel resistant to the economic parcelling of human life. She doesn't wear Lycra, just some old shorts and a Snoopy T-shirt her sister gave her. She's pretty fast though and getting faster, something that fills her with a solid, disbelieving pride, for this is quite a new thing for her, something James always did and which gave her a stitch after five minutes when she tried. She always swam but it's too time-consuming and there is something about moving through the world like this, going from one place to another, where she needs to be. In the space she inhabits when her feet hit the pavement what is behind her retreats, and what waits for her is unimaginable.

She gets to Waterloo five minutes early for the nine thirty-eight and swipes her Oyster card through the barrier without removing it from her bag.

On the train to Wimbledon she thinks about it more. Will going to work be different now she's been nominated for the Carson Prize? She knows her teaching career can only be enhanced, but that's not really what fires the glee. She's not a senior staff member. Lecturer grade only, teaching mostly on the BA though she's asked several times for graduate classes. Above her in the Faculty are a lot of Eng Lit staff who can't quite see the point of her. Or her discipline. They may pretend they don't but they view the teaching of Creative Writing as woolly, vague, not really on somehow. In prose or drama it probably has some value for skills learned: but poetry? She's fairly sure most of them think it can't be taught and even if it could, what the hell were you going to do with it? This while they're all obsessing over Milton or Auden, as if these literary figures were actually more like them than they were like her. James, who has always been supportive of and somewhat awed by her work, harbours reserves of particularly acidic bile for members of his profession who don't see that people like Alice keep them in a job. Tawdry, he says they are. Necrophiliacs, the lot of them.

Alice likes the idea that these people might now look at her differently, but it's her colleagues in Creative Writing she's really thinking about, the novelists and the playwrights and the has-been TV writer who are all paid more and given more research time than she is. And, of course, the poets. There are two others on permanent contract, a professor and a principal lecturer, both of whom treat her like a precocious child. Do they know yet? She doesn't even know if the list has been officially announced. The idea that they do and are waiting to congratulate her through gritted teeth delights her. But actually she hopes they do not know yet. The principal lecturer, Peter Shale, is particularly grand, even though he hasn't had a book out in years. He offers her nuggets of unasked-for advice and she wants to experience this with the added clarity of knowing what she knows. As she walks up College Road she feels as if she's carrying something small and sharp, like a letter knife, which she is going to stab him with.

No trumpets are sounded as she walks into the main reception. She goes up to her communal office but there is no one there. Disappointment. She laughs at herself and heads to the Health Centre for a shower, where she does find someone. It's a student, an American girl on the MA who has asked her to look at her work. She's just getting undressed from a workout and Alice feels uncomfortable, though she's never normally shy about her body. In other environments – Greenwich pool for instance – she positively likes being naked among other naked women. She finds their bodies in all their age and shape configurations beautiful, as well as enjoying the reduced and relaxing communality. There's something wrong about a student seeing her naked though but, as she can't say what exactly, and is annoyed with herself for feeling it, she strips off, chatting away, impressed by the rubbery bounce of the girl's breasts as they emerge from her sports bra. She is then a little startled by the almost complete hairlessness of the girl's genitals. Just a small, cursory tuft, half a catkin stuck on. This is something she has noticed before of course but never in such startling proximity. She herself favours some but not much pubic intervention and wants to ask the girl why she does this, whether it has some socioeconomic or cultural significance. Or is it just an age thing? Are all her female students thus denuded? And, if so, do any of the barely post-pubescent boys sleeping with them have any idea what a woman actually looks like?

Would Ruskin have found life easier, married to a girl from Wimbledon University?

It's a relief to be in the shower cubicle and on her own. She refuses to hurry though and exit before the girl. They chat again as they dry themselves and it is only halfway through that she realises what is happening. For as much as she has no desire to undress in front of her students, the girl is equally freaked. Her cheeks were red before but Alice assumed it was from exercise. But they're still red because, of course, she's embarrassed, as if she's walked in on her parents having sex. This does make Alice feel uncomfortable and, claiming a class she's late for, she dresses and hurries out.

There is no class yet. What there is is a lot of work waiting for her in the file on her desktop marked 'Pointless Admin'. She gets on with it, the big room still empty, trying not to wonder what the hell any of it has to do with teaching, because she still has to do it even if the answer is nothing. There is also something therapeutic about it, the pure drudgery sometimes having the effect she imagines chanting might have. It takes her from herself to a still, bland space, her tiny soul humbled by its interface not with the universe but with a megalith that seems almost as vast and incomprehensible: Institution. She emerges feeling recharged, very gently washed. And, even at its most pedantic and time-sucking, compared to looking after Ida it's a stroll in the park.

She can only take it for an hour at a time though and is relieved when Linus Frank pushes in. A sci-fi novelist about her own age, he's a nice guy, naturally open and funny, someone she could perhaps have fancied in another life. Ever since meeting his stunning girlfriend they've developed an easy friendship, during which they've never felt the need to meet outside the university or the local pub they sometimes sprint to after class. Today they chat about a student he wants to disembowel and then she wonders if he's ever had the shower situation. Yes, he says, and he was equally unnerved.

— But why?

— Easy. They talk about us.

— You think?

— The MAs. The undergrads are too busy doing E and shagging. We're way too old to bother with. But the grads do it all the time, trying to get inside our lives. I don't want everyone in my Modern Writing class knowing I've got a hairy back.

— Do you have a hairy back?

— Not any bloody more I don't.

She laughs, and it takes her back to that catkin.

— Female pubic hair.

— Great band. Loved the first album.

— Serious. Thoughts?

— Doesn't bother me. Let it grow let it grow let it grow.

— You're just being PC. Truth.

— Alright. Last girl I slept with before Goddess was a bit free-range. It was fine when she was naked. But I didn't like it sticking out the sides of her pants. Or on the beach. Wanted to take a strimmer to it.

— Why?

— Lines. Classical order. And it got stuck in me teeth.

— What about the other way?

— Nah, makes me feel like a paedophile. What about you?

— This is just a general discussion, young man.

— I mean how do you feel about blokes? Hair?

— On the balls?

— I suppose.

— I can't imagine anything worse than hairless testicles.

— And backs? I've always wanted to ask a woman this. What do you really think about hairy backs?

— How hairy are we talking?

— Right, Linus says, and stands. He hops to the door and locks it. He turns from her and pulls his shirt over his head, revealing a slim, tight, mole-patterned back with a fine gulley running up the centre. The lower half is mottled with hair, brown and curling like that on his head though not as thick. Alice stares at it through her laughter and begins to cough as Linus pulls the shirt back on.

— Fucking great. Lois says she doesn't care. Lying bee-yatch.

— She probably doesn't. I wouldn't either. I wasn't laughing at that. The situation.

— So you don't care?

— No. Save yourself the agony. Just be yourself, Linus.

— I will, Oprah. Right, then.

— Right then what?

— Get your bush out.

— Fuck off, she tells him, laughing even more now. And you can't speak to me like that any more. I'm a famous poet now.

Her first lecture is at twelve. First years or, as for some reason they are now called, Level Four students. She's never even bothered trying to work that one out and nor does she ever use the term, something that seems to endear her to them. She likes this bunch in return, for they seem more switched on than in past years, marked by the fact that a decent proportion of them actually turn up to her lectures. It's still a surprise to walk into the Lockyer and see that it is actually two-thirds full.

The class is a skills module. The students have to write different verse forms, a play scene, plus the opening of a novel, all to see what structures help which kinds of idea. She likes to teach it and tries to do the work herself that she sets the students, particularly enjoying writing villanelles and sestinas, ancient verse forms built around repetition. She feels like a singer practising scales when she creates them, though it is the sonnet that really grabs her. There are three in her latest collection, two Shakespearian and one Petrarchan, her favourite in the entire book. Something about the mixture of compression and the need to turn the whole thing round. The mere thought of writing a sonnet hones her, makes her cut through to the quick of a thing. She can feel one taking shape now, centred on the little tuft she can't quite shift from her mind. She stares out over the raked seating and is filled with the urge to ask all her female students to pull their pants down.

Maybe it's something they can include in the National Student Survey.

The next class she takes is as enjoyable as the first in the end. She's been dreading it though, so much so in fact that she's been unable to do any preparation. It's not a module she normally teaches on. It's Linus's, Writers and their Work, which does what it says on the box. He gets people to come in and talk about their writing. Today that writer is her and she feels like a rabbit in multiple headlights as she enters this smaller room, forty-odd second years looking out across six lines of tables. The first thing she does is ask them to join up and move forward, which they do grudgingly, like twelve-year-olds. She feels she's in for a hideous hour but it turns out not to be, largely because Linus is a hard bastard and has actually got them to read her book.

She starts to speak about how she got from an interest in reading poetry to seeing her first poem in print. She talks about the realisation that only in this particular form, the poem, could she explain to anyone any of the things that were important to her. This is a departure for her and for them because in the past she has only spoken to them about *their* work. The structure of their learning has left little room for her to enter the arena as an actual poet, almost as if it has nothing to do with her job of teaching them. She was employed because of her publication record but since then, she realises, she might as well have been anyone. She sees now that this connection between her own work and theirs is very important for them, and she has not been listened to with such complete attention before.

This quiet though intense scrutiny leads her on to more revelations about herself. They are structural rather than particular: how she wound up as the sort of person who needs to express herself. When one of the brighter students puts a hand up to say that there is still something very hidden in her work she is shocked, as she knows this is true but only James has ever seen it. When more students start chipping in she realises that it's she who is learning now, that she's never had such intense, focused feedback. Not even her editor has gone into it like this and the reviews certainly never have, the clipped but respectful paragraphs she's received in online journals. It's a new and exciting sensation, but challenging too, for she can tell that some of them haven't really understood what she's been trying to do. Or if they have they're not particularly impressed. She knows this must have been the case before but she's never had a bad review. She gets, not critique, but silence.

Get used to it, she tells herself.

It's just before the end that it comes to a head. It's been a fabulous, dynamic session, making her determined to bring her creative self to class more often. The hour has spun by and she is wrapping up when the boy from Estonia puts up his hand. The foreign students are often the best and this one is almost too clever, weariness hanging off him at the dim-witted nature of both students and staff alike. He hasn't said anything today, which has left her a little disappointed as she would have liked his take. The rest of the class are beginning to shuffle but she stops them.

— Juri? she says.

— They are all talking to each other.

— What do you mean?

— The poems. They talk, back and forth. Have different voices. Three voices. It's like they're written by three different poets. All mixed up. Why didn't you say anything about this?

His tone is accusatory but it is what he has said that pins her. She doesn't know what to say and blushes like the American girl, twisting with an uncomfortable sense of being seen. Found out, like Ida, when James asked what those After Eight wrappers were doing underneath her bed. For nobody has seen this before. Not her editor. No reviewer. Not even James. Her secret. The book has a shape, a body she thought she'd buried so deep nobody would find it. But this boy has. She is shocked and thrilled, this adding to the attention all these young people have given her, amazing even though they were told to read her book. She flusters a response, embarrassed by love of them all, and then thanks them, ducking out before Juri can follow her as he often does from other classes, battering her with points he couldn't be bothered to raise in the company of lesser mortals.

She grabs a latte from the refectory. In the corridor she sees Peter Shale walking towards her with the Head of School. The Head doesn't see her and so she can't tell if she's heard about the shortlist yet. But Peter does, though he pretends not to. He glances aside quickly, and it makes her smile all the way to her office.

The last thing to happen that day is something that takes her by surprise. And she doesn't know if it should make her smile or not. Linus tells her she has a message.

— Er, but wasn't it your rule that we don't dive across the office to answer each other's phones?

— Kept calling back though. Persistent bugger. Number's on your desk.

— What did he want?

— To speak to you, numbnuts.

She doesn't call back. She means to but has received about twenty emails since leaving her desk, most about the end-of-year show that it's her thrilling task to organise. When the phone rings she grabs it automatically.

— Alice, the voice says.

— Hello?

— Richard.

He's pronounced his name and left a space. As if she should know it. She doesn't, and after racking her brains, as she did last night when that package arrived, she's irritated.

— I've been reading your book.

— I see. But does she? This Richard's easy familiarity annoys her and she wonders if it's a prospective student with stalker tendencies. But then she thinks: interviewer. She'll be on Radio 4. Excerpts on the *Today* programme, a thing on *Front Row*. Great, she says. I mean, sorry you had to. Or something.

— Can we meet? I've called about five times today.

— I was teaching. Is it…?

— What?

— Are you…? But what if he's not an interviewer? How totally up herself would that sound? I'm sorry, but can you tell me why you're calling?

— Have you ever written a play?

— What?

— People on stage. Talking, mostly.

— No, I haven't and…

— Well, I want you to, so how about it?

— What? she says, shaking her head, needing, finally, to get to the source of this. Do I know you?

— Shit, the man says, and lets out a booming laugh. My wife told me you were a poet. Gave you some clothes.

— She did what?

— And your husband made me laugh my arse off. When can we meet?

She doesn't know what to say. He's talking again, how he Googled her the night before, found her poems on *3:AM Magazine*, *The White Review*, *The Other Room*. How they're so full of tension and conflict. He's saying the sorts of things Juri did but in greater and more practical detail. Her secret. Not any bloody more. She tries to get a word in but he just goes on and then she's distracted by the Head of School, pushing open the door. Her creased though still beautiful face is lit. Grinning, with her thumb up, she approaches Alice's desk.

7

SHE DOESN'T want anyone to see her. She stands outside the bespoke furniture shop next door, pretending to look at sofa covers. She's not embarrassed, though she might have been a week ago. She'd have wondered what people thought. Credit crunch biting? Richard not getting any work? Now she doesn't care, but she still doesn't want to be noticed. Private time. She stares at the sofa covers until she really is looking at them: for the kitchen room? Chloe Morgan did hers last month; they really brought the room up. She stashes the thought and looks round again, and when she's sure as she can be that no St Saviour's parents are around she goes inside.

It's the second thing she's done that morning that would not normally spring up into her life. The first was a little more radical than pushing open the doors of the Mencap shop and it needed to be planned. It worked well, and this easy facility for the furtive shocks her, makes her think of herself in World War Two, coaxing secrets out of lean Nazi officers. That would probably have ended in cigarette burns and a firing squad and she wonders if a similar thing is waiting for her now, at the end of this bizarre subterfuge. And it is bizarre, for she has never in her life followed someone.

She couldn't just lope after him. He would have been bound to turn and see her and so would everyone else, still standing outside the church. One thing she knows for certain is that people notice difference and, while she could have said to anyone that she was going to walk down into Greenwich, someone might have wanted to come with her. It was why she thought of the bike, digging it out of the garage and pumping air into the tyres the night before. She asked Michael to help, the son she'd been so terrified of seeing, whom she'd stared at when he slouched in with Richard. Not a dead flower inside her but neither was there the usual riot of cheap, colourful blooms that usually blossomed inside her ribcage when she so much as thought of him. There was nothing. She had to hide this though, and she did, turning away from him quickly. She told him he needed a haircut before banging on to Rich about how well Niamh was doing in music. This gangly girl living in their house.

She rode the bike across the Heath like some mad aunt, Niamh laughing on the handlebars. Outside the church she hasn't been to for a little too long, she stickle-bricked herself into a conversation with two of the more attractive mums, making sure she avoided Rachel Green, who cut her a quizzical glance as she leant the bike against a parking meter. She clocked him of course, early today, standing across on the grass with dancing, windblown hair. Same coat. When Dominic (not Dom, she has decided) came up with Niamh she wanted to lift him up and kiss him, something that might not actually have seemed inappropriate for such a small boy. But it would have brought James over. Instead she was polite but dismissive, which she could see he found a little difficult to understand. She rode that and chatted on until the hand bell sounded and the church began to fill, Niamh breaking out of her line.

— I love you, Mummy.

Amelia smiled and bent to kiss her, but could think of no reply. Instead she picked up her bike and pedalled off towards Greenwich Park.

Now she waits inside the gates. A beautiful day. She knows he'll come through there. When he does he passes less than ten feet from her but is so immersed in his thoughts she might have been naked. She's not surprised, imagining him like that, daydreaming about books, the American poet whose name didn't register. Thinking of this, she is scythed to the core, for the wife is a poet too, something tossed out casually when they were drinking tea. Nothing casual about it though for it was a marker laid down, an assertion that, in spite of donated clothes, she was in no way jealous of Amelia. Not a less successful woman but a different one. A caution too, an early refusal of friendship, as though she was putting Amelia in her place. She pictures her and James in the evening, talking about literature, the battered stovetop coffee maker on a chipped antique tile between them. Pious, she decides, and this includes James, though it in no way diminishes her almost physical need to know where he lives.

She waits to see which way he'll go before overtaking him again. If he takes the centre road he'll be heading for the main gates at the bottom of the hill but instead he cuts off towards the tennis courts. She takes a different path and waits beside a tree, watching as he turns out of the park through the small exit next to the White House. She follows and is then dismayed because he seems to have disappeared. But he must have gone down the grassy steps on to Hyde Vale. She can't go down them with the bike and not be heard so she pedals furiously to the top of the road, just catching a glimpse of James as he enters Diamond Terrace. Does he live there? Has she got him all wrong? No, she decides, and swoops down Hyde Vale and back up Point Hill, just in time to see him come out the other end of the terrace.

James emerges quickly and she's sure he'll see her, knowing she has to come up with some excuse. She decides on the antiques shop on Royal Hill but she doesn't need to use it because again he's oblivious, though this time because something seems to have happened. A phone call? Bad news? Whatever it is, he looks miserable in some deep, almost fathomless way. She knows he won't see her now so she locks the bike and follows him on foot, down Royal Hill towards Straightsmouth.

A red door, newly painted.

Number Seven.

The Mencap is nearly empty. This allows her to see it clearly and her initial reaction is surprise. It's clean, light, selling a lot of first-hand goods that are self-consciously Fairtrade or at the very least organic, though how can a shampoo be that? In a plastic bottle? It seems to all intents and purposes like a normal retail establishment though it is soon made clear to her that yes, she is in a charity shop. This by the staff. The middle-aged woman who smiles up at her from the till looks as if she could work anywhere, but the man beside her, in his fifties, is far less than five feet tall, one wall-eye closed, the other startlingly open, one ear encased in a medical dressing. Fussing behind him is a tall woman in a tartan mini-dress. She's made up to look like an extreme Amy Winehouse, with white pancake and black eyeliner applied, it seems, from ten yards away, a pair of Deely Boppers on her head. A good look for a teenager but this woman is in her sixties. From the curtain behind them a boy appears, no more than twenty, overweight with yellow-framed glasses. He's sweaty and chirpy, the kind who used to hang out with younger children, she feels, all of which fills her with the unnerving sense of having stepped into a fantasy novel. She's lived in Blackheath for fifteen years and never once seen these people.

The clothes are decent. She leafs through the men's first, sees garments that are clean, not that worn, far fewer on display than she would have thought. It could actually be Richard's wardrobe she's looking at, a leather jacket he'd especially like though she thinks it's hideous. She turns to the women's side and finds an even higher standard, though the seasons are mashed up, a brocade chemise from last spring next to a couple of peasant blouses she might have bought five years ago. Richard found them sexy. Told her she looked like a Flake ad, liked her to keep them on when he made love to her. She picks both blouses off the rail in turn, smiles and sets them back.

Nothing she wants. She almost expects there to be a raincoat but there isn't. She's disappointed, though there's something special in just standing amongst these honest but no longer wanted garments. Women have worn these. Been happy or sad in them, eaten and worked and snogged and drunk and had their periods. Their sweat has caked the armpits of the blouses. Their crotches have pressed into the trousers on tube trains and in cabs, the belts and skirts undone by amorous fingers. Now these clothes are here, cast-off, separated from their stories, which makes it dangerous to buy them, she thinks. She wouldn't know exactly what she was taking with her, something she realises she felt when she saw Alice's coat in the playground. Beautiful. But it wasn't hers, no matter that she'd bought it. It hung off her like a distracted boyfriend, still in love with someone else.

And the state of her hair. Alice just *has* to buy that shampoo.

Upstairs her eyes flit between kids' clothes, books, toys. She goes through these first, latching on to a funny-looking game in which a plastic, battery-powered elephant blows silk butterflies out of its trunk, for children to catch in coloured nets. It's for ages four and above and as the box is battered enough she decides to buy it. She takes it back downstairs, along with a cardigan for Niamh, which she doesn't give much thought to. She's heading straight for the till but is pulled up by the homewares section, arranged along the right-hand wall. It is much more like the charity shops she remembers. Three cheap wine glasses beside an overcomplicated corkscrew. An onyx ashtray in the shape of the sphinx beside a glass chess set with, the label states, three pieces missing. The whole effect being of detritus. Life shit. It makes her feel a little nauseous and she's about to turn away when a snow globe catches her eye. She used to have these as a child and she stares into a snowy alpine village she can almost believe is real, in spite of the fact that the woman in the centre of it is taller than the houses. She's wearing some sort of national costume and is singing, something Amelia can hear though there is no music function. She's lifted by the sensation and gives the globe a shake before setting it on top of the elephant game.

Outside, the wind has fallen. She drops her purchases off at home, finding another Laithwaites box to put the elephant game in. Then she sits at the computer in the nook under the stairs and logs into Google Earth. She stares down at James's garden but he isn't there. She wants to go back to Greenwich and stand outside that door until he comes out. Follow him.

Bump into him, say gosh, hello. She's desperate for this but instead she grabs her bag and hurries to Blackheath station.

Will work call the self she has lost back home? She knows somehow that it won't, for as much as she'll have to revert, act in ways she did before, these will be performed tasks. Just, in fact, as they always were. The mere busy-ness of it all will at least provide some respite and there is purpose in her step. Waiting for the train however leaves her static, with nothing to do, and she clenches and unclenches her fists with helplessness. She thinks again about how she followed him, something that seemed so natural, and now can't believe she actually did. But she so wants to see him and she almost thinks of phoning in sick and doing it again. She doesn't, but only because the train comes, and she forces herself aboard, holding on to a seatback until the doors close.

Is it age, this? A need to be found attractive by a man from *outside* before the long, slow slide? She needs to understand it, to look around as everything slips from under her. She needs to get a grip, corral this thing with understanding so that she can deal, decide just what to do.

So *what is it*? Have they met before? She wonders this as the train shoots on to London Bridge. Two sunburnt kids on a Spanish beach who connected in some incredible, unbreakable way, while their mums swapped recipes and their dads nodded grudging respect to Maggie Thatcher? Or is it that they haven't met but are actually meant for each other? As if there really is only one other human being on the entire planet you should be with? It certainly feels like that but she doesn't believe in such nonsense. So maybe it's just that she's bored. With her life. Marriage. But that's not true, the latter at least. Richard is attractive, successful. They talk, they laugh, they get on. They even have sex, the last time only two nights ago when he'd come home from rehearsals and told her he'd just spent the entire day watching beautiful young people kissing.

So what, then? What spun the ordered Rubik's Cube inside her and made this fractured mess? The four-oh was a year ago. Not that. She scours the recent past. First day at school, another legion of mothers, all just a little younger than her. Was that it? Or the girls' night at Sarah's where Jan's cosmetic surgeon friend told each of them with a shrugged matter-of-factness what they needed done. She shakes her head, sure it was neither, so moves the question on: how can she get it straight again? The frustration inside her is intense but she does know one thing: until she works it out she has to be careful. Not do anything else. *Following* him? Cling on, she tells herself, stare through it like the woman in that snow globe.

She's at the office by one. The steps outside are busy and she recognises some of the faces from their photographs. Inside, she blinks, as if it were an age since she was in a working environment, though when was her last job? Two weeks ago? A month? She finds it difficult to accept that she is actually there, and not at home, though when she finds Malcolm she is brought into the present. He's testy as usual, spitting bile into his iPhone, raking his free hand back through the long, wavy grey hair that marks him out as the outrageous old roué that he is. When he gets off he swivels his chrome chair towards her, man boobs contoured perfectly by his Paul Smith T-shirt, and tells her how beautiful she's looking. How he's dreamed of her. It's the usual stuff and she barely hears it any more. An old friend of Richard's, Malcolm has been professing his love-lust for years, and doesn't mind who's listening. Today it is Neil, the young, gay casting assistant, and he seems a bit shocked. She has to admit that he is going a bit far today, especially when he tells them what he did last night.

— Couldn't sleep. Went to this knocking shop near my house. Fantasy Massage, you believe the place is called?

— Jesus, Malcolm.

— Where for the niggardly sum of thirty quid I received the finest hand shandy my fifty-one-year-old todger has known. Shut me eyes, came all over your marvellous tits, Amelia.

— I'm flattered.

— The honour was mine. Fantastic tits, Neil, would even impress a woofter like you.

— In your dreams, Neil says, shaking his head, but Amelia smiles, for Malcolm does know what he's talking about in this regard. In pre-kid days she and Richard went to Andalucía with Malcolm and his then girlfriend, and she felt his unfettered gaze on her body most of the time they were there. He's even shown her a photograph he kept, her topless under a parasol, and which she's tried to grab and destroy but of which she's secretly proud.

— Right, Malcolm says, let 'em in.

She's a casting director. Freelance. At least a small corner of her is. She works – when she works – mostly in TV commercials and this is one, a cereal ad. It has been her job to find twin brothers in their mid-thirties, a task harder than more generic assignments for while there are many who fit that bill not many are actors and Malcolm is insistent that he won't use civilians. The client, one of the big ad agencies, would have liked to save the money but they like Malcolm so have agreed to his demands, so long as sufficient twins in the profession can be located. Amelia has done Malcolm a favour, having thought a little laterally. She hasn't told

Malcolm but, while at least half of all the twin groups are actors, some have brought along siblings who aren't. He won't notice, she tells herself, and once the client himself is seated she asks Neil to show the first pair in.

The idea behind the ad is good. Over The Hollies singing 'He Ain't Heavy' the viewer will be shown faked home movie footage of twins from birth upwards, all displaying fraternal unity and love. As adults they seem to do the same as they appear for breakfast dressed in identical shirts and ties. When they realise there's only one serving of cornflakes left, however, they resort to slapstick fighting, with bowls and milk flying everywhere. As Neil films them, the first two guys act this out and Amelia is mesmerised, not quite knowing why. She stares, letting them go on longer than necessary, until Malcolm draws a finger across his throat. Neil stops recording and she thanks the two guys, asking if they'll wait for a second. She leans into Malcolm, breathing Acqua di Parma.

— What? he barks.

— It's breakfast. You sure you want them in shirts?

— Yep. Off to work at the same place. They love each other.

— But what about pyjamas? More sympathetic? Or vests? Funnier? Shirtless, bit sexy?

— Nah.

— But you've been known to change your mind on set. You always change your mind on set.

— So?

— We don't want any surprises.

— Like what?

— Tats. Or, no offence to a flabby fuck like you, my love, but what if you say no, actually, let's lose the shirts. And they turn out to be flabby fucks.

— Good point. Lads, whip your kit off.

The next pair are so similar it's unnerving. They're dressed in identical suits and glasses, which really creeps her out. When they disrobe there is a slight disparity however and she sees this in two more of the pairs, and in one case markedly, their life pathways clearly written on their torsos. One of two lads from Ilford is honed so much he looks as if he's wearing sci-fi body armour. He's the actor of the pair and his vanity is not shared by his brother, whose paler body is normal, dad-like. There is more meaning in this for her but again she can't quite catch hold of it. She thanks them and the non-actor shrugs his shirt back on quickly, looking a little humiliated. His brother walks over and shakes all of their hands, not realising that his twin has left.

The session is over and the client is pleased. He's made his choice, which Malcolm will later veto as a matter of course, and he invites them all out for drinks. Malcolm and Neil accept, knowing an expense account is to be raided, but she says she has to dash. This is only half true but she's insistent and once she's sure that Neil has emailed her the casting she skips out on to Newburgh then Carnaby Street, where a loose throng of mostly Japanese and Scandinavian tourists are checking out the shops. She's the foreigner here actually for the bright, poppy window displays are meant to call to them, not her. She is momentarily affronted by this and on a whim she cuts into Kingly Court, and here she is whispered to. Almost immediately her body flies through the muted window of Carte Blanche and into the Strelli skirt-suit there, does so before she can stop it. Nor can she stop the relief, at being noticed. Tailored for. Or the pleasure: she'd look good in that. Really good, and what's more she could actually afford to go in there and buy it. The flush of pleasure spreads and she knows that she just might, next week perhaps or the week after, if only as an acknowledgement of where she's got to in the world. She won't do it today but instead will let the power of it build inside her until it feels as though she already owns it, that handing over the Amex is just underlining that. She pictures the carrier over her arm as she takes it home and then later, striding across the Heath – just the jacket, with jeans – towards appreciative comments in the playground that she'll brush off like lint. Her life will be bigger, more complete, the mere idea of which injects her veins with controlled, steady fire. She stares and can't deny that suddenly she is happy, light inside, though it can't simply be at the sight of these expensive clothes whose presence inside this shop is already becoming doubtful, as they transfer themselves to her. Can it? No. Something else has momentarily freed her from the spell cast on her and, for some reason, it is Malcolm.

Amelia blinks. The image of herself in these clothes vanishes as she realises something that is simple and obvious, but in that moment very important. She likes Malcolm. Really likes him. She loves him even, the feeling like a jack-in-a-box opening in her mind, surprising but immediately undeniable. This big, arrogant, largely objectionable man: he's part of her life. First he was just a friend of her sometime boyfriend. Contentious, swaggering. Then he was a friend of her steady boyfriend and then a friend of her husband, after which he became a godfather. He's become part of her, one of the pillars holding up her life, and in spite of his lurid patter she knows he'd do anything for her. For a second a cloud comes over because God, shouldn't she have been more picky? Sought out only the finest and most brilliant people to take up such permanent residence inside her? But

Malcolm is real. Substantial. His weight doesn't just come from chateaubriands paid for by hungry-looking thirty-somethings. And, unlike most people who exist for her only in their external shape, she knows him, has heard his *story*, which means she is linked forever to the person she saw at the end of it, the real person he pretends not to be, the last figure inside the huge Russian doll of him, so tiny it could fit inside her hand.

This feeling grows as she walks through Soho. It's a place she has, in the past, felt ambivalence towards. It has never totally accepted her, in spite of the fact that she doesn't just hang out there like most of the pavement candy but earns her living among its secretive, shoulder-turned streets. She should feel like a real insider but the people she passes look right in a way she doesn't think she does. They all know something she doesn't, so much so that she's often wanted to stop and ask them the secret. Malcolm is one. Richard another. Not trendy. Never that. But like Malcolm he walks down Dean Street as if the street needs him to exist, which it probably does. Whereas she feels like a visitor every time she goes there.

What's this? Glow for Malcolm and now Richard? So maybe coming out today has made her get a grip, see life clearly again. She clings on to the feeling, knowing it can help her if she lets it, turning it to James. What hooked her? That he was new, excited, unsure? Was it the potential in his life that took her? If so, she needs to look at her own, realise what she's got. And can go on to have. It's not Niamh's fault that she hates her fucking coffee machine. No one forced any of this on her.

Just having these thoughts stops her in her tracks and she gives out a laugh, thinking again about these two friends, one of whom she married. Substantial. Real. Successful now the both of them but never any doubt about that, not even back when she first met Richard in that grubby pub theatre where you could hear the bogs flushing during the quiet bits. And she needs that. Not money. She just needs to feel their heft, their masculine energy bowling through the world with great V-shaped washes in their wake. Malcolm is gauche, insecure and obscene. But he moves people out of his way, which James does not. He's one of the people flailing in the churned-up water behind men like Malcolm and Richard.

And there he is, sitting on a bench in Leicester Square.

She's cut through Chinatown on her way down to Charing Cross. Train back home. Dinner with Richard, their weekly date, the Argentinian place in the village. All day she's been dreading it but suddenly she's looking forward. Being with her man. Telling him about Malcolm's wet daydream. She sees James from behind and can't believe it, thinking perhaps that the point she has been making in her mind is somehow underlining itself. But no, it is him, and the feelings she's having unfurl further for what is he doing? Standing, walking towards that comedy club. Checking his watch as he stares at the window. Scales fall because how prosaic: stand-up. A night out with some laddy mates. He's one of these, she says to herself, staring at all the people in the tacky square she only ever walks through, hasn't stopped in for maybe twenty years. He'll drink pints of urine-coloured lager out of plastic glasses, call out a heckle from the darkness no one laughs at. She laughs herself, almost rubbing her wrists with the freedom she feels until she sees his double there, in the window, sees what he is looking at.

8

HANGOVERS. A benefit of this new life layout: they don't bite. Oh, there's pain, but not like there used to be, not enough to take over the day. It's just something else to carry, like Dom's school bag or Ida, who simply won't go in the buggy at all this morning. Even when it's just him and Dom, walking across the Heath, there isn't space for it and once he's alone, striding back down to Greenwich station, he almost enjoys the feeling. The world seems closer to him. Women check him out more. Something about being heavier, slower, all of his energy huddled in on himself. James Dean, he thinks, how the man used to look as if he was locked up in a house, peering out.

On the train he looks over his notes. At work he gives a lecture on Walt Whitman, a guest thing, something he promised before he got the sab. He leaves quickly afterwards, just nipping into the student office for some papers he agreed to second-mark. He walks down to Waterloo and on the train to Wimbledon reads them, the same arguments repeated either by fairly supple or more clumsy young minds. A lens, going in and out of focus, an image he should mention to Alice. Thoughts of his wife spike a smile and he lets his mind create images of her until the train pulls into the station.

Ten minutes later he's looking at her.

He's done this before. He'll tell her one day but for now it's his secret and as he takes his seat at the top of the lecture theatre he thinks back to Sussex. She was outside the library, handing out her writing magazine. They'd already met and she'd seemed nervous, the only undergraduate invited to join a postgrad Creative Writing class, run by a visiting New Yorker. He'd been intrigued, but unable, really, to see her. He watched her handing out her paper and it was a different person from the day before.

In the subsequent weeks these two Alices became so defined it was as though she had a twin sister. In class she'd be defensive, sometimes overly hostile about the work of the other, older students. When her own work was being critiqued she'd either insist it was their fault if they didn't see it or else agree it was shit, claiming she'd scribbled it down on the way there. He kept quiet and when she chewed up his own sub-sub-Carver efforts he could only shrug, knowing the class was tourism for him. Unlike her. For Alice it was obviously essential, something she was totally useless at hiding.

He saw her in the library, staring at her books so hard he thought the words might get broken off the page. On the grass with friends, similarly scruffy in their fleamarket threads and self-conscious piercings, the names of various festivals floating up as he walked past. Once he saw her alone in a nest of beach stones, another time kissing someone in a club on student night, her body swivelled very deliberately to the left. These unseen observations helped him understand her, made him vow that he'd experience this Alice. He set about breaking into her life and managed it, though even after that he needed to see her. And not be seen. For when they were together he knew how much she kept from him.

But Brighton was small. In London you didn't bump into people, or see them walking past. He didn't realise how much he missed these chance sightings until he got one. He was walking along the Southbank. She was working at the *Big Issue* then and he spotted her, his new wife, sitting on a bench, interviewing a famous actress. He stopped and saw that focus and was fascinated, wowed by her complete and serious competence, the body language that told him she was in no way intimidated by this almost comically gorgeous woman. The reverse looked true if anything and, as he watched, the actress seemed to fade, until it seemed as though Alice was talking to the air. He had the renewed sense of having found someone unique and set apart and when the actress stalked back over to the theatre he was filled with the urge to rush up, cover her eyes from behind and tease her, tell her what he'd seen. Instead he sat there, ripped open with love, as she packed up her Dictaphone and weaved off between the plane trees.

Today she is wonderful. She holds these young people, enthrals them with her take on Sonnet 14, her understanding so unlike his own. From within. The lecture lasts an hour and just before the end he slips out the back, intending to leave, but instead standing in the corridor because his fix has not been intense enough. Risky this as he's met a couple of her colleagues but he doesn't care, wanting desperately to see her moving through her working environment. He walks round to the front door of the theatre and finds a pillar to stand behind and at two minutes to the hour he hears the surge. Alice is carried by it and he follows, getting ever closer until he's right behind and can smell the perfume he bought her, drifting out from beneath her hair. He could touch her now. Or call her – for what, he wonders, happens to her face when his name is flashing? The idea dismisses itself: he isn't there to spy on her, catch her out. He has come to see her. Just that. He keeps step until she turns left down another corridor and then, as on the Southbank, he lets her walk away.

It's she who calls. He's back home, the last of the papers on the kitchen table. He picks up and tells her this-had-better-be-goddamn-important-young-lady-because-I'm-one-*hell*-of-a-busy-man.

— It is. Should I trim my bush more?

— No. Neil From Next Door would be able to spy on us.

— Different bush.

— Same answer, different reason. I hope. That why you called?

— No. I'll take Dom and Ida out for tea after school so you can carry on working. Okay?

— More than.

— And I was curious. What is it?

— What?

— I forgot this morning. Funny. Something that ridiculous happens but the next day it's just not in your mind.

— What isn't?

— You haven't seen it?

— Seen *what*?

— Look out of the kitchen window.

— Shit, he says, doing that.

And then finds, in the enormous box, a pedalo.

He's already gone through the night before. Opened that box and taken everything out. The gig, so easy. Like that lecture theatre, unloading itself. Now he can see how he could have made it even better. He makes notes on his laptop, just to do it while he's thinking, and then the gig is gone and *she's* standing there, smiling with her big teeth. He couldn't for a second see her without the backdrop of her house intruding, as if she'd brought the place with her. The husband was different: he couldn't imagine him in that kitchen, or anywhere actually. He was so immediate, so present, sweeping aside the TV guy like a cardboard cutout. He got to James before Amelia did and pumped his hand as though they were old mates. What happened then was irresistible, though he did want to resist it. He didn't want to go out with them. He wanted to be on his own, feel the echoes running through him. Instead he was hustled, battered first by Amelia's explanation, that she'd been walking through Leicester Square and had seen his picture outside the Store. Called Richard on a whim. He was then battered by questions from this Richard, which Amelia answered for him, the praise flowing down like ticker tape. It carried on to the members' club he was bustled to, the very famous one, still fêted as if he'd just conquered Broadway, some very well-known faces staring at him, wondering who the hell he was. Richard ordered wine he was never going to accept any payment for and then dinner, James's assertion that he'd already eaten falling like mud thrown at a castle. He pushed through, did Richard, knew what you wanted, and James felt as if he was riding on the man's shoulders rather than sitting beside him. It was irritating and thrilling, relaxing and exhausting, and when one of the most celebrated senior actors in the country sat down with them it didn't feel odd, or special. Richard chastised him, telling him they had a matinee tomorrow, that he should go to bed naughty boy. Instead the man ordered champagne, his leg pressed very firmly against James's as he leaned forward to pour it.

— What do you do? he asked, in a voice like a television commercial.

James was a stand-up. Not his own answer of course but Richard's, who'd been told what James really was but had clearly decided it didn't have the zing. He was brilliant, Richard insisted, something he found himself rising to in spite of his annoyance. The old actor laughed at his jokes, rocking, his teeth like a horse's, hand on James's knee as he fought for balance. Amelia prompted him, returned him to his set, so sweet she insisted but had he really called them? It wasn't a recording? He told her not and had them all howling, though it was then that it came to him, the other thing he'd revealed. Intimate details of his sex life to a mother from his child's new church school. Oh, he said to Alice, in his mind, Amelia Leigh knows I shoved my finger up your bum. He whispered all this to the actor who doubled up, was killed by it, then wouldn't tell Amelia what he was laughing at. All the while James shook his head and smiled, aware that he must be having an incredible time. But it was like being at school. As if he wasn't really present. Wondering just how the hell he'd got there.

They stopped the taxi on the High Street to let him out. He shoved a twenty into Richard's hand and made him take it.

The pedalo is blue. The top half. The hull is white. It is a two-person pedalo, not one of the really big ones he's noticed recently on the boating lake in Greenwich Park. Just a small pedalo really, nothing to get excited about. James walks round it and then goes inside, hitting the Skype key on his desktop.

— Bastard, is the word that he leaves on his brother's answerphone.

When Alice gets home at close to seven the kids are knackered, something she has very deliberately brought about. They trudge into the bathroom as if retreating from

Moscow and are soon switched off and out of their lives. James cooks while Alice tells him about her day, about seeing Peter Shale in the corridor, and what the Head of School said. She's energised and he's happy for her, knowing her job will be different now. She'll grow. And all the while she's speaking he sees delicious and illicit images of her, for he was of course in this day of hers. He asks how her lecture went, to see if her account tallies with his own experience of it, but she talks about a later one, in which she discussed her own work. She tells him about the student she saw in the shower and then asks him again about his gig, wanting to really hear about it. He tells her and she seems to resist what he's saying. Almost as if she doesn't believe him. To underline it he tells her about the TV guy but she doesn't seem to be listening.

— What was he like?

— Usual. Got his card somewhere. I can't believe I used to...

— No. The husband. What's his name?

— Richard. Why'd you ask?

Alice pauses and sips her wine.

— No reason, she says.

When they make love that night she is assertive and particular, eschewing all but cursory foreplay, in no way embarrassed about what she wants him to do. He's uneasy, as if this should be hidden still. Perhaps always. Less acknowledged. Snuck up upon each time. But within seconds it's as if he's on a rollercoaster and isn't quite strapped in, though she is, happily visiting heights with the assumption he's having the same experience. Which he isn't. He might catch up and wants to, but what he doesn't want to do is come until he feels a greater connection. Do women know this? he wonders. That men fake it too, though physical processes continue unaffected?

In the event he doesn't come at all, as an air-raid siren sends Alice out of bed. He hears the pad of her feet and the shushing sound she makes so that Dom won't wake up too. He hears a light switch click on and then Alice say shit.

— Chicken pox, she calls, from the bathroom.

The weekend is eaten. Gone. The plans they made to stretch themselves out into the metropolis they live at the edge of are cut like kite strings, the Miró exhibition that is ending soon floating off forever. But James doesn't mind. For this is family. This, at least, he saw. Signed up to. Weekends he never feels resentment about his past self. For at weekends he doesn't stand out. The semiotics of his role as child carer revert to the traditional: he's just one more grufty bloke at the Sunday morning soft-play, giving his wife a lie in. Time doesn't chug through him the way it does if he ever goes there during the week, but seems to pause for a bit. The other men nod but remain within the circles of their own duties, do not try to interact like the House Daddies during the week. For this he is profoundly grateful and he enjoys being alongside these slow, hungover men, the previous night written clearly on their bagged eyes and trainer-jowls. More importantly they are all effectively naked, stripped of their working clothes, and it's very hard to tell who does what. There's the odd tit sporting brogues and a double cuff shirt but most are in jeans and trainers, twenty-odd fleeces and hoodies puddled round the edges of the multicoloured space into which the various children hurl themselves. Soft-play. He thinks of his life before Alice, the girls he slept with, went out with briefly, had longer liaisons with. It seemed so real. There was pain at times but now he knows that he was never in danger of being seriously hurt.

Ida likes to go mental on the bouncy castle with the bigger kids. He's fascinated by this, unable to work out why there never seem to be accidents of any major import. The lot of them mingle like gluons in a magnetic field, not quite colliding for some reason. Dom will try it before going off on his own, calling out for James to watch him as, studious as ever, he makes it to the end of the balance bar. He'll build a tower out of big squishy blocks which Ida will demolish like a line guard, something he's finally used to now and will laugh at as much as James does. At the end of the session Alice will appear, bleary from sleep, thankful of the rest but a little jealous of the time they've spent together, interrogating the kids for detail as if that will make up for it.

James doesn't care what he does at the weekend. Bungying around Greenwich? Going to the Tate? Kew? The Chelsea Phys or the Museum of Childhood? It's all the same, individual environments barely impacting on them. It's the light he's looking at, the changed light, the world refracted through the four of them. Through Dom. Ida. Dom and Ida, their growing relationship, Ida slowly but surely inculcating innocent Dom into her secret, wicked society. Dom and Alice, ever so slightly going the other way, his need of her a little further from the surface than it was, her need of him growing as he moves away from her. Ida's need for him greater than Dom's has ever been. It is this he sees and they could be anywhere, so having a sick child makes no difference. It's the weekend and he's happy.

He and Alice take turns to stay in with prickled Ida. The other heads out with Dom. This makes James realise they should do this more. Divide and concentrate. Dom emerges from beneath his younger sister's inverse shadow, enjoying being an only child again. Alice takes him to the swimming pool, returning a little lovestruck, amazed at his current proficiency. James shoulders him to the park where, with his first ever delivery, he bowls a yorker that takes out the middle stump. His eyes grow bluer. His smile wider, his freckles more pronounced. In the Saigon he reveals an easy charm with waitresses and wows a middle-aged couple by demolishing two soft-shelled crabs and half a steamed sea bass. James is awed, trying to put himself in his son's place at that age. Or any. Success, he tells himself as, incredibly, Dom makes a fair go of the chopsticks. He can see no future in which this engaging, intelligent boy doesn't get everything he wants. All that needs to happen is for life to be fair, to treat his son with gentleness. There is a man this child should turn into, if only the world he lives in will allow him to do so.

— We should get Ida ill more, Alice says, over dinner on Saturday night. James laughs at the construction and then gets serious, wanting to say something about Ida, how she's levered a position in their family they must not let her keep. When she came along he wondered how she'd cope behind super-bright Dom and was relieved that instead of being a shrinking violet she tore into life. But now Dom is in the shade. He wants to talk about this but he doesn't, stopping because Alice has turned away. Has pursed her lips, about, he is sure, to say something. Important. Tell him something. He's worried, knowing that she is being careful, trying to find the exact words to carry over to him the thought that has occurred to her, as if it is something delicate that may get smashed. Or smash him. He opens his mouth, the fear growing, remembering a similar look on her face as they ate breakfast together in his flat, in Brighton. She'd placed her fork down very carefully and stared at her plate, something like misery on her pale, serious face. He'd swallowed, felt sick, sure he was about to be dumped, preparing to fight the tears that jumped up ready to flood on to his face.

— I love you, she'd said, almost to herself, nodding as the words came out.

It can't be that. Those three words are not so razor-sharp now. They have been rounded down by being washed back and forth between them. So what? He holds his breath but never finds out what his wife was going to say to him. For Alice turns again, this time towards Dom, who is standing in the kitchen doorway.

— I don't feel very well, he says.

Ida looked like a twilight constellation. A total of nine spots appeared at intervals across her roundish, clean body. Dom is far worse and the speed at which he is covered is amazing. That night he is simply feverish, a dose of Calpol enough to settle him. By morning however he looks like the Milky Way, swirls and clusters of tightly packed though always individual papules covering him. They begin as distant pricks of red that speak of immensely distant cultures, but most soon develop into swollen gas giants about to go supernova. And they are, eventually, everywhere, covering his face, neck, scalp and stomach, Dom tearing at himself as if trying to rip off burning clothes. They then spread to the gaps between his toes and the recess of his belly button, before moving inwards to his palate, his tongue, his anus and testicles. Pulling back his foreskin James finds them there too but his son's misery is not yet complete. When they appear on the inside of his eyelids James rushes him to A&E where they burst, Dom's crying so pure and unstructured that even in that self-absorbed space a sympathetic silence develops, a ring of shuffling senior citizens and glassed Lewisham residents staring down as James holds his son to his chest and tries in vain to comfort him. The threat of blindness sends Dom through quickly, to where drops, and more pain, are administered, as if to a lizard boy in astronaut pyjamas. The doctor unpeels and checks him over, James unable to believe that his son's skin will ever be normal again. A complete covering of ointment sends his howling to an even deeper level and nothing James does gets close to him now. All he can do is drive him home, to Alice, the mother need having surfaced again, and he clings to her as if trying to re-merge with her very body, bury himself inside her so that she can subsume his pain. And she would do it if she could. He can tell that just by looking at her. She would take him back inside and once again withstand the pain of giving birth to him, if it would only give comfort to him now.

At midnight they appear in the bathroom together like conspirators. Macbeth and wife. Should we do it? Really? If it were done when 'tis done, then 'twere well it were done quickly. A double dose of Calpol? Their voices are lowered as if they are being monitored, exist within some parental Panopticon. They nod, feeling both wicked and brave, then watch as, finally, he falls asleep, whereupon Alice bursts into tears. James leads her into bed and then just stands at the top of the stairs like the captain of a storm-wracked ship. He closes the house down, double-locking the front door, bolting the back, which is when a thought scuds into him. He's immune to the pain his son is suffering. He had chicken pox himself, though he has no recollection of it. And the thought that his own parents did for him what he has done for his son sends a kick into his own stomach and soon he is crying to see his father, senile now, homed, holding him to his chest as he held Dominic.

In the morning Dominic is a little better. Physically, at least. His spots are still there but he's able to accept them, his scratching focused down to individual points, one of Alice's socks on each hand. He's still very tired though, and confused, it seems, at the very nature of life. Still he clings to Alice, whining when she even leaves the room, staring through James as if he isn't there. On Tuesday however he cannot do this. On Tuesday it is James's turn, for Alice needs to go out. Under normal circumstances Alice would get lecture cover but today she has three interviews lined up. One is for the *Poetry Review* and two for the BBC, including a short reading of her work on *Front Row*.

— I'll cancel, she says, at the door, having offered ten times to do this. But he tells her Dom will be fine, that he won't remember this when he's at Harvard.

— I'm his dad, he says. We do it like this. You just get Ida to Treetops.

— I'll make it up to you.

He just nods, too exhausted even to make a joke of it.

— Dad, Dom says, when it is finally just the two of them. And he is, marginally, happier. Is that a pedalo in our garden?

He gets no work done. He had imagined Dom sleeping on the sofa all day while he looked at his poet's early work. Trying to locate the very first signs of the later shifting into his famous fluid style. He expects Dom to crash and he does, two minutes into *Antz*. But two minutes after that the doorbell rings and he stumbles into the sunlight.

Neil? He fucking gets it this time.

But it's not him.

— Hi, she says, lifting sunglasses.

9

THE QUEEN OF ROYAL HILL is not in sweats today. She's in the kinds of clothes Amelia Leigh wears: new jeans and fitted linen grandad top, from which her collarbones protrude as if she left the hanger in. She actually looks like the posh girl she is and he is a little maddened, put down by what he can only describe as *breeding*. Alice is thin, but not in this drawn-up way that oozes wealth, parents in the Cotswolds, in the way that some other people ooze hip no matter what they wear. Her whole body is a tag, an evolutionary label, hardwired to tell him things.

James also realises now why she never made it as an actress. Creamy skin, green eyes, American teeth. But the jaw is too pronounced, goes back too far towards her ear. It makes her look hard, giving away the fact that while she has the apparent knack of wearing whatever emotion she wants on her instantly sunny face she lacks the necessary ability also to hide what is there behind it. And that is a deeper lake of emotion to which the common outsider has no admittance. It is, he decides, what really fires his instinctive resistance to her, a resistance that surely is not unique to him. She does not or will not connect. Cannot simply be in a room with someone. There is, at all times, an inability to hide the fact that within nanoseconds she has found many ways to dismiss whoever she is looking at.

She lifts her elbows to set her shades back in her hair and asks again if she might come in. It jolts him and he stops frowning at the fact of her existence.

— Yes, though…

— Chicken pox? I know.

— Is there a cross painted on the door?

— I saw your wife. On the way to nursery with your little one. So cute.

— Right.

— And it's just that I've got this cream. Homeopathic. It worked a treat with Theo.

— I see, James says, and stands aside for her.

When she moves to the left James is confused. He soon realises that she has her Bugaboo with her though, which she swivels towards him. It contains a child. Not the aforementioned Theo but the daughter he's seen so often at playgroup in St Luke's, younger than Ida by six months and surprisingly Munsterish. He helps bump the pushchair over the step and then waits for her to get the girl out. Instead she straightens to check out their home, a chin-led boxing process she hardly bothers trying to hide. Once she's done this she relaxes and he's annoyed at how informal she seems to think she can be. Were it the White House he'd opened the door to she'd hover, pay compliments, wait like a squaddie to be told she could stand at ease. But she needs no instruction here to make herself at home. He gets it again, a quick kick, not least because the house is trashed again.

— Tea? he asks, wanting an excuse to move away from her. In the kitchen he thumbs out a text. *Now I am pssd off. Ta v fing mch. And wht the fx her name again?*

Thomasina, comes his wife's reply. *No really*.

She takes the tea, setting it down next to her phone on the Persian even though her daughter is tromping around like a mobile gas rig. With half an eye on it he waits for further mention, and production, of the ointment she claimed was the purpose of her visit. She makes no reference to it, however, even though her back is to the sofa on which Dom is still lightly snoring. As she chats it begins to feel as though she's holding it behind her back, will only hand it over when he gives her something. And she does want something, though he's no idea what. Maybe, he thinks, as once again she grills him on Alice and her job, it's just to know what their house is like. So she can place them. Or has she come round because of Dom, having seen a window – no holidays booked, no birthdays coming up – in which it would be convenient for her girl to get his pox? Whatever it is, she's trying to soften him, chatting now as though they are secret allies, the two humans left in *Invasion of the Body Snatchers*. She moves towards cattiness, begins to diss Greenwich in a way that is oddly familiar, makes him wonder if she's been listening at the window during one of Alice's rants. It's disconcerting because he has the dirty sense of agreeing with her. But why dirty? Has he misjudged her? Is she shy, overcompensating with her sun-powered, gleaming energy? Insecure rather than solipsistic? It occurs to him that she might have just seen Alice in the street and had the impulse to be nice. She's no way of knowing that she interrupted him and perhaps just wants a little texture in her day, as he surely does in his when he's got Ida. So he's the one with the problem. Has he ever really spoken to her? His assumptions are based on an instinctive wariness of her presence that he doesn't know the reason for, plus the impulse he and Alice give way to sometimes, to rip people to bits. A phobia, that's all, and when she turns to smile at Dominic it seems to vanish.

— And he's okay? she asks, removing the sunglasses, her blouse riding up a little. He's aware of a scent. Patchouli. Not sprayed on; from a shampoo or shower gel, a telepathic amount. He nods and helps the daughter wind the lift on Ida's play garage before turning back to his guest.

— Getting better. It was pretty awful, though. Apparently if you catch it from a sibling it can be far worse than...

— No. She smiles. I mean I'm glad. Of course. But at school.

— School?

— He hasn't been going long, has he?

— No. A month and a half. Second intake.

— And it's St Saviour's, right? On Blackheath?

— Yes.

— God, you did really well. Brilliant Ofsted. It's as good as the Prep, they say. So I was wondering. I mean. If you don't mind my asking. How on earth did you get him in there?

He talks about this at the gig the following night. He likens himself to a naïve old lady who's let in a conman with an eye on her savings. How focused she was, stripping him of everything she wanted. Leaving within thirty seconds of discovering their route into primary school nirvana.

It's the Comedy Store again, though this time the one in Mile End. When Carty phoned that afternoon, James laughed.

— Something going round?

— Nah, mate, you're not a stand-in tonight. They bumped someone.

— For me?

— They do now and then. Put people in their place, stop 'em coming back with the same old crap. Word's out you did well.

— I did, he says. And I want fifty quid more.

Once again he shows up less than fifteen minutes before going on. The stage manager acts as though some holocaust has narrowly been avoided but he just shrugs. And once again it all unfurls. He intended doing a polished version of the first set. He thought about it on the tube: where he could have set things up better, a couple of lines he could add here and there. But instead, just like that, he asks the audience if they can help him out with something. As they nod or tell him no, get on with it, he checks them out, sees a more relaxed crew in front of him. Something about the fact that most will already have travelled home from work, that that won't still be hanging over them. He himself is relaxed and takes his time before telling them about the Queen, sketching her first before getting them to guess her name. He tells them to think up the most ridiculous fucking thing it couldn't possibly be because that would be just too much, but still no one gets Thomasina.

He jams for ten minutes about her and the mummies go mad. They clench their fists, calling out *yes*, their own particular nemesis springing up into their minds. James says button it: they're as bad. They're the ones who push five-hundred-quid buggies when they live in an ex-council flat, call their kids Atticus or Holden because they've only ever read one fucking book their entire life. Turning the focus on himself, he tells them of something that happened last month. The post came and there it was on the mat. Like Death, it had finally found him, his name on the front – somehow – so *there could be no mistake.*

The Boden catalogue.

And the same thing happened to Munch, the day before he painted *The Scream*.

At the end he hushes them, gets them to really listen. Does serious in a way they instantly buy as he announces he's got things to show them. Beautiful things. When they're totally silent he reaches into his shirt pocket and steps off the stage, approaching the audience. The items he pretends to extract are, he explains, Ida's, something that sets the front row smiling as they all know her very well by now. But then he holds up his hand, whereupon they recoil in a Mexican wave of hilarious though very real disgust when he tells them what they are. She insisted that he keep them when they came off, he explains, and put them under her pillow.

For the Chicken Pox Fairy.

Only one person isn't dying with it, leaping back as he walks the crowd with his cupped hand, pretending to offer them round and then sneeze them out into the crowd. Suit boy, sitting near the back on his own.

He's just nodding.

10

THE INTERVIEWS go well. What will be made of them by people listening or reading she cannot tell. But for her they seem good and this is a surprise for does she not deflect gaze? It was why she hated James so much in those classes, barely saying anything about her work but seeing through it – and her – in a way that made her feel sick. But she came round to James. His painful noticing. Isn't this, after all, what I've been waiting for? She thinks about that as she exchanges the high portal of Broadcasting House for the bustle of Oxford Circus, tripping over a memory. That job for the *Issue*. How she had to stop because she couldn't stand pretending to be interested in mundane people with no idea they were mundane. How she felt particularly demeaned to realise that they actually assumed she was interested in their drivel, that it wasn't just her mortgage payments that explained her desire to sit in front of them. Now she knows she was jealous. I suit this, she tells herself, looking back at the austere building. I am someone to be interested in and this, by God, will not be the last time I am interviewed.

Half an hour later as she walks on to the concourse at Charing Cross, Thomasina Davis springs to mind and Alice nods to herself, knowing how the woman draws people to her, thinking now that she understands why. She is completely unapologetic. She inhabits her role fully, her previous life almost impossible to imagine. Like Alice in those interviews she never talks about anything that does not come back to her chosen profession, as if she had been born when her children were. Having fixed on her job as mother she goes about it with the rapacity of a bond trader. Alice doesn't want that kind of life but there are many jobs she wouldn't want and there is real purpose to Thomasina, unlike most of the other mothers she encounters who are all, to some degree, embarrassed, their energy drawn in and rounded off, as if their husbands leave them in a huge, adult crèche every day, which is what Greenwich is in many ways. The only thing she wonders at about Thomasina is her husband. She's beautiful, slim, does a credible approximation of charm. Alice thinks of the man she met, a chirpy but doughy sort of man, nothing but an extra to Thomasina's lead and clearly feeling very lucky to get even that tiny part. The way she interacted with him, the way he responded, told her that his purpose was simple and clear: not only to provide but to defer, as Thomasina went about sculpting their lives. It occurs to her that in Thomasina's mind their roles are reversed, that she must think that, like a housewife, he's got the drudgy life, while she's the glamorous high achiever, the Greenwich stay-at-home CEO, organising her peers, leaving them gasping at her accomplishments. But, so single-minded, could she not have got what she has from someone more vibrant? Or equally normal but who could have offered her something *more*?

Alice takes the train back to Greenwich and tries to remember the answers she gave. She also thinks about James and the time he saw her, interviewing some actress. How, when she noticed him, she was ice-cold, razor-edge furious, until she realised that he hadn't followed her. It was a chance thing. What had happened next though was crucial. As she packed up her kit she'd waited for her name, his arms, knowing that it could ruin everything for him to break in like that. She'd steeled herself as she walked away, down towards London Bridge, only to be intensely relieved when nothing happened. What a man. For her life to be suddenly in his hands, and for him to let it go. She'd beamed all the way back to Hackney.

And never spoken of it.

She's on the following night. Seven thirty-five. Before the start she thinks about telling James she doesn't want to hear it, going through the motions of diffidence. But she doesn't, and nor does she disagree when he tells her how well she came over. She just wishes him luck with his gig.

— Won't you be late?

— Don't care, he tells her.

When he's gone she eats a bowl of pasta and then waits, pretending not to, for her visitor.

When Richard Leigh arrives there is a moment of recognition because it has to be him and anyway the first thing he does is state his name. This however is mixed with the certain knowledge that this cannot be the person she spoke to on the phone from university. Since then another man has formed himself inside her thoughts and the difference between them is so vast it takes a while to remove him. This Richard Leigh is, for a start, very badly dressed, sporting combat trousers and a burgundy silk shirt, above which is a denim jacket, over which is a leather jacket. She has a vague recollection from her early youth that this was once fashionable but it is so long ago she can't be sure.

Amelia's husband? The man seems at once like an impostor, in no way capable of playing that role with that woman. And at the same time totally suited to her.

— Meet Annie, he says, indicating the pretty teenage girl next to him.

They had agreed he would come to her house. No mention was made of going out. Richard, however, insists, telling her that Annie is the daughter of a friend, but more importantly in this context the babysitter of his children. And, on this night, of hers. He has already paid her and she is very capable. When Alice protests that her children are already in bed and don't know this Annie, he tells her all the better. When she tells him that her eldest has chicken pox he winces but then insists that Annie will call if he so much as murmurs.

— Look, he says, you can't talk properly with kids around. As a creative person you must know that.

She knows no such thing but arguing with him seems far too difficult, there on the doorstep, with this paid girl hovering. She hesitates, which means she'll do it, and then rushes the girl in, glancing at the unwashed pasta pan and her plate, but knowing she'll be back before James gets home. She turns the TV on, apologising for it, and then asks Annie if she's hungry.

— Thanks, she tells her, two minutes later, as she's tying her trainer laces. Wondering what she's being thankful for.

They're going to Café Rouge. Okay? Alice nods but this is a disappointment because, despite its being the nearest eatery to her house, Richard hasn't chosen it for its proximity. From the way he asks she can tell it's because he likes it. Chain restaurants are no-fly zones for Alice and this one in particular makes her wince, the *faux* antique metal Gitanes plaques manufactured, she is sure, somewhere near Beijing.

She's always found its alleged Frenchness risible, cloying, so much so that now, when actually in France, she won't go to the places it is a copy of because they don't seem authentic either. She feels instantly uncomfortable, something reinforced by Richard's hand on the back of her neck as he steers her across the road. It's an instinctual thing, she can tell, a luvvie-tick, something he's hardly aware of. When they enter the restaurant he keeps it there, looking around as he signals a waiter.

— Four, please, he says.

The waiter takes them to a table near the middle of the restaurant, leading them across a space so centrally planned that she finds herself desperate to find some evidence of individual human input. It's hard. The waiter is in uniform, his apron clearly folded down to an agreed length. Even his black shoes – surely his own – are without a brand mark or label. The chalk boards are pre-written to look as though they are not and the menus are, of course, laminated. The walls are bolted with more silly froggery and the music has, she is sure, been chosen by committee to most effectively stimulate the easy purchase and consumption of hygienist-designed, pre-portioned food items. So it's Norah Jones. She's dismayed, not sure she can stay, until phew, there it is: a wedge of folded cardboard beneath a table leg, the wobble of which was not – by some middle management oversight – predicted at head office.

Alice reaches a hand for the nearest chair-back but a little more pressure on her nape from Richard steers her on towards a table in the window, dirty, as it has just been vacated. But when the waiter asks if they'd like to wait for it to be re-laid Richard doesn't seem to hear, sitting and gesturing for her to do the same, ordering a bottle of house red, nodding to Alice as he does so, then nodding to the waiter when she shrugs fine. The waiter starts to leave but Richard holds up some of the used plates for him, which obliges the kid to clear the table right away instead of fulfilling any of his other, more pressing duties. When it's done Richard then expands, answering Alice's unasked question about who is to join them. It is no one. This man just needs space, the table soon seeming small enough even with just them. After that he settles, not speaking yet but very consciously reconfiguring his body to his environment, realigning himself as if driving a hire car.

She waits, mildly astonished by the seriousness with which he seems to be taking the simple business of beginning to talk to someone. Should she be more aware of herself, like this? Doesn't she just sort of blunder on? She looks around, at an old couple getting up to leave. The woman searches for a waiter, then jabs her index finger down towards the tip. She thinks of her house, her children sleeping, and though it's only a minute away it's as though she's on a different planet.

— We're going to win awards, Richard says.

It is a pawn pushed two squares. Alice doesn't know if this is a timed game or not. So she waits. When he says nothing she just shrugs again, to which he responds by reaching into the deep inside pocket of his leather jacket. She finds herself with no idea whatsoever what he might pull out but it is books. Her books, and not just the current one but the previous two also. These, she knows, are easy to come by on Amazon, and damn quickly at that, but the fact that this double-jacketed man has actually bought them makes her feel uneasy. Shocked, as if she's being confronted with incontrovertible evidence of infidelity. She blushes, sitting up, the desire to leave almost sending her from her chair.

She takes a breath and is about to speak, but stops because Richard hasn't seemed to notice her response. He's fanning pages, after which he nods.

— This, he announces, is beautiful.

It's from her first collection. A short poem about giving birth, written long before she ever did so. It's really about creativity and what she owes to those who've gone before her because, as the poem reveals, she is the screaming baby being carried away from her mother to be cleaned. She is then carried from the room completely, towards an unknown fate, blinking at the blur of shapes and colours. Now she glances down at the poem and sees that it has been annotated, barely a line free from strident pencil marks she is extremely curious to know the meaning of.

— I won a prize for that.

— I'm not surprised. Which?

— Listowel. It's in Ireland. Best Single Poem. It's my husband's favourite.

— Not mine, says Richard, closing the book and setting it aside.

He does not open her second collection and this miffs her. Was there nothing in there to grab him? What about the title poem, about which London Underground enquired, though she never heard back? Or the beach one: how the pebbles will be sand one day? As soon as she thinks of it she winces, knowing then that it is crass and that he probably thought so too. Why did she never realise? She takes a series of short breaths and is relieved when the waiter appears with their bottle, setting down four glasses, two of which Richard hands back. And would they like to see the menu?

— Do you still have cassoulet?

— Yes, though if –

— I'll have that. Alice?

— I'm not hungry. Nothing for me.

Richard looks across at her, about to argue, cajole, but deciding against. Instead he takes the wine from the waiter before he can pour it and nods him away again, glugging out the thin-looking red into small *ballons*. An hour later it is still untouched. Even the cassoulet has been set aside, its limp beans cooling to a pallid mess amid the twists and chunks of duck and sausage.

— So what do you think? he says. Brightly.

Alice frowns. What she thinks is nowhere near as important as what she has been feeling. In fact she can't think, just as she can't in her arguments with James, not until the morning when she unpicks where he was right, usually on all points, and where he was wrong – usually in the way he approached those points. What she feels is raided. Robbed, Richard as Malcolm McDowell, grinning at her after he has taken her most precious possessions and smashed them to bits in front of her. It's a breathtaking feeling, her outrage almost too big to contain, given an unreal twist by the fact that he has chosen to do this here in this mundane virtual reality, surrounded as they are by a crowd of shockingly normal, subdued people. People who will shortly forget this average evening and never think of it again for the rest of their lives.

What does she...?

Alice blinks and looks down at the books on the table between them. The first thing he told her was why he read them. Amelia, mentioning her. A whim to look her up, online. How stunned he was. So far so fine, but, while he's read it, he doesn't give a shit about her poetry. He's been looking through it, not at it, as if what she's written is mere ore. Juri: *the poems are speaking to each other*. This is true but it's not all they're doing. What Richard has done is take this element only, giving each tranche of poems a human character, people who could be on stage talking to each other. What she expected she cannot say because she didn't expect anything, his approach so out of the blue that nothing came when she tried to imagine their conversation. But it wasn't like this.

She wants to laugh at him. She wants to tell him there is no way she can do what he's asking though she pauses for a second, startled by other feelings, mingling amid the violent ones like undercover cops at a protest rally. She's flummoxed by the effort he's put into this. Into her work. A fluke maybe, resulting from a chance encounter with James, but since then he sought her out. He tracked her down, so impressed was he by what he read. Is it two days or three that he's had to look at her poems? In that time he's sketched the structure and basic story of an entire play, identified how the dialogue she has created could move within the two time zones of theatre, stage time and narrative time, both of which he's explained to her. He's seen where the immovable tensions and conflicts that give her collection its hidden nucleic power could change and ebb, reform and intensify, push to a resolution.

So why isn't she pleased? The last poem in her collection returns the reader to the first, a refusal to let the reader out. What Richard has done is break that, suggesting a way in which an irreversible change could take place, a movement in time complete with room enough for a fifteen-minute break for fucking ice cream. The mere fact of his effort nearly has the effect of sweeping her away but no, this need for an interval makes her hate him again. And the medium he's talking her work into. Kind of him to show a bit of interest but he's mashed her, traduced the secret output of her heart into a brash and less considered thing.

— Is there something wrong? asks the waiter.

— No, Richard says. But Alice wants to say yes and it's very wrong. He hasn't eaten that because he's been feeding on me.

She wants to run shivering into the street, but one thing keeps her there. Alright, two things. She's too shy to run into the street. The other thing is that, though she hates this implicit dismissal of her work, she can't deny that this proto-play he has outlined could be very good indeed.

— Just think about it. I've sold it hard. And it doesn't have to be like this. The three women, they don't have to meet at the dad's funeral. It could be, I don't know, the lawyer's office. That's where they have to decide who gets the house, everything. Who gets to live on. From the father, who takes it. I mean I think that's great but come back with something else. You're the writer. Just go with the idea, that's all I ask. Nothing happens, we shrug. But if something comes out it could be great. It will be great. Legacy, who gets what, we're all interested in that. A play about three women who have decided that only one of them can, you know, live. Syria? Nazi Germany, whatever. I really want you to write this play, Alice.

He sits back and smiles again. As if noticing his wine for the first time he sips it and winces, setting the glass down immediately. Alice is about to speak. Tell him no. Politely but firmly. She needs to nip this in the bud, can't let it inside her. She's not a playwright. Or maybe she'd like to write a play but she can't rip this book of hers up to do it.

— When you're in the Louvre.

— Yes?

— Looking at the *Giaconda*. Are you looking at it?

— Of course. Of course I am.

— Or are you just thinking what a good play it would make? How you can cut it up into pieces.

He laughs and frowns, no idea what she's talking about. She's about to explain and then ask why on earth he thought that she might be interested. But she doesn't get a chance. Richard stands. For a horrible second she thinks he's seen how angry she is and is coming round the table. But a man has blundered in. She turns and sees him as he moves towards them, knocking into at least four empty chairs as he negotiates the tight space, which scrape and make half-turns like cogs. He's a big man. Not tall but overweight. He has longish grey hair and a flushed, thick-skinned face that expresses some kind of outrage, as if someone has just backed into his car. He approaches Richard without noticing the last-hit chair performing a delicate pirouette on one leg. It revolves, twice, before dropping gracefully on to its back.

— Who's this? he says.

— Alice, Richard replies, with no other explanation.

The man then sits at their table. With no explanation he reaches for her untouched glass, downing the wine to a third without looking at her. It's then that she realises that nothing is wrong. The outrage he exudes is just something he carries. Richard sits too and smiles at her, after which the man launches a volley of unprovoked invective so virulent and unfettered that it astonishes her. Actors are mentioned, and producers, a cameraman. None of it is put into any kind of context, though Richard seems to know what he's talking about. Alice just blinks, staring into the cavern of his mouth with its crooked teeth, gold at the distant back like nuggets in a cartoon mine. His blinged fingers shove his hair back, his big shaking body something separate from him, which he must consciously manoeuvre as he snorts and fizzes. Alice thinks of her kids. Any kids. How could a child possibly turn into this? This big, loud, totally self-absorbed man?

Richard starts to reiterate his request to think things over. She blinks and turns to him, about to reply. But she doesn't, because – and she can't believe this – he doesn't mean now. He means later. With growing amazement she realises that his body language is now indicating that their meeting is over. She's being dismissed. She's furious, not having asked for any of this, wanting to tell him what she thinks, but knowing she can't, the other man almost tapping his feet with impatience. She turns back to him, sees him smile and lift his chin as if to say go on dear, chip off. Grown-up time now. She swears, deep inside, tries not to snap as she stands, spits goodbye and walks away, halfway to the door before she thinks no, fuck it, she's going to tell him. Richard. And grab her poems from him. But when she turns back all he does is raise his hand, not quite meeting her eye, already having moved on to this friend. The door is closed on her and again she turns, face closing tight, her hand going to her bag for her phone which, to her shame, she hasn't checked once.

It isn't there.

— Shit.

Alice hisses, even more angry now, utterly flaming that she let him rush her out of the door like that. As she hits the street, forcing herself not to run across the road, which he would see from his position in the window, she pictures a waking Dom, blinking into the face of a stranger. Who's probably forgotten his name. She swears again, glancing back into the restaurant, the other man laughing, wagging his finger at Richard. She walks as fast as she reasonably can, knowing she will sprint the second she is out of sight. But she does not sprint. Instead she stops dead, caught by something so shocking that for a second she cannot believe it.

Her. This Annie. This alleged babysitter. She's there. Right in front of her. On the 386. Back seat, laughing at something, phone stuck to the side of her head as the bus sways by.

11

SHE THINKS JAMES. Must have blown off the gig. Either that or he's got back by ten-fifteen somehow, even though he wasn't supposed to be on till quarter to. He's sent the girl home and is waiting, not unreasonably wanting to know just what the flying fuck is going on. She winces, but it isn't her husband she sees when she pushes open the living room door.

Silk butterflies fill the room, swirling up to the ceiling, descending gracefully towards Dominic. Her son is scampering around with a net in his hand, trying to catch them, one hand hitching the pyjama bottoms that are a little too big. The butterflies are being ejected through the vertical trunk of a plastic elephant, a just-this-side-of-copyright version of *Dumbo*. The elephant is grinning, as is Dominic, who squeals with delight as he manages to catch two at once before turning to Alice with a series of quick, two-footed jumps.

— Look, Mummy.

She is. At the butterflies and at her wide-awake son, but mostly at Amelia Leigh.

She is standing from the sofa, her expression a mixture of embarrassment and friendliness, a little apology thrown in. Alice's internal response is wild, beginning as she is to shake, demand, scream for an explanation – until it becomes clear.

Dominic must have woken. Totally chagrined, she knows this, even as Amelia starts to tell her, quickly, trying to get it out before Alice says something she might regret. He woke and Annie could do nothing to calm the boy. She called Alice but the phone rang inside the house, after which she called Richard who, as is his wont, had his phone turned off.

— I thought it best if I came, Amelia says. He knows me.

— Yes.

— So I whipped down in a cab. I sent Annie back to my two.

— Thank you. My God. I'm so sorry.

— Don't be. Annie said you didn't want to go out.

— I just rushed – I...

— Richard should have phoned, should have asked you. He doesn't think. But anyway I came down and just thought it would be silly trying to get him off to sleep again.

— Dom, Alice says, dumping her bag. How are you, love?

Fine, of course. As for herself, she's relieved, which makes a sickly mix inside her with the sheer humiliation. She wants to slam her fists into the side of her head, scream at herself, *This is real. You are not a child. You cannot bounce around the world like this any more. Get a grip on yourself.* She thinks of the times she's left the car key in her coat pocket and gone to work, James livid at being stranded. But this is worse: her *children*. To escape from herself she focuses on Dominic, pleased at least that scabs now cover most of his spots, which means his torment is nearly over. She tries to cuddle him but is stung when he turns back to the elephant, flipping a switch at the base, whereupon a motor cuts out and the trunk flops to the side. He takes it off and then proceeds to gather all the butterflies, dropping them back into the body of the elephant before reattaching the trunk and hitting the switch again. Alice watches like a spare part, Amelia explaining that she found the thing in the garage, got sneered at when she suggested her two play with it again.

— What a lovely house you have.

More chagrin for Alice for this is an original, felt comment, not an automated response, pointing up the lack of any such statement from her at Amelia's.

What happens then is not what Alice wants. She cannot say no, though, cannot deny Amelia without telling her of the feelings she has just been having while talking to her husband. Amelia wants a lift back home with Richard but when Alice describes the man who usurped her she frowns, says she doesn't want to interrupt them.

— Those two. Best friends. Go way back. They've got this film script. Mind if I wait for him here?

— Of course not. Though how...?

— Malcolm, she explains. They'll bury him with his phone on. They'll put an extra battery in the coffin.

Amelia phones Malcolm and tells him where she is. An hour later Richard arrives, laughing at his wife when she calls him an idiot. She chastises him but with zero conviction and Alice can tell she's the type of woman who actually likes being treated this way, as if by an adult child. Boys, she'll say, to her friends, in response to other examples of thoughtless masculine behaviour. For himself he insists no harm done, grinning at her when he says this. He makes no mention of before, has no idea he upset Alice. He treats her like an old friend and Dominic too, attempts to overwhelm him with a huge, faux-uncle shtick, calling him 'big man' and 'fella', from which, Alice is so proud to see, Dominic instinctively shies. He seems to have got the measure of Richard and finally withdraws to her, curling up on the sofa by her side instead of showing Richard how the elephant works. The two of them then watch together as their house is taken over by these big people. Big with their voices and their bones but in another way too that makes her want to hide from them. They are somehow big in the world, bringing their rather metallic version of it into their little nest. The successful couple, so shiny, so pleased with themselves. Their confidence so thoughtless. So blithe. It exhausts Alice and repulses her and she wonders if they were always like this. Or if they were real once and something happened to them, something she and James need to be terribly aware of, to avoid. No, it's unthinkable that they could end up like that, though she still wills these people gone, even when she is offering wine which Amelia turns down, finally pricking some antennae in her husband. Guilt, perhaps, for what he's done tonight.

— Go on, he says. I'll drive.

— Don't worry. Really. And we should be going.

— No, Richard insists. Not before James gets home. I want to hear how his gig went.

They find out later, Dominic asleep in Alice's lap. He's surprised, of course, to find them there, then laughs when they explain, cracking another bottle, a really good one he's been saving. As if it's nothing. Alice watches as he talks about his set. They laugh of course and Alice does too, though she knows he's only acting this uplift. For his voice is a fraction too loud and his eyes slide over hers as he sits, joining her as a team to combat these invaders, rigid arm slung over her shoulder. An over-solicitousness about the state of her wine glass further demonstrates that he is angry, something she expects to come out once the house is breathing a sigh of relief. But he's so furious that when it is just the two of them he doesn't say anything at all. He just shuts the door and focuses on what he's doing, closing up the house without a word, jaw tight, then insisting that it's he who carries Dominic upstairs, as if her previous failure in his care means she can no longer be trusted with even that simple task. She watches as they ascend, arms folded, feeling helpless, like the time she smashed one of his mother's statuettes and he insisted on sweeping it up. She's hurt by but also somewhat admiring of the ruthlessness with which he's treating her, this cold, brutal anger. She doesn't argue with him or even try to justify herself, knowing for a start that he's right, but also what she'd unleash if she did. Nor, however, does she apologise, which she knows she should, because that too would bring it all out, something she can't face right now: the forgiveness ballet will be at least an hour long from past experience. A dangerous time. For in the forgiveness of unbalanced error too much ground can be conceded, a relationship reconfigured in ways she can't accept. She will apologise but when she's ready, and knows what she's prepared to give up. Instead she takes another tack, one that she knows is lazy and, worse, a deferment: she pretends not to know how he's feeling. It's a gambit she knows he sees through, and they skirt each other like diplomats whose countries are about to be at war.

She's cleaning her teeth. Performing it for him as he slouches against the changing table, arms folded, doing a very poor imitation of mild interest as he smiles at her.

— A play? You didn't tell me.

— Oh. No. There's nothing to tell. Richard had this stupid idea.

— Richard. Right.

He tells her casually that, well, she should think about it, and goes to bed, is asleep by the time she gets there.

In the morning she's confused. Back in time? Her consciousness isn't dragged into the daylight by a scream from their room or small knees climbing on to her hipbone. Instead it emerges of its own volition. Dominic was always going to sleep late but for some reason Ida has too and Alice finds herself blinking, then pushing at the duvet as though she's coming out of hibernation. She's delighted, smiling to herself, knowing that it won't take anything here: if she lays it straight down. Capitulates. She'll cringe, ask why he married such a klutz. He'll accept this and then they might even do it, get one in, a quick stolen penny from the jar in this rare piece of squeezed-out extra life. But they can't. Can't because he's not there. Or rather he is but he's not lying next to her but standing, his laptop bag slung over his shoulder and his cycle hat in hand.

— Oh. James? Where are you going?

— Work, he says. British Library. Need to go. Bye.

— But...

— What?

Blinking. She mounts an elbow.

— I mean. The kids...

— Yes. Told you. I need to get some work done. I had Dom three days last week.

— Yes. Shit. Just woke up. Right. Of course it's okay.

Only it isn't. She has a lecture at eleven and a seminar immediately before.

Alice follows James downstairs, thanks him for the tea he's made, trying not to show that she's squeezing her mind for a solution. Trying not to show that she's wondering if he really did tell her, or whether he's just gone for this. Has he? Seen a door and dived through it? She doesn't know but if she pulls him up he'll slam her with what happened yesterday. *Leaving their children while she...* She's caught, and it is more likely that she did fuck up, just assumed James would have Dominic, being on sab and all. But why? She doesn't know. She has no idea why she's only just thought of this or, more importantly, how on earth she's going to fix it. No one can cover for her, not this late on. She racks her brain though all the while she stays calm, following James down and into the garden, wishing him a good day, even unbolting the back gate as he gets his bike from the shed.

— I'm sorry, she tells him. Good time to say this. He's leaving. Just has to take it.

— What for?

— Dom. Yesterday. Totally useless of me. And that game; it's like we're some sort of charity project.

He laughs, tells her it was no big deal, then goes, hitching his bag up as he bumps down off the pavement, a quick glance back and a short hand up for Neil who is walking up the street with the *Mirror* beneath his arm. She shuts the door.

— Mummy? Dominic says, behind her. Bed-headed. Shocking-looking in the context of the early-morning garden. Where am I going today?

There is only one answer, and it is school. Alice knows this immediately, even as she begins to ask him how he's feeling, trying to do so without giving away the consequences of his answers. She nods without hearing, knowing that, after they've dropped Ida, he has to go, that there is no other choice. Guilt batters the decision, hardening something inside her that even then she feels will never truly soften again.

In the church for Thursday assembly this firms again and then sharpens, the perfectly modulated surprise of the other

Reception parents on seeing Dominic intended to tell her that he's *back too soon.* Some say it's okay, that their child's already had it, as if she'd even think of bringing him in if he was still infectious. This conjures no more than irritation but when one woman tells her that *her* son was far more tired, needed much more time to recuperate in the post-viral stage, her mouth goes dry. Dominic *is* tired. Especially after last night. She grits her teeth, though, knowing that most of these women stay home, never have to walk over the burning coals of self-hatred just to complete the simple though essential task of getting to work. She steels herself but when Dominic's line partner refuses to take his hand she feels sick and wants simply to throw her arms in the air and give it up, all of it, her life, pull her head down from the parapet and sink back down into motherhood completely. Instead she swallows and hugs him and then turns, which is when she spots Amelia. Who looks terrible. Haggard, as if she's been up all night, pale and staring and slightly mad. An attic-room version. Has something happened? She feels she should go and ask but she's no time and she slips out before Amelia sees her.

The lecture tanks. The room is too hot, the transition into summer taking the building managers by surprise, again. Scant rows of near-horizontal students look like victims of a sarin attack. She finishes early and goes back to her desk, though she stays for less than five minutes before packing up, leaving by the back door so she isn't collared. The only person she sees is the pretty American girl, who smiles, blushing a little as Alice hurries by. She remembers her tuft and wants, in that moment, to see it again, thinking not of her students now but the women who drop their children off at St Saviour's, the variety of shapes beneath their pants. Would she be surprised by these post-childbirth fannies? Or guess each one correctly? What would the knowledge do to her relationship with them?

— Alice, the girl calls after her. Have you got a moment?

— Sorry, she says. Not now.

She'll get to the school by two. Take Dom out early. She'll buy him a milkshake in the village and she pictures this on the train to Waterloo, desperate to get back to him. It feels as if he's her only child again and she thinks of that time, how a whole new store cupboard of love opened up inside her, one she never knew was there. Which could have stayed shut forever until its contents went bad. She pictures them, just the two of them, getting an éclair in Jade, or Hand Made Food. She's proud, making a fuss of him, has to keep herself from grinning. The idea seems like more stolen time and the guilt she felt begins to flow out, for she can patch this, make up for the hurt he doesn't even know she's done him. She laughs: he's probably having a great day anyway. He really missed Milo this week. As for the other parents, they're probably chastising themselves, resolving in future not to treat their offspring like minor royalty. To be more like Alice Hart. The thought sends her back to James and she wonders if, actually, his cold shoulder really was caused by Dom waking up with the strange girl. He goes on about mollycoddling, makes a show of being slapdash, the *never did me any harm* line.

No, it was the play. That she didn't tell him Richard had approached her. He's never intruded into her writing before, though, so why's he angry now? She has no idea, especially as it was just a passing whim that she's already rejected, a decision she needs to tell Richard of.

Or does she?

At Clapham Junction she sees a poster bolted to the side of a café. The train has struggled to this point with the resentful sluggishness of a teenager, its stops and starts and lack of any discernible purpose leaving Alice frustrated. Powerless. Not today. *Please*. She checks her phone just to distract herself and sees a text from Anna, an old friend from the *Issue*. She blinks at the message, a simple invitation for a drink. When was the last time she went out with someone? Not Linus for twenty snatched minutes in the Grove, or coffee with the other mums after drop-off? Someone like Anna, or Mark and Em from Sussex? Someone from *before*? The text reads like a note from a girl she met on holiday, whom she vowed to keep in touch with, meaning it at the time until she came back to reality. *Yes*, she replies, *love to. Just let me check my diary when I get home.*

The poster catches her eye like an old acquaintance: she's looking at it but without knowing why. It's advertising a Tom Stoppard in the West End and she frowns, wondering what he must feel, to see it. What would that be like? To be so identified, for a sign to say *go to this place to see writing by this person*, and for that person to be you? She'd wince. Want to hide. She can't shout about her work or have anyone else do it for her. Though, once again, isn't that the old Alice? Pre-nomination, pre-*Front Row*? Is it really so unthinkable that she should be out there, hawked about the world like Stoppard?

Yes. It is, and it makes her realise something. Her own chosen literary genre is, of all of them, the least popular. She blinks, aware that she's always known this, but suddenly understanding the implications. Very few people intersect with her writing. None could ever be described as the *general public*. As far as she knows, no one outside a university has ever even read her work, and when she told Amelia what she did she was stared at as if under glass. This, she now sees, was probably the point, was almost definitely why she chose the genre, the fact just as important as the possibilities that writing poetry offers her. To stand up tall, and not be seen. Talk, and not be heard. The idea of the contrast makes her feel grubby. To be so overt is unthinkable. She's disconcerted to realise that her work so far has not been about reaching out but pushing away. The controlled yet violent scream *I'm not like you*. In a language you don't speak.

There is also the fact that it is hers and hers alone, no director or actors kicking her work between them. She shakes her head at the idea of seeing something she's written and not recognising it, some clumsy performer muddying the waters or, perhaps worse, someone brilliant pulling attention from the words, like Perlman playing Tchaikovsky. That Thomasina used to be an actress apparently and she winces at the idea of passing a character she'd created over to her. Or that famous woman she interviewed outside the National. Whether she was good or terrible is not the point; it's the theft she'd cringe at, the assumption of ownership, each glance or pause, each sigh or eruption an attempt to reduce her. The attempt of someone without much depth to take what she's created and pass it off as her own.

And yet. Alice is shocked. Ashamed, and not just of the bitchiness inside her towards women she doesn't really know. She goes back to the idea of putting her work out there. Is she really so afraid of the scrutiny of normal, intelligent people? Who might know her better? She's angry with herself and she tries something out, for no other reason than self-admonishment. When talking to Richard she had, in spite of herself, a flash: people on a stage. It was put there by his sheer enthusiasm, snuck in beneath her radar. She goes back to it, stares at the three people there until they do something she does not intend. They begin to talk, or at least one of them does. She reaches for her notebook and another does the same, and then the other, the last. She stares at the resulting scrawl and laughs, but then adds to it, just the logical follow-through of what has gone before.

But then she scribbles more. And more. She is still doing that when, miraculously, the train slows, people already standing, pulling down bags from the overheads, folding newspapers. They're pulling into Waterloo. She didn't realise they'd actually moved on from Clapham Junction. She stands too, grabbing her things, stuffing her notebook into her bag as passengers begin to pour on. She edges against them, struggling out on to the platform before heading towards the Costa, hurrying in the way she hurried home last night, as if in an egg and spoon race. Careful not to drop her idea. It makes her frown because, last night, when she thought her kids might have been left alone, why the hell didn't she just sprint across the fucking road?

The Costa tables are all taken. She grabs a coffee from the Burger King instead and sits amid empty cardboard cartons, a pile of abandoned fries like pick-up-sticks. She scribbles more, transcribing, moments, snatches of dialogue, words scudding across the page like the result of some lexical suicide bomb. Soon a heavy, muddy river is churning through her and it's a struggle to pull herself out as she claws through her bag for her phone.

— Office, the voice says.

— Yes, she replies. It's Alice. Dominic's mum. In Reception?

— Of course. Glad he's back with us.

— Yes. He's much better. Thank you. Only I forgot to tell Mrs Mason this morning. He'll be going to After School Club today.

The woman seems to hesitate and then says fine, I'll tell her, and Alice hangs up, knowing that she now has another forty-five minutes before she absolutely has to get the train. Head down, she carries on until something strikes her, something nebulous and disconcerting. A mirage, a false creation proceeding from her heat-oppressed brain. Glancing up across the whirling concourse, she sees a flash of blond hair which, for one mad second, she thinks belongs to James.

12

PREGNANT.

Amelia finds out this way: a head-rush as she's topping the stairs, a swirling dip to the knees as if her brain is being boxed. Vomit. It rushes out of its own volition, gleeful like kids into lunch break on to the ridged carpet where it seems to float, resisted by the Scotchgard that even now she remembers discussing with the salesman, turning to Richard to ask if it warranted the extra expense. He just shrugged, she recalls, but his indifference was clearly misguided, for is it not, now, showing its worth? When more vomit follows, it too seems uncertain which element to inhabit, standing above the carpet as if in doubt about something. For a second all Amelia can do is stare, her brain pulling its boots on to catch up with this. When it has, a third and final lurch sends out the rest and she gawps down through a tangle of horror that surprises her for it is not, immediately, the fact of her condition that makes her want to scream. It is the Scotchgard. When James came round it was like seeing with different eyes. Not his but hers, her real eyes. He probably didn't even notice the Nespresso machine but she did. The Scotchgard is the same. When did it happen? When did she change into a person who could care about whether or not her carpets should have a protective film sprayed on? Answering this question seems, in that moment, far more important than moving, and she watches as droplets fall from her lips to join the soup. Was it when she realised that she'd failed? When she saw her teenage dreams fade, and then vanish? When she also realised that this real world offers compensations to dull that blade, mirrors to turn to when you haven't got a self to look at any more? Yes, though it didn't happen all at once. It took years, a piecemeal pawning of herself with the things surrounding her until she was all gone. How did she let it happen? She wants to get a brush and scrub, not the puke so much as the Scotchgard.

But she does want to scrub the vomit. Oh, yes. Re-focusing on it, she is jolted and wants it gone, now, while the football highlights Richard recorded earlier are still playing. For she knows what it means and it's not the puking, nor the dizziness: but the two of them together. An unmistakable physical memory, not just of unborn Michael. Or even Niamh. For with them she was already forewarned, thanks to a man whose name she has not said for fifteen years. She hears it now and then, or sees it, writ large, and whenever she does the ship of her thoughts turns, pulled as if by a compass to the unsafe zone at the edges of her internal world with signs reading *Here Be Dragons*. And she is warned off, normally, pulling hard on the rudder at the first twitch to keep herself on course. But not today. As she wipes her mouth on the inside of her wrist and turns back to the stairs, Actor Twat fills her thoughts, just as he did at Alice's, as if sprung from a panto trap door.

She'd been so buzzed to get Annie's call. It nullified the hundred different plans she'd been concocting to get inside that secretive little cottage with its poorly painted red door. The elephant was one, a perfect Trojan Horse, she thought, but how to take it round? If James and Alice lived in Blackheath she could have knocked and said, hi, look, I was on my way to the Mencap but do you think your two might..? But Greenwich was a long way to carry a plastic elephant. So what about following again, Alice this time, doing the false bumping-into that she'd nearly done with James? A good idea but in no way guaranteed, as Alice could well suggest coffee in a café. She's guarded, Alice, careful, plays her cards so close to her chest that she can't even see them herself.

Dinner, then, the irresistible Newtonian tactic. It could take weeks, first to set up their side and then to wait for the equal and opposite reaction. She was planning it though when, out of the wide blue, Annie called. A play? A fucking what? With Alice? Richard had told her nothing, just said he'd be back late. She felt exposed, discovered, as if he'd landed a knight in front of her queen when she didn't even think he was playing. But what could she say? Richard would shrug, go yeah, grabbed a book of hers, fed up of shepherding luvvies through the classics. Sure I didn't tell you, hon? That would be it, unless she was willing to take it further, which would leave her wide open. She was hamstrung, scared, but that all vanished when she realised what Annie was throwing her.

— Oh, actually, Amelia, I think he's settling down. Don't worry, I'm sure I can cope.

— No, she almost bellowed. I'll come.

— Michael, she said, two minutes later, yanking off his headphones, I'm going to leave you in charge of Niamh for half an hour.

Actor Twat came into her mind when James came through the door. As his eyes opened, as he adjusted himself to their presence there, she wondered what he could see. Did she show it all on her face? She thought not but was still wary for even if James had no idea, his wife might pick up on the inexplicable seethe that happened to her in his presence. From now on she would be more careful though fortunately Richard was in Man Mode, acting as if this Wendy House were his. She could retreat, and look at James, asking herself again: *why*? It really did feel like a disease, something from outside of her, without meaning. *Diagnose*. So, Amelia, you've been having these symptoms for about a week. Have you ever felt anything like this before?

Yes.

And when was that?

Some years ago.

With whom?

With Actor Twat.

She'd had other lovers. She had actually been living with a boy when she met him, though that was what Dan was. And she a little girl. These things were clear the moment Actor Twat turned his beam on her, said hi in that tentative, almost horrified way, a smile that showed a depth of sadness she'd never seen before. They were in the King's Head on Upper Street, where she'd gone with a group of girlfriends that included Dan's sister, who sent daggers at her for the rest of the night as she, quite simply, ignored them. What they didn't realise however was that she was not being unfaithful. Dan was packed from that second, their relationship over in a flash as AT counted out change on to the bar for his pint. Dan himself couldn't understand, try as he did to reason with her. She couldn't just throw it away. Weren't they going to get married? Have children one day? Hadn't they spoken about that? But she could hardly even hear him. If we had kids, she told him, bags piled up in the waiting black cab, I'd still be leaving you.

She'd known him four days.

He was three years fledged from drama school. She was his acolyte, carrying him along on the litter of her belief. It was a role she accepted because she'd known from the moment she met him that, somehow, he was more than her. She was normal. A good-looking lass from Beverly with decent bone structure and a big laugh. He, however, seemed not to be from any recognisable natural place, created instead in some hatchery from raw feeling. And he had a destiny. She moved to London with the desire to join, engage. She pressed herself up against the city, looking for an opening that was her shape. Her 2:2 in English had taken her from shop girl to assistant manager at the Agnès B in Covent Garden – not great, but no more than she'd expected. And okay, at least until she met him. For his life seemed preordained, a place picked out for him right at the very centre. It didn't matter that he was penniless, something he didn't care about one bit. For he was special. Genetically A-list. There was something about him, his body containing truth somehow, as if the universe had parcelled up its secrets in the cleft of his pectorals, his sunken stomach, distilled them into the corners of his slow, liquid eyes. You felt, when you looked at him on stage, that you were improved. Knew more about yourself than you ever had.

And he was always on stage. Even in bed he was hardly there, so unlike Dan, so present and competent, so loud and appreciative. Actor Twat in contrast just lay there accepting her benedictions, a passivity that would have bored her in another man but only served to call her on. Afterwards he'd sometimes weep, something which, she didn't realise, was mere rehearsal for a deeper passion. She should have realised, of course, as anyone so out of their league should realise. It was only later however that she did, and in doing so understood what it was that left her so flogged by wanting this limp, ineffectual person. He was a future. A life in which she might turn out to be someone other than herself. He was a door, her passion a projection to the other side. It was love as *The Apprentice*, a golden life waiting if only she was noticed which, as it transpired, she was not.

Pregnant.

She found out this way. Head rush and her legs went, and then she was barfing Guinness over a pub garden fern. She was in support. He was slumming it in pub fringe to get a lead, spending more time trying to get the RSC in than on learning his lines. The pub was in Kennington and she'd gone to pick him up, only rehearsals were overrunning so she was doing what she'd been doing for most of the time they'd been together. Hanging out. Waiting. Basking in her position: *girlfriend*. She'd had the drink because an old lag at the bar bought it for her, telling her it was the best damn drop of porter in this godforsaken country. She'd taken it outside, sipped the metallic fluid waiting in ambush beneath the creamy surface and then stared at the splattering result. The risks they'd been taking. Her fault. He'd reach for condoms but she'd just tell him to be careful, wanting to really feel him, aware that if he did suit up he sometimes never even came.

She stared at the dripping plant, and her arms felt hot with happiness.

— You okay?

Was it the first time he'd said it? The words didn't register. She turned and blinked up at the big, confident man with the deep smile. The director, so she'd been told.

— Yes. I don't know. I only had a sip, I promise you.

— Here.

A handkerchief. Clean, such as a dad might carry. She smiled and took it, and held it to her mouth.

Did he see her? She never knew for sure. She suspected he did. The rehearsal room was upstairs, with a window on to the back. He could have been looking out. Either that or he might have finished and been walking out to find her. And seen. And known it. And if love is a projection towards a future self then her puking killed his own because it was no future he wanted. He did it that night. She hadn't told him, was going to wait until she'd done a test. Or longer, when she'd seen a doctor and was sure. Find. The. Right. Moment. She'd already sketched out pictures, mocked up a mental storyboard in which she was the cool young mum, their gurgling tot passed around the family of actors at Stratford, the subsequent albums full of pictures of Coriolanus or Hamlet, babe in arms. But he was too selfish, he said. Too focused on his career. Not able to give her what she should have, not able to adore what was so clearly adorable. The words were like razor blades, somehow untethering her body from her mind so that she could only watch as her hands grabbed hold of him, clinging, fighting when he pulled them off, his pain so much worse than her own it seemed, tears cascading down his face as they did later, in his first big movie, the same scene enacted though with Helena Bonham Carter this time. Another rehearsal, the end of their devised piece the perfect opportunity to explore what it felt like to ruin someone. Take them from their life, give them a peek at a different one, then ball them up and toss them into the breeze.

He moved house without telling her. His agent wouldn't give her his new number. After that she never saw him again, apart from the twelve consecutive nights in which she sat in the back row, staring at him in the Nazi uniform that seemed so fitting, watching him dissolve into a madness she felt she herself was sinking into. After the last night, and another no-show by him in the bar afterwards, she turned once again to this Richard.

— Want your hankie back?

— Keep it. The tears too. Pointless on a vain cunt like him. We should have done *The Mirror Crack'd*. He'd have been perfect.

She never told him. Her secret. Nearly did, nearly asked him to take her in fact, but by then she could sense that something might happen between them. He was funny, large, his soft certain bullishness an incredible comfort after Actor Twat's manic doubt. She allowed herself to be drawn, pulled down this side road rather than returning from whence she came, glad, at least, that her old self was gone. She asked Dan instead. Met him outside the Royal Free on a wet October lunchtime. He was quiet and wouldn't touch her. Afterwards he took her home to her new flat and asked if he could come inside, asked if there was any chance that...? No, she said, and watched him walk away. Watched to make sure that he was going. Then, for just a second, she was tempted to call out after him. So easy it would be to start up again with him, just until she was back on her feet again. Doubt stopped her being so cruel. For didn't he just want her again so that he could do the leaving, dump her as soon as he'd got his pride back?

That night she let Richard Leigh kiss her for the first time. He did it seriously, with care, a masculine tenderness that promised to know things and take care of them. Her included. And she accepted, even though she felt cheap. Relegated. Passed from Real Madrid to Aston Villa.

She saw the madness of it too. Hold on, a voice cried. Take stock. She pictured herself single like most of the other girls at the shop, each of the urbanites heading down into the Men's section a potential drinks date, dinner perhaps with some of the older ones though Nina said they all had hairy backs once they got past thirty. Was it terror that stopped her: the raw fear of having to negotiate the tube stations and the busy cafés, the Covent Garden crush or the empty staff room, as a single person? Or just that, whenever she needed space, time alone, whenever she needed to feel free, Richard just backed off, said sure, call me if you want to hook up? During these times she played at being single. She told people she was; even snogged a guy at Dingwalls in Camden Lock. But Richard was always there in the background. Not judging or, it seemed, even waiting for her. Quite simply he never provided a reason for her to finish with him, and, as time went on, gave her plenty of reasons why she shouldn't. He was not in the same sphere as AT. But he did live in London. Really live in it. He took her to pubs that didn't look cool but which after ten minutes she would see were very cool indeed, full of people she envied for the fact that they could, in public, relax. Some of these people were ones she recognised from the TV. But Richard wasn't manic and bitchy about them. Nor was he earnest and attentive while in the company of people who could help him. People liked him, well known or not, it was as simple as that. Something about him made them want to touch him, men mostly, their arms draped over his denim-jacketed shoulders as they were introduced to her or rubbing his balding head when he finally got himself a buzz cut. Women too, one a pencil-thin starlet he'd known at drama school who sat on his knee the whole time as if he was Santa and then grabbed her by the shirt when he went off to the bar.

— He's my mate, alright? And he's great.

Kidding? No, certainly not.

— So don't mess him about, okay?

She nodded, startled and a little choked, but only thought about it later. How could she mess him about? Even in Dingwalls she had the feeling that he wouldn't have minded. She was his. He knew it. Eventually she gave in and it felt like such a relief. It's just me, she told herself, head on his big chest. I have boyfriends. She didn't know then that this was the last one she would have, that time would then grab her by the lapel and rush her through it until she was kneeling at the top of the stairs in a big house on Blackheath, picking lumps out of the loop pile.

They saw each other more. He picked her up after work, soon on nickname terms with the other girls, who subsequently came to Amelia for relationship advice. But it was his friends they hung out with. Her choice, for they were more interesting, outrageous, larger-than-life people including one called Malcolm who was an assistant director on TV ads. He was the only person who was in no way protective of Richard, his first words whispered to her five minutes after he'd nodded an uninterested hello at one of Richard's parties.

— Pay you a hundred quid to suck those tits. Five minutes, hundred quid. Upstairs right now.

She blinked at him.

— A grand, she said.

— What?

— You serious?

— I fucking well am.

— Prove it, then. A grand in cash and you can suck my tits. Both of them, one after the other. Five hundred quid each.

— Too much. You'll let me do it for free one day.

— In your dreams, she laughed – which, as he would later describe with such relish to Neil, was precisely the case.

Was it Malcolm who got her that first job? Or one of the swirling group who were their friends? Helping at a cattle casting, some precocious pre-pubescent bitchette needed to play a sweet English girl in a classic for ITV? It wasn't Richard. He never helped, not directly, though he made suggestions, offered advice with a *why-ask-me* air. Soon she'd left the shop as you leave a bland dream. After three weeks as a casting assistant she could barely remember the names of the people she'd worked with there, the only thing to last a pair of sleek black leather boots she'd bought at the Christmas sample sale, which had Malcolm saying that he really might consider paying her the thousand after all.

Promotions. Different jobs. A partnership and then freelance. Years heading out into the world, taking it by the horns, catching sight of herself in city windows now and then and liking what she saw. A little afraid even, as if it wasn't really her. So when did it change? When did her real self detach, jump from the train of her life while she wasn't paying attention, to be replaced by a part-time version? And, more to the point, now that she has woken up to that, how will she get herself back again? How must she act now? What must she actually do?

The immediate answer is clear, a neon sign a thousand feet high standing up in front of her.

Clean. Up. The. Puke.

There is no more. She waits but her stomach is empty and so she pushes herself to her feet. She scurries to the bathroom, though not to clean herself. Beneath the sink she rummages for Dettol, grabs sponge scourers too and a plastic bucket, which she fills with warm water before hurrying back on to the landing, eyes and ears down the stairs again. She's been lucky. Ten minutes later and Richard would have been up here too. All she needs to do is get rid of this evidence and she bends again, pleased to hear a quiet roar from the TV, a goal, though mightn't that send Richard up, the game won or lost and no longer worth bothering with? She takes a deep breath, swears, and then returns to the bathroom where she grabs a loo roll and, from under the sink again, the dustpan and brush. Back at the vom pile she balls a fist of paper and tries to slide the puke on to the pan, hoping to get the sharp edge underneath the sickly-smelling slurry. It won't work, not really, so she scoops up a small handful and then another, glancing at the Dettol, hoping to fuck that it will mask the smell. Not too much though for that would be giving it away. In fact it's bound to, or at least draw questions, and she racks her brain until *ting*. Wine. Red, which she'll say she spilled, tripping on the top step. All she has to do is go downstairs, grab the glass that she's just taken a sip from, bring it upstairs and...

— Mummy? the voice says, behind her.

Niamh. She's standing in the doorway of her room. Empty water glass in hand. Her mouth a little O. Amelia stares up at her, not knowing what to say, the pan full of vomit shaking in her hand.

— Are you okay, Mummy?

She nods. Furiously. She swallows, does her best to smile, whisper-hisses *go back to bed*. But even she can hear the desperation and it doesn't get past Niamh. The girl is worried. Frightened. A year ago maybe it would have made her turn back, withdraw. But not now. Now it pushes her on, tells her this is something big, something that can on this occasion outweigh parental instruction, can countermand it like chocolate biscuits on a bank holiday. There is resolution on her face as she slips forward, past Amelia, dodging the outstretched hand that tries to grab her ankle. At the banister she leans over, opening her mouth before Amelia can stand and stop it shut which, in that moment, she would gladly do forever.

— Dad, the girl shouts. Daddy. I don't think Mummy's feeling very well.

In the weeks and months that follow, Amelia will think back to this moment. Such a trivial thing for a new life to be founded on. And another to be ruined by. The chance emergence of a girl from her bedroom. Different futures stretched out in front of her kneeling form. Her real life, the Amelia she could have been until her death, and the one she now inhabits. The former is snuffed out the instant Richard comes pounding up, looking first at Niamh but then transferring his gaze to Amelia, and the floor, a frown on his face but only for a millisecond before a smile burst up from underneath it.

— Oh, my God, he says. Knowing it.

She feels like puking again. So hard that the thing inside her splatters out on to the floor between them all.

That night he picks her up like a child and carries her into the bedroom. He puts Niamh back to bed and she listens to him cleaning up the traitorous vomit, after which he locks the house up, something she has listened to so many times, the click of the mortise lock in the back door, the beep of the alarm. It used to be a comforting sound. She expects him then to go through to their bathroom once he's remounted the stairs but he doesn't, just padding up to the side of the bed, the shuffle of his clothes coming off, belt buckle thumping on the floor. A draught as he gets in and there he is, spooning into her back. He doesn't ask what's wrong. Doesn't bring up dodgy takeaways, something going round the school. He just whispers I love you and moves yet closer, the fat cock she'd been given pause by all those years ago swelling between her buttocks. He makes no move. He just continues in tenderness towards her, running his nails against her scalp, kissing the space behind her ear. Yet it is there, rock-hard, and she feels sick again. He wants to underline the point. Print it in bold with a bullet point. She cringes, about to push him away, tell him it must have been something Alice gave her from the fridge, looked like it had been there a few days. But then she thinks no. She turns into his arms and kisses him. Tentative at first, then more deeply, her right hand ducking beneath the duvet. Gripping him. He begins to initiate foreplay, his hands going down beneath her legs, but she stops him, swivelling her hips up, licking her palm and then slicking it across the top of his cock. Still holding him she lifts her groin, guiding him inside her, sighing, pulling his mouth to her left breast, the one he favours for no reason she's ever been able to tell. He isn't prepared and as she starts to move he begins to come, upon which cue she slides out from him, quickly, doing panicked, directing his semen on to her stomach, a globule landing atop her right nipple and dripping down her breast. She hops out of bed, cleans herself up in the ensuite and then gets back in beside him.

— Close, she says. Naughty boy.

As if it mattered. Said as if she didn't know it was already a done deal. But I'll bluff it out, she tells herself, during the standard acceptable period of cuddling. Then she turns into her own space and swears she'll get through this. Never say a word. Pretend ignorance. Just get it sorted and the puke won't have meant a thing.

But in the morning she can't hide it. She wakes first, as she had planned, glancing across at the mound beside her, Richard's head beneath the pillows like some fallen, buried statue. There is no moment of forgetfulness, no coming into realisation. She's awake in a moment and out of bed in another, desperate to make it to the bathroom. If only she can. But there it is, back in her hands again, and then there is Richard, holding her hair back over the sink, a mirror-grin so wide there's no pretending any more. Which is when she begins to cry, falling on to her knees, burying her head into his broad, hairless shoulder.

— But it's okay, he tells her. Talking to a child. I'm really happy about it. I'm not just saying that. I'm really, really happy, love.

She can't answer. She just shakes and wails until, once more, Niamh too is standing over her.

That day he is everywhere. Spinning his solicitousness round her. He stays home. Just wants to be with her, he says. They are awkward as newlyweds, bumping into each other, speaking at the same time: no, you go on. Really. Amelia is self-conscious, as if she's starring in Am Dram, Richard's performance even more see-through than her own. It's so incredible, he says.

But is it?

He acts as though he's blown away. She stays quiet, watching him, letting him make their lunch, then a casserole for later, saying he can't remember if she can have pancetta or not. She tells him she's sure it'll be fine while all the time the suspicion seeds. And then flowers inside her. To begin with she can't believe it. Won't. But she can't cut it down. When Michael comes in from school the two of them head out into the garden with a football and she walks over to the French doors, palms against the glass as she watches them. Niamh is at some friend's house and it's odd to see them together. Her two males, the gangly youth and the big man he's shadowing. She stares at the boy and has a memory, the abhorrence she felt in her teenage years for boys like this, faces of such Icelandic turbulence she was terrified of getting too close to them, wondering if the rest of their unknowable bodies looked like that. Echoes of her love of her boy fight these thoughts but no, it was for someone else, a small, sweet child, like Dominic. She shivers and turns towards Richard. And nods. For it's still there: the self-consciousness, as he dribbles round Michael and puts the ball into the back of the net. Michael doesn't notice but once again she sees it: Richard is acting this. He knows she's watching him but he also knows it's not in a casual, normal way. He's pretending to be with his son but he's not: every molecule of his being is focused on her, to see if she's guessed yet.

That he knew.

A gasp. Small, silent. Now it's Michael's turn to get the better of Richard, kicking the ball through his legs and running round him, Richard's response being to lift Michael screaming by the waist and throw him over his shoulder. Amelia blinks, turning away for a second as she wonders.

Has she been had?

They agreed two. Even before Niamh was born they made that commitment, signed that verbal contract with each other. She's not imagining that. It came from her, sure, but he agreed and was keen to or so it seemed, appearing to join the happy ranks of the mentally snipped, though he always winced at the suggestion of making that a reality. He gave away baby toys to his sister. He whooped when they finally got rid of the pushchair. He raised his eyes in horror when teased by friends about having another, made cracks about keeping his mobile phone in his boxers. The Ark was full. They'd pulled the plank up and sailed off. The four of them.

So where does the suspicion come from; why is her mouth set hard?

He's hinted. She didn't really take it in, but recently he's made comments about how gorgeous she looked when up the duff. He's moaned about how quiet the house seems. On the appearance of the new babies of friends he has genuinely cooed, rather than just taking a peek and then mouthing some obvious platitude like the other blokes, hand in the cooler for a beer. Again she blinks. Michael is attacking Richard now, grabbing his legs, trying to tip him over. Were these comments outriders, sent into the domain of her intransigence? To see what fire they'd take? And, if so, did she play it wrong? Did she cut them down with too much force? When she snapped back that he'd better find himself a fat mistress then or told him how she loved the peace and quiet, did it warn him never to try to persuade her? Did her implacability tell him not to play his hand or else she'd be eternally vigilant? Did it force him to resort to other means? Has he done this to her deliberately?

— Fuck. She says the word aloud, her breath misting the window in front of her. She squeezes her eyes shut, a collapsing hollowness inside as she plays it out. Last year, totally sanguine about her coming off the pill when her rosacea got so bad people were always asking if she'd just been running. The patch then making it worse. Getting her pissed at the school auction last month. Not being able to find the johnnies when they got home later, joking that Michael must have swiped them. The look he gave her at Alice's when she said she didn't want a drink, how he leapt on that. And then, when they got home, how he poured her a nightcap immediately although it was so late, clinking her glass deliberately so she'd down some. Knowing, from that beer garden so long ago, what the reaction would be.

He was testing me. He did this to me on purpose.

Did he?

And now he's watching.

Richard lets Michael up-end him, but grabs his ankle when he tries to run off to score. He stands, the boy in a head lock, his free hand ruffling his hair.

And grins at her.

The next day he also works from home. And the next, though not, he asserts, because of her condition. The rehearsal space was double booked, so he just thought… The actors stumble in as if to a soup kitchen, after which Malcolm appears, to hash over the film script. In the intervals Richard touches her, kisses her, makes clear to her his joy: so she can have no doubt about it. Then it's Sunday. The following day she thinks she'll get some respite because Malcolm, as usual, has demanded a second call for the cornflakes casting. But even here she gets no space for Richard shows up just as lunch is being called and takes them out, picking her up at the end of the day as well. Dinner, he smiles, with Annie organised and everything. Annie, the girl Amelia now despises, whom she can't look at, for if the lazy bitch had filled Niamh's water glass as she's been told a thousand times then Amelia might have got away with this after all.

Richard glows. He expands. His pride is so big it surrounds her, filling the house with an odd heat. She, in contrast, seems to shrink until she's like a Japanese wife, all tiny steps and bound feet, timid, watchful. Sure he can read her thoughts. Can see the dread deed she is harbouring, the thoughts that churn inside her like badly oiled machinery.

Kill it.

Kill it.

Kill it.

Kill it.

Kill it.

The words thump inside her skull like an in-car sound system. They are so close to the surface of her thoughts that she's sure he must be able to see them. But it just makes him nicer. More appreciative. Meals are cooked, shopping done. He can't walk past her without running a hand across her bum, brushing the back of her neck with his lips. This response gives her nowhere to go, nothing to push back against. She wants to tell someone but who? Her friends, of course, but which of them wouldn't think that he's not being brilliant, supportive, that her fears aren't just paranoia? They all would because, of course, they are not her friends. They are *their* friends. Her own have faded into the past. She can barely think of one single person who sees her as existing on her own, who can even picture her without Richard standing there beside her. So what can she do?

How can she relax his smiling, velvet guard?

The following evening she slips into his lap. The kids are doing homework. Richard is looking over a play script.

— Howzit?

He smiles, eyes up in surprise. She hasn't touched him in days.

— Good. And you?

— Yes. Good now.

— Now?

— Richard, love. She pauses, sucks air through her nostrils. You might not have known this. I didn't want to say anything. But…

— You're not really sure about this?

She nods, a shameful secret, out at last.

— I *wasn't* sure. I mean… God I can hardly even say it. A baby. It was a bit fucking shocking, you know?

— Tell me about it.

— And it still is. But I've been thinking. And I'm happy now. I'm really happy. I wouldn't have chosen it but it seems so right. It's going to be great.

— I know. Yes. I mean I was just as –

— But we can't tell anyone. She points at him, teacher-like. Not yet.

— Of course. Twelve weeks, isn't it?

— Yes, though it might be earlier. I'm no spring chicken and they might want to get a scan done early. But not until then. *Okay*?

He nods and she kisses him, knowing that she's done it. She's lied her way to space: a couple of months in which to get it done. A visit to a clinic, private this time and definitely on her own. Then back to the toilet bowl, crying when she calls him at the theatre and asks him to come home…

But later on he smiles across the table at his family.

— Kids, he says, setting down his fork. Plates of half-eaten spag bol sit on the table in front of them all like jangled thoughts made real. He looks from Niamh to Michael and then back again, waiting for their attention. As usual, neither takes long to give it to him. How wonderful to be in this man's orbit, how fixed in their happiness her two children are. He leaves a beat and, as he often has in the past, she expects him to make some general announcement of his own contentment, an affirmation of their qualities, the sort of thing that makes them both blush, Niamh especially unable to hide the rush of joy. But instead his hand reaches across to hers, and takes it.

— We're going to have a baby.

She stares. Cannot believe what he's just said. Wants to pull her hand back but how can she? All she can do is watch as he somehow manages to keep it in his and pull the two children into an embrace before turning suddenly serious.

— Though it's a secret, okay? Until we've had a scan. For now keep shtum because we're not telling anyone. Not *anybody*, okay?

Michael is embarrassed. The few steps back to sex between his parents are just too much for him. Niamh, in contrast, able to short-circuit that or having no problem with it, claps and squeals in both real and performed happiness, her genuine excitement mixed with relief that her mother is not dying from some hideous disease as she'd no doubt begun to assume. Amelia is able to take back her hand now and she watches them, shaking her head, the suspicion that once again he's played her seeming to melt her skin from her body. She knows what will happen, and less than forty-eight hours later Rachel Green leans in as the bell goes.

— I hear you've got some news. Won't breathe a word of course but *huge congratulations*.

Other mothers look at her. Niamh's teacher winks and squeezes her arm, while her traitorous daughter behaves as if nothing has happened at all.

13

SHE GETS THE feeling a lot. That he is there. She finds herself looking around whenever she's in a crowded place. It was him asking about her play; it made her defensive. She's clung to her work since she was eight, identifying even then its importance to her. To have anyone else care about it too much or question her motives sets off alarms. Even if it's James. Her work was always something he respected, the bedroom with the 'Keep Out' sign on the door. And he did, unless and whenever she invited him inside, before which she always made sure that the sheets were straight and there wasn't too much shit strewn over the floor. It was how she liked it, needed it even, something true from the first moment she found out that connecting words together properly mattered to her. The problem then was that her first writing was done in the most raw and public of spheres: school. She'd write something and it would be dissected, given a mark, as if any teacher could grade how close she'd come to understanding the flurry inside her.

Eventually she couldn't take it any more and what she did caused problems. She wrote a story and found she couldn't pass it over, perhaps because she'd put herself in it for the first time. She was looking for her father. He, like all the fathers, had been taken to an old castle and by the time she found the place the most terrible thing had happened: she'd forgotten what he looked like. Men were everywhere, working at mundane tasks, but which was he? Despair filled her until she realised: she still had his photograph, she used it as a bookmark. She pulled her book from her bag but when she went to open it a hand reached down and grabbed it. A woman. Thin. Not dressed in rags like the fathers. She lifted the book away and Alice could do nothing as she plucked out the bookmark and tore it into pieces. She flung these into the wind and Alice chased them out across the winter fields that sloped down towards a slow, twisting river. She snatched uselessly, sure the wind would take the pieces into the churning water. But something happened. A bird swooped down. It thinks it's food, she thought, but then another came and another, until there were as many birds as pieces and each bird caught one. She watched as they landed, and then cleared. And there he was, her father, smiling at her again for one brief second before the breeze picked up again.

Back at the castle there was no one. But it didn't matter. She'd never lose him now.

— No, she said.

— You mean you haven't done it? That's unlike you, Alice.

— I have. I just. I don't want you to see it, miss.

— Why ever not? Your last one was so good.

Questions from the Head. Questions from her mother, pointed, she realised years later, towards some secretly suffered abuse. But it wasn't that. She just couldn't let anyone see, and after that she wrote two sets of stories, ones to be marked and others for herself. Eventually managing, as she explained in that lecture, to unite them and become a real writer, her words seen but never losing the ability to hold her deepest secrets and hold them tight. And now James seems to mind what she does, which creates a landslide inside her for why did he not see in her latest collection what Juri from Estonia saw? What Richard Leigh feels is going to win them awards? Because he doesn't read her work for what it is but as a way of looking into her? Because he is, in effect, intruding? She tells herself this is nonsense but can't shake the theory that the work means nothing to him, that all he does is look at it like a code-breaker, trying for some advantage.

She can't write with him looking at her. The house is a dead zone, no signals getting through. Instead she sits in cafés in Greenwich but this doesn't work either so she gets on the train and finds new places. Random coffee bars, pub gardens in parts of London they've never been to together. There are hidden benches on the upper levels of the South Bank from where she watches a square fountain with rooms that appear for a minute and then drop away, reform in different configurations as squealing kids jump through them. It's like her life. She has to keep changing shape, has to keep moving around so that no one can get a handle on her. If they did, it would all stop; she'd find herself pinned. Only by slipping out of James's grasp can she be herself, and only if she is herself will the writing work.

She looks after Ida, takes Dom or picks him up. She goes to work, pushing through the term, which seems grindingly long, in spite of the fact that she is, to some degree, fêted. There is a piece on her in the university magazine. She's booked to appear at two local literary festivals. And all the while the date of the prize announcement draws near, after which she will either stay at this new level of respect or take yet another leap up, which is why she has avoided the Head of School, wanting to know where she stands before putting some pressure on, asking about the possibilities of advancing her career. Peter Shale can sense this and still looks sick at the sight of her, a yellowness to his over-shaved skin. She will be promoted, there can be no doubt, but could she actually leapfrog him to Reader? Yes, and he knows it.

If she wins.

But as much as she knows all this it barely registers inside her. It is the play that matters now.

It's funny, this new modus. If writing was always a way of being herself, she's found a different self to be. Writing poetry she feels tiny, engaged in a shut room with the very smallest units of communication. Sometimes during these moments it has felt as if she is as close to being completely alive as she can be, but given this, how can this rushing thing be true? For now, writing her play, she feels not as though she is uncovering herself but making an opening through which something external to her enters, and is transformed. There is little conscious intervention. She doesn't screw her head up for the exact word. She is more like a translator, working in a language that seems more and more natural. And it's brilliant. She's sure of this. She works away in disparate, nameless places, amazed at what is appearing in front of her, until her mobile alarm goes off, whereupon she packs up and hurries to the nearest train station, yomping hard across the Heath to the school, or home, always just about getting where she needs to be on time. The spaces between her various lives are minuscule.

And as the play grows she waits, in trepidation, for James to ask if he can read it. Until then they are on hold. With poems it's easy. She says no until they're finished, knowing she'll lose the drive to make them work if she gets validated for them too early, or lose the confidence to finish them if she can detect any lack of interest. She does however have work to show him periodically, corners of herself to open. Her finished poems are like bridges they can cross back and forth but now there are no bridges. For the play is not finished. And she cannot let him in until it is. She waits for him to mind this, tell her they're not speaking any more. But what will she say when he does?

For now, though, she can relax because he won't ask. They've entered something she's previously been terrified of: a normal way of being. Dom and Ida get where they have to be with a minimum of fuss. The correct homework is done, fancy dress costumes made, weight and height measurements taken and medical charts remembered. Lunches are packed. Music courses applied for. Parties are gone to, hideous occasions in church halls where exhausted parents shepherd confused and barely interested kids through a tedious rote of supervised playing, as if they don't get enough of that shit at school. Vaguely appropriate, secretly inexpensive birthday presents are bought, wrapped and remembered. In this back-and-forth, this tag parenting, they are, she realises, parcelling up their children's lives with the efficiency of divorced people.

It's because he's busy. They cannot swing, letting each day be itself, throwing things up to be responded to. If they did they'd be swamped. James is head down into his sab, opening and closing the BL, with his gigs to think about too, which continue to secretly anger her in a way she still can't put a finger on. She has to admit that they are beginning to add up financially, a small though surprisingly significant boost to their shared income. The regime of their ship relaxes somewhat: fewer home-made sandwiches at work, the odd takeaway bought or impulse lunch out on Sundays. More tangibly a new TV appears in the living room to replace the ancient portable, Pat the Telly, so named because you had to whack it now and then, too small to show the score when Murray was playing. How odd, she thinks, that by standing in a room talking her husband can improve the quality of their electrical appliances. She stares at the thing, as discreet in size as the store allowed but so modern it looks embarrassed, like an early party guest in Gucci, desperate for others to arrive.

Ah, fuck it, she misses him. That's what it is. They have very little time together and when they do have dinner there is so much outside stuff to be sorted, agreed on, mostly to do with the kids. There's the prize too, which has begun to seem like a weapon. He advises her on how to navigate the treacherous waters of academe, not to Reader he thinks but straight to Prof, something she's sure is far too weighty for her. She in turn talks about his book, whether he needs to ride it to another department, and they sound like each other's life coaches rather than two people who fancied the fuck out of each other and were finally brave enough to admit it. He doesn't ask about the play. Has he realised how his questioning clammed her up? Is he now doing what she wants? Or is it that he has so much on that he doesn't care, his poet running around in his head so fast she can almost see him mouthing iambs at the table when he's pretending to listen to her.

Ask about my play, she begs him.

She feels lost. Abandoned. She can't help wishing that, when she does glance up from this café table or that, he really were standing there staring at her.

So why not stare at *him*? She could go to one of his gigs, though the idea scares her. Seeing him out there, shorn from the context in which she experiences him? She'd shy from it, made uncomfortable by the essential dishonesty that is comedy. Spinning their lives, twisting, all for the big laugh, idiocised faces turning round him. And it wouldn't work anyway because he'd be nervous, just as he always was, something she put down to the fact that she was able to see what he chose to reduce things to. That or he'd curtail himself, his energy if not his words. So don't tell him, laughs a voice, but she won't do this. The venues are small. She'd never get away with it and the kids would dob her in anyway, at least the fact that she'd been out. Then she thinks that actually what should happen is that he should invite her, just as she should invite him to read her growing play. They are living in their own circles – not a problem as they always have – but where are the intersecting vectors? The zones in which to take their relaxation and their joy? Until they open up again she feels both exhilarated and horrified to be chained up alone, to her play.

She dives into it again. The outside world is seen through a film, her children's voices muted, their kisses less felt. She barely looks in the mirror before leaving the house, is surprised without tampons for the first time in years. It happens on the train to work and there's no loo paper left in the swaying toilet. All she has to get her through the next ten minutes is her notebook and she tears out and folds a couple of pages, a sestina she's already given up on. Back in her seat she thinks about her blood, slowly obscuring the words she's already moved beyond.

One morning she notices, leaving Ida to her nursery toast, that her dress is inside out. She hurries away before one of the staff makes a joke about being in a rush that morning. She was not in a hurry, just not alive to the correct alignment of children's clothing. She feels like a submarine on action stations, all non-essential operations shut down as she drives on to her target.

As Richard harries her.

He sends texts. Emails. Leaves jokey voicemails asking if she's doing anything. He wants to know if she wants to meet up, run her ideas by him, the effect like one she recognises from some part of her life, but cannot get a handle on. She resists, refusing to even tell him that she's working on this play of theirs, knowing that could very well let some virus in. They haven't met since that first time but still he tries to contact her, not for one second taking her silence for the dismissal it originally was. Is it arrogance, the fact that he just assumes she's doing what he suggested? It irritates her that he is right, and probably knows it. And at times she wonders why he is even bothering. Is it really that he was blown away by her writing? Or is there something else? A need with new people in his life to corral them, fix them as part of a universe in which he is the centre, the kind of guy who is always throwing parties, generosity masking some need to pull everyone towards him? Something in that but she hasn't got it exactly. There's something he can, but she cannot, quite see.

James, in contrast, is hovering. She can tell he's thinking about it now, and is reining in his curiosity. She should want to finish it so they can connect again, just as she wishes the cramps in her belly would ease. But as she rips through the last scenes, scribbling them so quickly that the words look like heart blips, it is Richard she wants to show it to, him she'll call when it's done, or send a muted text to, wondering if he wants to meet. And she still won't show it to James because it won't be done until Richard has read it and talked to her, until he has agreed with her about what she has made in these short, frenetic weeks. Not a finished thing. But a real thing. Ragged and raw, she is sure, but something strong and vital, which now exists the way a mountain does, a fact in the world. Brought about by her and him, by her with his help.

The night she finishes her play Alice goes to bed early. James is out. She has a dream. Or is it a dream, going over as it does something that definitely happened? Can we dream true things, exactly as they were? If not then she can't have dreamed but remembered, yet it felt so like sleep. She was building a Spitfire. They were his thing. She bought a kit and secreted herself at intervals, refusing to let him in on the surprise, even though he did his best to circumvent her. Still she held out though until it was done, built and painted, a beautiful thing that she had actually enjoyed making, surprising herself in that. She couldn't wait to give it to him. Only she never did because, the day before his birthday, her father walked out.

She wakes up and gets out of bed. She goes through her play and puts this in, this Spitfire, puts it in throughout the play for no other reason than that it should be there. After that she feels sweaty, and cold. She hears rain and opens the curtains, stares down at the sheet of light stretching out of the kitchen window, the overhead left on for James. Their garden. Their wall. The pedalo, still there. Something of a feature now, its soggy cardboard box slouching round its shoulders as it leans against the wall. She feels like crying. She wants James there, wants to be crying in his arms. To tell him sorry. About what she does not know, but she wants to clasp his knuckles to her forehead and beg for his forgiveness. She almost calls him but does not. Instead she dresses quickly, and stands at her children's door. Silence. She pulls on her trainers and then her mac before slipping out into the damp night.

14

— RICHARD, I don't want this child.

Amelia says the words in a strong, clear voice. She speaks them to the wind on Blackheath. She speaks them to the trees in Greenwich Park, once to the inside of a café window from a cruiser table, the businessman next to her making a hurried finish to his latte. Why not to him? Her husband? In bed perhaps, the darkness enough to leave the words disembodied, as if not coming from her? Is it fear of what he'd say? His broad, male shock? His disappointment? No. She stays silent for the simple reason that – of course – he already knows how she feels. She's told herself she's being stupid so many times but the fact won't go away. He's been three steps ahead from the start. If she admits it overtly she'll be playing into his hands. He's already shown her some of the weaponry he'd use to shoot down her objections, having thrown an au pair at her the very day after she puked, upgrading the offer to nanny two days later. She just nods but feels more tightly bound by this show of support. He's trying to block every alley her mind would use to duck away from this and the next thing he does is so audacious it literally stops her breath.

Sunday morning. Often he reaches for her for a session of sleepy, limbic sex. The kids, sensing this, no longer barrel into them but stay out until called. Today however he slips away, leaving her to push herself to a sitting position, hand reaching automatically for the radio before she pulls it back. Instead of vaguely important chuntering on Radio 4 she blinks into the silence, a car driving past on the Heath road like the slow tearing of fabric. She glances around at their room, her room really for she chose the carpet, the William Morris on the walls, the chests of drawers and duvet covers. They came from Heal's in the sale while other items – dressing gowns, pyjamas, candle holders – were all netted from different posh catalogues, the ugliness of their packing materials still seeming to hang around them like dirty secrets. She wonders why she bought any of it and what it says that there is nothing old, no dodgy heirloom furniture pieces or scraggy T-shirt from her student days. The room is like a squash court in which images of herself bounce back and forth, images she no longer wants to see and which are made worse because – and this has never occurred to her before – they could belong to anyone. Rachel Green has a bedroom like this. Amelia went there once, took a wrong turn on the landing, staring inside in shock. Dumpy Rachel with the boudoir of a beautiful woman, almost identical to her own. It made her feel cheap and it does again, an added claustrophobia pushing her out of bed.

She heads to the window and pulls aside the velvet curtains, whose weight used to so delight her. Her eyes rove over the empty Heath where James disappeared that time. In his place stands Loser Man from round the corner, flying his remote control plane. Again she wonders what horror he's escaping, how doing this for so many hours could seem like the way to spend your life. Though at least he's good at it. And what does she have to distract herself from the emptiness that has seemed so suddenly to surround her life? She watches as the little machine nosedives towards the ground, certain to be smashed to pieces until it levels, skims the grass and rises. After that it just rolls and banks and, bored, she turns to watch two people on the pathway, walking towards each other. A middle-aged man and a young woman who, from Amelia's position, also seem destined to crash. They don't of course, walking past, and Amelia screws her eyes up, wanting to see some sign of recognition, a hello or a nod, the homeopathic hint of a smile. But there is nothing. Nothing at all, as if they didn't even see each other, are walking across the Heath alone.

Amelia shivers and pans her gaze to St Saviour's. Each day she's been there, at least one person has made some veiled comment, slipped a secret congratulation into her hand. Her only response has been to smile, from a thousand miles away, unable to get past a thought that turned her stomach to clay when it came to her. James. When she first saw him it was with a sense of seniority, the finishing line getting closer. But as she stared around the playground last week she realised that one day he'll be gone while she'll still be there, putting together the Christmas box, reading the Monday Mail, trying to remember the log-in for ParentPay. Her child will be born in just over eight months, will start there five years later, which means she'll be going there for twelve more years. She could barely compute this but she forced herself to do the maths. On the last day she ever sets foot there she will be fifty-three years old. The knowledge hit her like a blast of pure heat and she could barely stand, the ring of the hand bell seemingly aimed at bringing her into line not the kids. She needed, for some reason, to see him. She spun, barely hiding it as her eyes scrabbled through the bodies until they latched, fixing on to him as she asked herself the question that had been building for the last few days. Will she be free of it now? Filled, as she is, with a far more dangerous horror? She thought back to the moment she first saw him and wondered whether it could have been anyone, the first vaguely shaggable man she clapped eyes on that day. No. For as she moved towards him she could feel it, still there, her gaze desperately eating up the side of his neck, his lips when he turned and smiled at her with an ignorance she still had no idea how to break.

He finds it easier now, to let go. He doesn't even kiss Dominic goodbye but just ruffles his hair and tells him to have a good day. Which he will. Amelia stared at the line of children, amazed at how happy they looked. The place has become another green zone for them. Seeing this has made James relax and when he brings that girl of his he won't look shredded the way he did those first weeks. Nor will it seem such a shock to him. It'll be a routine more than a rush, something that has already begun to happen. He chatted with his peer parents, some play date being organised. He too seemed happy and she wanted to tell him to beware, to stop right there, because if he doesn't he'll spend the next eight years marching round the place like a kid's pet beetle, getting closer and closer until he can no longer move.

He saw her. Headed over. They were friends now, weren't they, and the thought struck that she could kiss him. She could just do it and he wouldn't be able to stop her. She did, on his bristly cheek, after which she turned to look down at Dominic, a delicate sunflower stalk waving from the clear plastic drinks cup in his little hand. For the first time she saw that the blond hair has fooled her: it's Alice he looks like, not James. He really is her child, and in his energy too, so like her, something that will remain true forever, she thought. Unlike her own children on whom she has left no mark at all. Whom she bore and raised for Richard. Bending to look at the sunflower, she wondered, what if you were my son? And what if you weren't there? You didn't exist? She wondered if it would matter and the answer was no. So many other children. She blinked and it was as though Dominic was disappearing in front of her eyes, transported to a different school that popped up in her mind: for all the curtailed children. Very much like this one but for one small difference. The children line up at home time, but no parents ever come to collect them.

Amelia pulls on her dressing gown. Downstairs she finds orange halves, piled on the kitchen island like bright, gutted fish, the recycling bin crowded with supermarket croissant boxes and strawberry punnets. Another surprise: Michael, whom Richard has somehow hacked out of bed. He hasn't showered and she can smell the teenage stew, Niamh shifting her chair to be away from him.

Richard himself is in the centre of it all. Big, hearty, delighting his groaning children with his ribbing and jokes. In spite of herself she nods, perching on a stool to watch him. For this is Dad. This is epicentre, pure male hero, living up to absolutely everything he has ever promised his family. For himself he seems to inhabit the room more fully than anyone she has ever seen, so is this a drug for him? One he needs to re-supply himself with? Is this what he gets from his job as well, so many lives resting on his shoulders? Amelia blinks at the impact he has, his expansive proximity like gravity, making them move when he moves, their eyes following him as he pours the juice, so orange in colour that it looks artificial, dollops out yogurt and muesli, Michael reaching automatically to take the honey spoon from him as he has since the age of two. Chunks of the past fall out on the table and she sees him when Niamh was Dominic's age, Daddy of Daddy Hall, whooping as they pulled out of the drive, pretending he was stealing their car. On his shoulders, saying he'd lost them, asking strangers if they'd seen whoever was riding up there. The songs he made up, a lullaby for Michael, adapted when Niamh came along. She swallows, sickened again for no reason she can think of, the feeling only getting worse after breakfast when he helps Niamh with her violin. He gives such simple and strong advice that she improves her playing immediately, fired by his vast, love-soaked certainties. Amelia watches it all with the knowledge that her husband is not some evil control freak intent on ordering and ruining her life. Instead he is perfect. Ideal in some *Woman's Own*, daytime TV way. She can find no fault with him at all, which leaves her with snakes of self-loathing crawling inside her arms for what does it say about her that she is really beginning to loathe him?

He loads the machine, washes up the juicer. She does not help, in spite of all the work she knows he has stacked up for later, play scripts and set-design proposals to go over, which will keep him at his desk until midnight. He mends a kite surf harness with Michael while she mooches, seething, fighting tears, deliberately slovenly, wandering upstairs again, aware that there is more activity in the kitchen now, some meat searing, a blender sounding. She hears this from the bath, after which voices call out to her which if she strained enough she could hear. But she doesn't. Nor does she respond, expecting someone to come up and tell her whatever it is. Instead there is more clatter and then she hears the door close, after which she wraps herself in a towel and lies on the bed, alone it seems for the first time in weeks. She should plan. Plot. At least steel herself, but instead she takes the soft option of sleep, though it turns out to be more than self-avoidance. She wakes to inner determination, planted when she was comatose by some unknown force. The pulling images of domestic glow from an hour ago are gone. She is not part of them now, but herself again. It can't go on. She has to put a stop to this. Who cares if people know? They'll claim a miscarriage. It's her body. Hers, finally. After waiting for it so long. She'll tell him right now and what, actually, can he do about it? What country does he think she's living in? She's filled with a buzzing glee, tempered by curiosity at the fact that sleep seems to be the only place where she can find herself these days. Only there are her true feelings able to align. How can she find such clarity when awake? she wonders, before stopping what she is doing.

Voices. Muffled, from below. Not just her family. They have a different energy: there is a stranger in the house. She dresses quickly and arranges her features into a cautious welcome, adaptable to whoever she encounters. But she is still totally banjaxed to see the vicar standing there.

He's not religious, Richard. Oh, he's in church with her every now and then, making the old dears' hearts flutter at coffee, cooking up hotdogs at the fundraising day. He helps carry the Christmas tree in and is happy to rattle the Christian Aid tin now and then. But she's heard his comments to the Prep dads at parties: hours on the knees saving thousands in fees. Though he's not completely mercenary. He's drawn to the decency. He loves the effect on the kids, even if they do subsequently turn their back on it, which he fully expects and will be relieved by. And perhaps he likes the fact that his wife has something about her, something set back, that she does in her moments genuinely believe all this though not in some gurning, do-good way she sees in a lot of the other mothers. For her it is a truth, if one she doesn't very often contemplate. It has spoken to her since she was Niamh's age and used to go and stare at the carved Christ in the Minster. There is a God who had a Son and He did the inconvenient thing of showing us how to live. She never really questioned it because the feeling was so real, staring into His gaunt, haunted features, so like Actor Twat's now she comes to think of it. The gap between her own life, and His, is the hidden electricity that powers her. And now, as she hovers before this most sinful of acts, Richard has chosen to rub her face in that.

— Amelia, Graham says. Hope you don't mind me invading. You must blame your husband, he was quite insistent.

— Yes, she tells him. He can be like that.

It's lamb, of course. Cooked to perfection. Richard's roasts are beyond compare, not a potato that isn't both crunchy and creamy, always some secret added spice lurking in the carrots or leeks like a test guests try to pass unasked. Today the meat is a little pinker than he'd normally do it, blood running down the cliff face when the carving fork compresses it. Graham opens his mouth with relish, long teeth visible that he can hardly wait to use. He's thin, is Graham, with the unhealthy pallor of the late-adopting marathon runner. Amelia sees him in various local locations, sunken chest visible beneath his perforated vest, grey head bobbing as though he's being flogged.

— Wine? Richard asks.

The bottle is already uncorked. The vicar nods and Richard walks over to the cabinet and takes out glasses: but only two. One for him and one for the vicar, who looks at him with slight reproach before asking if Amelia won't be joining them.

— No, Richard says. Amelia… isn't really drinking just now. Unless, sorry, you want a small glass, love?

— I see, the vicar says, nodding. He reaches forward to the water jug and fills Amelia's tumbler. She just stares as, smiling at her, Richard glugs out the Rioja.

It passes in a blur. She feels as alone and betrayed as she ever has. The vicar glances at her during the meal, trying to make benevolent eye contact, but turns away each time, aware that something is happening here. He focuses instead on Richard, who appears not to pick up on her distress, carving darker bits for Niamh, letting Michael have some of the wine she herself is being denied. Without making any sort of fuss about it she gets a glass and pours herself a decent measure, but she can't even take a sip of it and nor can she eat. All she can do is stare at her husband, wondering what she's done to deserve this. Wondering too what he's got lined up next for her.

It comes when the vicar is leaving. They show him to the door and Richard pulls out his phone, apologising: he really needs to take this. It leaves her alone with Graham, something she doesn't think anything of at first because he's been playing the fool a bit, infected by Richard's bonhomie. Scales fall now though and he looks at her. Still. Focused. Throwing off the fact that he is a normal person. He doesn't even thank her for lunch. It's as though they're back in church, completely alone together as she opens her hands for the wafer.

— If you need to see me. He's staring at her. Not with pleasure. It's as though he, too, can see inside her. You know where I am. If there is anything you want to talk about, Amelia.

She watches him stride off towards the church on the big green space.

Her legs are weak. She leans against the wall. A movement beside her and she turns to see Michael pick up the snow globe she bought in the Mencap shop. He shakes it and then stares for a second at the singing woman with her blue, slapdash eyes until, bored, or embarrassed that he should even have been interested in it, he shoves it back on the windowsill. The flakes whirl, though they are not flakes. They are shards of grit and gravel and it's her they're scything into, scouring her skin, biting into her eyes. She can't move. She can't even lift her hands to protect herself.

For two weeks she's blinded. Torn. She wants to storm at Richard, just do it, scream it all out at him. She can't, though, one reason being that he's never there. He's made a tactical retreat. He's working hard, often home late, some issues with Malcolm that he doesn't share. She's harrowed and frenzied, a nightmare witch-woman staring back whenever she dares look in the mirror, misery filling each of her sunken pores like some inverse version of collagen. At school she shoots her gaze around the playground: at the women. They come to and fro with such apparent complacency but have any of them done it? Had a little human removed from them? What is the worst thing you have done while coming to this place, this church school, still professing what your presence still claims to profess? She wants to ask but she's no friends there. Not really. She can see that. She only has fellow cast members in the play they've all been acting out. The play with no ending but which is happy, happy, happy all the same.

Graham is there. He comes in to talk to the children, lead prayers. She avoids him, cut by the realisation that, of course, Richard was right to bring him home. Shove him in her face. For no one forces her go to church. And she does go. She says what is required of her there, and more. She also sends her kids to this haven, angry when her motives are slyly questioned by atheist parents with children being chewed up in the state process. So the least she owes that pale figure by the altar is to run foetus murder through the filter of His gaze. This time. The first one grieved her, but she never doubted it was the right thing. She was young, she was naïve and terrified – but now? She'll live in the same house. Still work, though it'll be harder. What other reason but rage at being short-circuited does she have for wanting to poison the seed inside her? And if she does it, will she be able to walk into that church again? Accept the quiet stillness that moves into her? Or will that gap between His life and hers be so wide there'd be no point ever trying to close it?

Again she's desperate to talk to someone. Rachel Green would listen but she wouldn't understand. None of them would, these women she's been drinking coffee with for so many years, jogging, laughing over dinner tables in one or other of their comfortable houses. Alice. Perhaps she could talk to her. She's more awake. Hasn't bought into the whole package. She wouldn't judge. She wants to approach her but something has changed: she's even more remote than usual. Has she guessed the reason why Amelia wormed her way into their lives? She hurries off each day, whether at drop-off or pick-up, pretending on at least three occasions that she didn't see her.

Term draws out. Summer parks itself on the Heath, the grass fading like a TV with the colour down. Picnics sprout after school, which she joins as Niamh plays rounders with her friends or lets Year Six boys teach her skateboarding, unaware as yet of any of the complications this sort of thing will one day bring. More women congratulate her, it's not secret any more, and she doesn't bother to deny anything. For to her great astonishment she is already changing.

Her skin first. It's morphing, given some strange, elfin smoothness no beauty cream could replicate. Not only that, but faint brown blotches appear on her arms like leopard spots. They are beautiful things that seem to mark her out among these other women, and her face is changing too. Not ragged now. In the past few years it has thinned, something she was proud of, beginning as it did to give her the appearance of one of those early-middle-aged women whose beauty is faintly forbidding. The sort of look that asks men whether, at their age, they have done anything to deserve a woman like that. A slight reversal has taken place, however, a refilling of her features. In contrast to how she feels she radiates health, something she needs to be careful of for isn't it just another Richard ruse? He knows that in spite of the initial puke phase she liked being pregnant. He knows how beautiful she became, how lightsome the two of them looked together at weddings or parties, how the eyes of both men and women alike were drawn to her. No, she won't be seduced by it, even though she's beginning to see some effect on the one person she wants to really see her.

She and James are the same age. They could have been mates at school, got pissed, lost their virginities together: but all this time he's treated her with deference, as though she's a different generation. She's been unable to break through that. Up to now. She tells herself it's her imagination at first, some stupid teenage hope that the crushee is getting the sickness too. But no, she can tell: there's definitely something different to him, his body responding to her own in a way it simply didn't before, even if he doesn't know it. He's looser, easier, coming over to the house after dropping Dom, the lack of any excuse other than a coffee in no way embarrassing him. For the first time she feels as if she has some power over him, the fact of her fecundity slithering beneath his guard, and whispering to him.

As Richard stays distant. Ever so slightly cold now. An error? A miscalculation? The erroneous belief that playing the vicar joker won him the hand? During weekdays she'd have said yes because she'd have had all that time to herself. But at weekends he has his proxy to keep an eye on her. Niamh has eschewed any formal activities. Michael is going to Millwall Dock every Saturday for sailing lessons. He gets himself there, finds his own way back. Someone feeds him. But when summer day trips are mentioned Niamh shakes her head, doesn't care that all her friends are going. She wants to be at home.

— With you, Mum, she insists.

It's the baby. Arm round her shoulders, Richard explains this to her. She may be ten but she's still nervous, terrified of being kicked into the long grass. Amelia knows this is true, and that she also wants to join in. She talks about it endlessly, asking baby questions she has to rack her brains for answers to, pointing through the window of that kids' shop in the village. She suggests names, writing a list of possibles on the fucking fridge in two bubble-neat columns as Amelia irons. Did Richard put her up to it? Or did he just know she'd be like this? Amelia isn't sure but her daughter's constant attempts to imagine the baby's arrival make real the notion that, left to its own devices, it really will. She's not some fifteen-year-old in binge-drink denial.

She needs to think about this, and one afternoon on her way to the grocer's she stares at a bouquet of prams outside the Costa. Christ. To be the mother of an infant? Again? The idea in its concrete form shocks her even more than before and she stops, staring in dismay at the determination with which a seemingly animatronic six-month-old waves his arms and legs. She's moved on. She's cast off skills in favour of others. She is a mother, but of a ten- and thirteen-year-old, and while her performance in these roles has been less than perfect of late they're roles she can deal with. To go back in time? Some of it seduces. The slowness, lack of rush, the drawing back into the immediate self that must of necessity occur when looking after a baby, the casting off of any responsibilities beyond care for the new arrival. Relief in that, but when she sees *The Very Hungry Caterpillar* lying on the seat of a Phil & Teds she pictures all the previously wrung-over experiences. Staying home. Cooking mush. Shaking pre-prepared portions of milk powder out of plastic cubes into obsessively sterilised bottles. The crawling and then toddler phases, a year and a half when relaxation for one second could mean burned fingers, scalded skin, frantic searches in galleries and shopping malls. The tedious bits are too bewildering to face again, while the wonderful moments would just be ghosts as she willed her child to grow, walk, talk, read, write, get dressed, wipe their bum, and then do that most important thing of all: learn to be on its own. All so that she can get back to the moment when her life stopped, all so she can be herself again, like skipping forward through scenes on a DVD to the place you fell asleep at. No. She's too old, and not just in her body. She simply can't go through with it again.

But neither can she do *it*. Have it sucked out. Not on her own, or at least she can't make that decision on her own. Not again. The first time, she realises, cost her more than she ever knew. A self, in fact, the one she might have lived to be without ever having got together with Richard. The individual life that was waiting for her before he came to claim her. AT would have dumped her eventually, pregnant or not. True, but if he'd left it a month she might have got over him without the shoulder Richard offered. She would have had to cope. She has a sense of her, the person she could have been, and the woman is so real she can imagine her out there in the city, working, serious. A little, perhaps, like Alice. With a decent haircut. She has a fantasy of meeting herself one day and of the two of them staring at each other, that other Amelia taking her baby from her arms and holding it awkwardly for a moment before handing it back, turning quickly and striding down the street, or running.

But to do it on her own... She imagines telling Richard. Just saying it. *Sorry, pal.* Would he freak? Fear bucks inside her, for what if he did more than that? What if he packed his bags? She feels loose at the mere idea and wonders if he'd leave her, find someone else, someone younger, only too willing to sprog for him. She'd get the house, but what would it be? A shell, echoing and deteriorating without its heart, which she now knows to be him. And she'd have no money to keep it, not really. She'd be alone, frazzled, and about as attractive to future partners with her two kids in tow as the small lake of vomit that flagged all this.

She swallows. But then takes a breath because he wouldn't. Not to the kids. However he punished her it would not be that way, though she still can't do it. Not alone. She can't stand up to it by herself. It's too much to bear. She'd have to justify it, first to herself and then Graham, who will know what she has done, whatever the story. And not just to him but to the pale sad statue in the church who certainly will know. She wants to but it's too much to carry, not least because this thing was done to her. She can't get round the thought. Consciously? Subconsciously? What does it matter? Richard – or something in him – saw that she was emerging from the life he'd made for her. He could see her blinking in the light and was terrified of what she might do. So he did what he did, which means that he must accept his share of the responsibility for what she is going to do now. And she will have this abortion. She will, and she won't care who knows about it. And somehow Richard will agree to that. She just has to think of a way.

Where is she? What day has she arrived at? She blinks, sees that it's Saturday morning and that she's at home with Niamh. Niamh is bored but not willing to say so, fearful of her mother's moods. Amelia watches her slouch around, then pick up the snow globe as her brother did, though unlike him she is fascinated, staring inside as she moves it. A shiver runs down Amelia's spine. She hurries across the room and snatches it, snapping at her daughter to do something, anything, read a book, play her violin, she doesn't care what the bloody hell she does. Niamh backs away and Amelia stares at the thing in her hand, wanting to be able to shake it clear. It cuts her deep inside that all she can do to stop the confusion is nothing.

Or is it? She strides over to the sink. She pulls a knife from the rack and stabs at the base, prising up the plastic dome. She lets the water and the snowflakes run out as the question comes.

Why is it never men in these things?

She drops the dome and base in the bin. Then she walks back to the windowsill and stands the woman up there on her own.

15

— Is THE PRODUCT damaged, sir?

He's on stage again. A thing he does: make calls to people. Live. Channelled through the particular venue's PA. He's getting known for it, sees the odd face he recognises in the audience: his fans. He gets a nice little thing in *Time Out*, calling him a 'mobile-toting psycho dad'.

He's stopped phoning home because Alice has started to sound a little acidic and, as he's further up the bill now, he goes on later, when the kids are asleep. A shame though as they're naturals, Dom's space knowledge particularly hilarious. In a competition with three plucked-out students at the Laughter Lounge he beat them all on planet order and light year distances, which took James on a particularly satisfying riff about St Saviour's kicking Imperial College out of the Russell Group. Dom then told off a physics professor for a rather loose explanation of how black holes are formed.

— But what about the helium? his five-year-old son had screamed.

Ida was just magical. She sang, told the first half of jokes she'd heard from Dom, too cracked up to go on. She made fart sounds. When she refused to kiss him goodnight at the

King's Head, a woman in the audience jumped on stage and did it for her.

Today he's at Glastonbury. And, because it's a daytime gig, he's able to call Park-Gear.

— No. It isn't damaged. As far as I can tell. What it is is a pedalo.

— I know that, sir. We manufacture and supply a variety of pedal-powered boats made from roto-moulded polyethylene.

— Pedalos. To parks, would that be a fair guess?

— Usually, sir, but –

— Or seaside resorts?

— Yes, though –

— While I have a garden the size of a Subbuteo pitch. Which is in no way a public amenity. Nor do waves lap up against the flipping rhododendrons.

— Well, you ordered it, sir.

— I did not order it. My idiot brother ordered it. All I want you to do is remove the useless thing.

— It is not useless, sir. From my records here you have a Mark 126 Clipper with a top speed of over five mph as well as a side independent pedal system. That allows both drivers to pedal at their own speed.

— Oh, can you not just take the silly thing away?

— We'll have to charge you.

— *Charge* me?

— For the van coming out. We're in Milton Keynes.

— Where else? he wonders, before taking another tack. Actually, forget it. I don't want you just to take it. But you've made a mistake.

— Sir?

— The order note says it should be orange. And it's blue.

— I see. We must have been out of orange ones. That must have been why we —

— Oh, no, you don't, James tells her. My brother ordered an orange pedal-powered boat made from roto-moulded polyethylene and that is what I want. You will come and replace my blue Mark 126 Clipper with an orange one. *Okay?*

To which four hundred people in the Comedy Tent roar out their approval, after which he decides on this occasion to break his rule about phoning Alice, first getting all those there to *really hush it.*

— Hi, love, he says, as if he's strolling down the street. I just thought you'd like to know. I've solved our pedalo problem...

He pauses.

— Sort of.

The one person he doesn't phone is his brother. He's fed up with these games. It's his turn now to play the next joke but he's long since tired of it. He's got a family now, a life. He's going to phone and tell him, though not when he's on stage. Send an email maybe. Meanwhile he's totally busy, more so than he's ever been. He loves it, though not when his publisher calls, from a world he can barely remember.

— When are you going to send me something, James?

— Soon, yes. He buries his head in his poet on the train back to London, making notes until Chris Carty phones.

— Great gig, his agent says.

— How the fuck do you know?

— Just heard. Jay Farrell was there. He called.

— Who?

— Jesus, Jim, you *have* been out of it. What are you doing Friday night?

— Why?
— The Big Time, Carty says.

James arrives at the studio half an hour before he's needed, having eschewed the offered car which he knew would leave him hanging around for ages. He gets there 'late', the studio manager in a fluster, hurrying him in to have his make-up applied by a nice woman in her early thirties called Jill. Her soft thumbstrokes on his cheekbones remind him that his wife hasn't touched him with such intimacy for longer than he can remember. It makes him wistful, a little confused, his subsequent performance on the comedy panel show just as relaxed and natural as his stage appearances have been, owing to the fact that he'd much rather be at home. He's not really there at all in fact but in a place of missing Alice, and he's the undoubted highlight of the thing, his answers coming as afterthoughts, a comic though very real bewilderment at the ridiculous waste of time that is the proceedings.

The show is all about how many facts you can tell about the life of a famous person without the other panellists guessing who you're talking about. It's the sort of thing you do out of desperation when the car breaks down on the motorway and he's amazed anyone has turned up to watch it voluntarily. Or that it's going to be on TV. He doesn't bother hiding his belief that this is a huge waste of everybody's time, something he demonstrates by his lack of any preparation, making his stuff up as he goes along, something he knows the other comics do not, even the one who's famous for ad-libbing. When it's his turn to guess he doesn't really do that, just picks what he thinks might be funny and talks about himself. And he is funny. Because he doesn't care if he is or not. He steals the show, and Suit Boy appears afterwards, as if by magic.

Jay Farrell.

— Let's talk, he says.

James shrugs, reflecting on the nature of chance, and timing.

— What about?

— Projects.

James nods half-heartedly, remembering this moment. He assumes, as he learned to assume, that the man means in some nebulous, always to be deferred later time, and is about to walk off. But he doesn't. He means now. He leads James away, as the other comics try not to stare, and soon they're in some private bar above a restaurant where famous people who hate publicity go to get papped. They sit in retro buckets of cream leather as wine is ordered. Oooh, fizzy wine. Not actual champagne, though. Oh, actually, hell, yes, it bloody well is. With a year on. He wonders if it's on the licence fee.

— If you could do anything on TV, James, what would it be?

Thinks. He wants to laugh as Suit Boy pinball-flippers the sides of his chair. It's all so fucking ridiculous. What's the man asking him for? Why not that lot downstairs? They'd chuck tons of stuff at him, but he hasn't the faintest idea. He's never even thought about it, at least not for years. Old formats and pilot ideas come back but they're stale, worst of all normal, and he doesn't even think about repeating them. His mind is blank and he wants to shrug, say nothing, though he doesn't do that. Instead he nods, frowns, leans forward into the man's thin, tight, nostril-dominated face.

— Well, James, don't keep me in suspense.

— I want to take a pedalo across the English Channel.

Suit Boy throws his head back. It's the first time James has ever heard him laugh.

At the British Library next morning he thinks about this. Frowns, then shrugs, as if remembering a film he saw, not his own life. But not for long. It pales, shrinks beneath the austere frown of knowledge bearing down on him.

God, how he loves this place. From the heavy doors at the entrance that seem to warn incomers of the increased gravity within, to the smooth desks and wide, solid chairs. The quiet, so masculine and unapologetic. Historic somehow, even though the building is new, seeming to radiate from the cool smooth stones and the undemonstrative bookshelves, as if the silence too was brought over from the original space in the British Museum. Being there is like slipping into a pool. The day seems its correct length, hours stretching in front of him like stairs, which will take him into the future. Not a great future. His endeavour, like that of all the people there, he suspects, will not change the world. Yet it is the particular path he is cutting. With the help of the books, the chairs and tables, and the silence of course, he is going to create a pattern of thought that has not previously existed. The poet's work is like a rainforest, explored by some but not, in James's opinion, correctly mapped. When he emerges from it, people will know it better, and get more from visits there.

There is focus to him now, a measured correctness that seems to hum like a well-oiled machine inside him. This interface is real as yesterday's visit to TV land was not. He enjoyed it, can't deny that, but from the periphery of himself. It was like sleeping around in Brighton before he made love to Alice for the first time and felt her slightly concave breastbone beneath his own. Alice. Her again. He sits up straight and takes a breath, some small panic coming to him. When he got back last night her hair was wet. She was sitting in the kitchen with wet hair. They made love in the pitch dark and his hands kept finding parts of her that he wasn't trying to reach for.

He goes on until lunch, sitting in Humanities 2 as usual, only mildly distracted by the silent flirt-fest taking place across the stacks, a web of eye contacts weaved above copies of Bukowski and Hłasko, Woolf and Webb. Distancing himself from it, he takes his home-made hummus and carrots to the café outside the Reading Room, allowing his eyes the freedom to roam around the airy atrium. Even the public space is wonderful, a superior sort of light stretching up to the distant ceiling, imported from Tuscany perhaps. How lucky is he to live like this? How many people get to do this for even a proportion of their living: sit, think? He shakes his head and a small laugh escapes his lips and then it's time to get back to work. For some reason it's harder in the afternoon. He tries to concentrate on Action Poets but he can't snap back in and ends up staring at the ceiling, his mind crisscrossed by thoughts and ideas, fragments of understanding he can't nail down, bits of comedy that he leaves alone, not wanting to explore them until he's actually on stage. He's angry with himself. He packs up at six with fewer of the stairs climbed than he'd hoped, knowing he won't get any more done tomorrow either because the mummies have him.

It feels like this sometimes. Not that he is spending a day with his daughter; but with them. That he is a trader from a far-off land, bringing spice into their padded cloister. They'll cajole him. Get him to explain what a sabbatical is. Again. And it will be even worse than usual today because Alice has betrayed him. With a wince she admitted that she unthinkingly let on to a few that he's doing stand-up now.

With his academic work he can bore them on purpose. But not now. How they'll pull at him doesn't bear thinking about and another horror waits for him too, something he doesn't usually have to endure. But he's swapped days with Alice this week and will have to take Ida to Twistin' Tots. *Sic.*

Twistin' Tots is a 'dance' class. While children from ten months to three years sit, either bored or just unresponsive, their mummies wind bobbins up, as if their children will ever see such a thing, do Matthew Pinsent impressions and, worst of all, march up to the top of an imaginary hill and down again. All in a dusty room above the library, run by a girl from the local music college whom he saw once outside the pub near Greenwich station throwing up. He can't do it. Not with the conviction that seems to be required. He can make an arse of himself in front of any number of people but standing up and saluting to a bunch of toddlers is beyond him, especially as those toddlers would much rather be charging around on their own, smacking each other over the head with the tambourines.

Why is there never a class that offers that?

He won't go. Fuck that Alice paid for the whole term. He'll spend the day alone with Ida. What they'll do he's no idea and he's still no nearer deciding once they've dropped off Dom at school. When Amelia Leigh invites him for coffee he accepts, as Ida seems pretty keen and it will give him time to think. They cross the grass and he feels himself relax, interested in this woman now he's spent some time with her. She is, he realises, as are many of the mothers of older kids, quite hard. Hard*ened*, a mother now not a mummy, difficult to imagine gurgling at a baby or singing 'This is the way the lady rides'. Is this because the seesaw has shifted: she has gone from being needed entirely by her children to needing them instead? He's not sure with Amelia but with a lot of the others he's certain he can spot the calcification of rejected hearts. This of course is waiting for the lovesick mummies he normally hangs out with and for a second he feels sorry for them. How will they cope when one day they too are spurned, when the soft, uncomplicated beam of child love no longer shines on them? When they too must re-cross the bridge back into adulthood?

Amelia finds a box of toys for Ida, who for once is content to root through them on her own. He chats away with her at the breakfast bar and again finds himself interested as she talks about her work. He's embarrassed too though because only now does he realise that she actually has a job. It simply hadn't occurred to him before. He asks about it and she tells him of a recent casting, of twins, and of two who looked very similar until they took their shirts off. How one had really let himself go. He shakes his head, insisting that it's the other way round, that the fit one has done that. He's stayed the same, vain, single, a bloody actor. His brother has probably got a family, kids, a grown-up job. When he gets a bit of time he can hit the gym and get it back, but what can the other guy do?

— But *you* haven't lost it. Porked out.

— Because I'm vain too. I can't accept what I am. Anyway, did they get the job?

— No. Malcolm – he's the director – he said the thin one was too earnest, was trying too hard.

— Well, there you go. Problem with me is that I've got the twin inside me. I can't get rid of him. I don't know what you'd see if I took my shirt off.

When Amelia leaves him to write a quick email, James checks the place out again. He re-evaluates his initial impressions, liking it more than before. And to his surprise he's no longer jealous. He feels somehow a part of it, a sense almost of ownership by association. It feels more human too, with a relaxed messiness he didn't see before, some kind of sailing harness left on the living room floor, music scores on the sofa. It's just a house, he tells himself, where a family goes about its living, though there are differences from his own. There are no unpacked cardboard boxes filled with files or toys, no vertical stacks of CDs waiting for a rack. There is in fact nothing at all temporary, which seeds envy again, though not of the house *per se*. It's more for the fact that the place is finished, that this is almost definitely the last house this family will live in. They are happy, just as his family is, but in a permanent way. He doesn't want a big house, actually. He just wants to be free from the desire for one. What would it be like to walk past an estate agent's window and feel no temptation to look inside? Not even to see them? He shakes his head and makes resolutions concerning drills and rawl plugs. And he really will find out about that loft conversion.

There's a stack of snaps at his elbow. He moves them aside, flicks through the cook book they were sitting on, and then gazes at the pictures themselves, lost until his mind readjusts. A couple. Amelia and Richard. A version of them smiles out at him. They are standing on a sunny, bleached backdrop of too-white houses, multicoloured flowers tumbling down the walls. They are tanned, dressed in shorts and T-shirts, both with small red scarves around their necks. Richard is thinner. Amelia is leaning into him and James knows immediately that this is pre-kids, though not because of their youth. There is a voraciousness on both of their shaded faces, a lack of any concern whatsoever beyond the time they are having. No small person is off to the side, asking a question, demanding a drink. And nor are there any kids back home with grandparents, sucking thoughts across the ocean. Their children are nowhere, un-thought, the twinkle-in-the-eye lie no more clearly shown than here. The way these two people cling on to each other shows that they are simply of themselves, swimming around in each other in the moment the camera found them, caught within an almost embarrassing fuck need that is nothing at all to do with procreation. James laughs, thinking for some reason of those pictures on the news sometimes: of plane crash victims. Taken moments before they boarded their craft, their doomed faces smiling out into the lens as if forever, making it almost impossible to conceive of what has happened to them.

He slides the shot off and sits up straight. Amelia is alone this time. Sitting beneath a parasol. Topless, one breast demurely in shadow, the other startlingly sunlit. He glances up the stairs. Then back down. Footsteps. Guilt scuds into him but he's also surprised that Amelia should leave these out like this. He slides the top shot back and pulls the local free-sheet towards him. When Amelia comes down she smiles and he thinks she glances at the photos, something he pretends not to see, concentrating on the paper instead.

— Right, he tells his daughter, when he sees the feature on the front page. He thanks Amelia and they leave her. Forty minutes later he's looking out over bright, slapping water, amazed that only now is he losing this particular virginity.

He's never been to a lido before. He didn't know the one on the other side of Charlton existed. But there they both are, after a simple twenty-minute bus ride, the ease of which chastises him. They should do this more. Make the most of the places near them. As the trees and clouds shine up at him from the wet, stippled poolside he thinks how many times they have stood in front of Stephenson's Rocket at the Science Museum, or a plastic dinosaur next door. South London, he's a convert. He gets a locker token and leads Ida through to the Men's.

Five minutes later a toe dip shows him one area in which the local council has chosen to save money in these straitened times. The water is Atlantic-like, though he's no choice but to enter it. Ida has her armbands on and waddles towards the shimmer like a duck, which she obviously thinks she is. Seeing a ten-year-old perform an illegal dive bomb, she runs after him and does her own version, a rather dainty effort actually but which still takes her deep below the surface of the water, James's stomach flipping before he manages to leap in and grab her.

— Again! is the predictable demand.

With him in the water Ida jumps in repeatedly, arms high, furious if he disobeys her instruction not to catch her. When she resurfaces there is a confused look on her face that turns into wet blinks and giggles, and then she scrambles back towards the side. Again she refuses assistance as, like an emperor penguin on to an ice floe, she tummies out, her aquatic bravery soon drawing attention. She shames other, far older kids, whose mothers urge them to *look at that little boy*. James doesn't tell them that, just occasionally, she too is like this in the pool, just accepting the plaudits, which increase when he announces that Ida is – *ta-da!* – a girl. No one thinks this, owing to her general attitude and on this occasion the swimming trunks she likes to wear instead of a bathing suit, in imitation of her brother. James has no problem with this of course though some people do. He can see it in the slight confusion of their expressions, which often they don't try to hide, an irritation at the correct order of things being reversed. And suspicion of him. Ida herself is confused, as she often is when the mistake is made, for she's in no doubt of what she is. He shakes his head. If his daughter were stark naked, he thinks, all he'd have to do to get people to assume she was a boy would be to put a blue hat on her head.

Bored with this game – him, not Ida – James persuades her off to the slide. She resists but has fun on this too, and then is content just to drift, various floats and rings knocking around them. She grabs his thumbs. She kicks her legs and beams and as the ropes of light dance around her happy face James reflects that Dom too considers swimming to be the pinnacle of his existence. Is it a return to the pre-state? Or the mixture of danger and safety perhaps that allows them to fling their delicate bodies as hard as they like into the forgiving medium, just as long as they know that hands will be there to grab them? It could be either but there's something else, which he finally gets, knowing that Ida is liable to do anything at all if his eye is off her. It's just that. In the pool the child knows it has its parent's attention in a way it rarely does. A lot of it is direct eye contact for they are, unusually, at the same level. Even when it isn't there, it is replaced by touch, by arms and legs, shoulders. Ida has him completely, something which, for a second child, must be even more important. He simply cannot choose to turn away from her and he enjoys this too, is captivated by it. So why does it bother him at other times?

God, he's happy. He wants to be nowhere else. He looks around and realises that, as usual when he's with Ida, it's mummies who surround him. But again there is a softening of his attitude. Because he doesn't know these ones? They don't notice him, as taken by their own kids as he is with Ida. They are less childish in their discourse with their children too for some reason and their bodies seem different. No longer cow-like, they look natural, touchingly human, made beautiful by sheen, their rolls and overspills liberated by context. A pregnant woman's bump breaks the surface like a geodesic aquadome. A fat fake blonde's shoulder-mounted snake tat glides through the water as if through some Amazonian tributary. Wet hair straggles down shoulders like tomb ivy and among all these bodies he places Alice's. He blinks at the mirage, as if he can really see her, suddenly aware of her form in its communal maternity. He's always seen it as her own body, its swellings and subsequent shrinkings pertaining only to her, his interaction with it still and exclusively with the unique person, with Alice. But now he pictures her within this social context and her body is somehow lost to him, what he sees not her at all but a metaphor for her new belonging. As mother. Is sex, then, between two people who want no future children, just nostalgia? He shifts position in the water and scans the pool, trying to spot pre-maternal bodies, not easy at this time of day though he spies a couple of teenagers. But nothing connects. It's as though he can't even see them, and he has a realisation that he never would have believed. He was scared of the body Alice would acquire after kids, worried he'd always look from it to younger, tighter forms. Or back to Alice's body in the past. But as he slides through the slick water to warm up he knows that the reverse is true. His desire has caught the bus, followed him into this matrix. He is part of this community. The bodies of the teenagers are adult-looking but his response is neutral and he remembers that he always fancied young mothers, was made red-faced and coy by them, found it impossible to be around when they were breastfeeding. He always wanted to be here and now he sends his eyes out yet again, sieving for the ones who would have caught his gaze, the slimmer ones, spotting two or three. And they are attractive, something he feels in a way that is not lustful as it would have been when he was twenty, his own near-nakedness putting them all in some sort of club.

One shape does rather get him though. Very thin, from behind. Standing in two feet of water, T-rex back, tied blue bikini bottoms caught in a wedgie that shows him a taut, elongated buttock with a thumbprint birthmark halfway up. Keeping a blank half-eye on it, he gets a flash of dark blonde pubes as an index finger pulls it free. And then the woman turns, with that knowledge that someone, a man, has been watching her, James a little too late to turn away.

— Hello, says the Queen of Royal Hill. Beaming.

They spend an hour together. Are mistaken by an old lady for husband and wife. *Shoot. Me. Now.* The woman's prattle is constant and, as usual, she shames him as a parent. She has every pool accessory imaginable including goggles, beach ball, diving rings and – he can see himself on stage – underwater camera. She even produces wipes from somewhere for her daughter's nose, while all the time dribbling on about her life, discussing problems faced by couples she assumes he knows, then carrying on regardless when he says he doesn't. There are issues with building work she is planning. Or has she had it done? It's unclear and he wants to ask but before he can she moves on to a nanny-share dilemma of such labyrinthine complexity he gets lost in the detail and expresses strident sympathy for the wrong side. Her neighbours come in for a pounding next followed by the Co-op near the station whose crime, it seems, is ontological: not being a Waitrose. After that it's the new flats near the station and how John Warner's last Ofsted was abysmal. This fact is of greatest import to her, so much so that she actually stops speaking for a while, and he breathes a sigh of relief, remembering now why he and Alice charge into London at weekends. To be lost. Un-flag-downable. He wonders why he couldn't have just been polite and said hello, before going off to the far end with Ida. She probably wouldn't even have noticed, though, he thinks, and would have followed. But she's good with Ida, or at least interested, praising her 'language skills' as though she's some sort of genius, her own squat *Gruffalo*-child barely able to mutter an intelligible word. The girl is trussed up in a floating jacket and sways with the gait of an overweight US marine.

He's had enough very soon and tries to cajole Ida out to the shower, promising more chocolate than she usually has in a year if she'll only come *now*. It doesn't work though and, by the time he's managed to drag her out, Thomasina is coming too.

Squeezing shampoo into his hand. How are you guys getting back?

— On the *what*? she almost yells.

Surprise: it's not a Chelsea tractor they find when they hit the half-filled car park. A silver VW estate 'does' for Thomasina and Co. James moves muslins and Mumsnet printouts from the front seat, thankful for the ride, actually. There is something far worse about going home on public transport than coming out on it.

But soon James begins to regret it. Ida cracks a yawn and he thinks bollocks: she'll crash. It wouldn't have happened on the bus. He wouldn't normally mind but it means she'll wake when they're back in Greenwich and he'll have lost his space, the hour when she sleeps in her buggy. Sometimes he sits with the newspaper. Today he was planning on getting some work done, in the park with an americano. He sighs, the afternoon suddenly seeming incredibly long. But as it happens his worries are unfounded. Ida, like Alice, normally bombs the moment the seatbelts click, but today she's hyped about being on his lap. Something forbidden. She looks around with glee, drinking it all in, and he's relieved, only half paying attention to questions about Alice until it's his turn to hit the ball back.

— So your husband. Sorry, I...

— John.

— Right. He's in...?

— Acquisitions.

Please do not try to tell me what that is.

— And you live in the Ashburnham Triangle?

There is silence. It was a simple, innocent question. Not a question at all, really, as he knows the answer, but – oh God – it seems to have hit some nerve. Thomasina turns to him, then away again. Her wide mouth opens and then closes, before she swallows. She's about to reveal something. Shit. It's one of those moments. He's stumbled into it, like a trap. She wants to *share*. He winces inside and braces himself, but she can't just plough on. She needs prompting, but he does not push the cracked door open. Instead he pretends to be obtuse. He does this to avoid stickiness but more because he does not believe for one single second that she can have any problem that was not auto-generated, a self-indulgent phantasmagoria created to shift the focus of the world towards her. What could she possibly say that he might sympathise with? He smiles and shrugs, as if his question needed no answer, turning to point out some police horses to Ida. He then turns back to Thomasina, who is flummoxed, brought up short by the failure of her intended manipulation. She jerks upright, shaking her head until James pretends to notice.

— Sorry. Were you going to say something?

— No. No, I mean, yes. I… She shakes her head, reducing her concern to nothing. John's work, that's all. He's not really enjoying it at the moment.

James sympathises but he is of course delighted that job satisfaction is not part of the fucker's no doubt very generous package.

— I love my job, he says, brightly and out of nowhere.

Five minutes later Thomasina bumps her nearside front over the kerb outside her house, letting it fall down again with a squeal. James has been pointing more things out to Ida to keep her awake and in doing so has made a mistake. He should have asked to be dropped off at the top of Hyde Vale. But he didn't and, *too late*, he knows what is going to happen.

— You guys coming in?

— Oh. No. I really need –

There is a steel in Thomasina's voice as she interrupts.

— Oh, do, she says, pinning him.

It's a show-off thing. James sees this immediately. The perfect middle-class mother has shown him a crack in her life. She has let him know that some issue exists between herself and her off-the-peg spouse, which is something she now regrets as he pocketed this information without giving her anything in return. She now has to backtrack. She knows that a man like James can only look at her and the chub-hub together and ask what the hell she gets out of it. She's keen to show him now and, yes, he's got to admit, her package is impressive.

The downstairs is a knock-through. Vast sliding doors lead out to a garden of multiple levels, coated in a variety of highly expensive outdoor surfaces. The marble kitchen plazas inside are not just black, as he has often seen, but glow with a deep, iridescent inner green, hewn no doubt from a singularly exclusive chunk of Italian hillside. They are frowned down upon by broad Danish units in perfectly mismatched colours and a steel fridge the size of a henge. On it are home-made reward charts for both sleeping and getting dressed, the sort of thing he and Alice gave up on because they always forgot about them after two days. Other than that there is surprisingly little kidography, and an edginess that impresses him. It makes Amelia Leigh's place seem a little homey and he wonders if there was an extra need here, for Thomasina to show him another, alleged side to herself. He's not sure he buys it but he does smile, thinking again of the husband, how none of this *Wallpaper**-über-style can have come from him, with his lumpy suit, deck shoes and tucked-in yellow polo shirts at the weekend. He in fact is the only thing that probably makes the place look shit, and James wonders if Thomasina winces every time he comes home.

Ten, no more. Take the coffee – great machine, give her that – and scarper. As Thomasina begins to make it he smiles at her, then goes in search of his daughter. She toddled off through a side door which, on entry, seems for a second to be a secret portal into Hamleys. A playroom is on the other side of it, about the size of his entire floor space, the carpet showing scenes from *Winnie-the-Pooh*. Most of the toys he can see are wooden and all in some way educational, though the teeny trog has clearly not taken advantage of them. She is there, in her Bugaboo, having been transferred sleeping from the car, head lolling. But it's not that which stops him dead.

It's Ida.

He was going to get her out of there. Put her in her own buggy, knowing she'd nod off ten yards up the street, perhaps even give him two hours for his poet. But swimming has cleaned her out. With horror he sees that, for some reason, born no doubt from an innate desire to screw him over, she has crawled in with the other child. Has fallen asleep beside her.

James stares, panicking, knowing that if he doesn't get Ida into the Maclaren then Thomasina will extend her invitation. Perhaps even suggest lunch. He'll be stuck, petrified by the dark queen. He starts to move but a laugh behind his shoulder stops him dead.

— Aaah. Sweet.

— Yes, he agrees. Though…

— Look at them. Bless. No denying it, is there? We love them to bits but it's great when they're asleep.

— It is. Really. I usually…

— Get shit done? Another laugh, short and ironic. Me too. Stuff you can't if they're awake, yeah?

— Absolutely. So…

— And not just a bit of tidying up. You can find yourself for a bit, if you're tough with yourself. If you let yourself turn off from them. For a bit. Read a book. Stare at the wall. It's like going back in time.

An insight. James nods, about to agree with her. So she'll understand if he has to… But when he turns to her he sees it again: that look on her face. As it was in the car, though it seems more real now. Raw. Opened, peeled back. And real. The actual person behind her performance? She looks at him and her expression develops, a level determination that tells him she won't let him escape this time. A focus that fills her features as that chin rises and her sharp green eyes find his.

— Fancy a fuck, then? she says.

16

TORTURE, THIS. Waiting. Alice can't take a breath without wondering: what does he think? She's no idea because she hasn't heard from him. Not a word.

So did he get it?

She pictures the padded envelope, the one she stuck her notebook in. She remembers the rain whipping the windows of the 386 as it barrelled her up to Blackheath. She shoved it in his letterbox. The right house? Of course the right bloody house, after which she couldn't wait but ran all the way back home. Did something happen to it? Did Amelia get it, keep it from him for some reason? Or was it one of their kids who maybe left it somewhere, meaning to tell him but then forgetting? She takes deep breaths, her brain clenching and unclenching as she tries to imagine different scenarios.

One day.

Two days.

Three, four.

After a while she just thinks no, he got it, he had to have fucking got it.

So why hasn't he been in touch?

What did she ever do before this play? Now, spat out the other end, Alice blinks and looks around the house, sees the mess that has steadily grown like ivy snaking into a ruin. She sorts clothes. She actually puts them away. She dusts and hoovers, empties the back of Dominic's drawer of clothes a good year too small. She looks in shop fronts, stares out of the train window for the first time in weeks. Depression would take her now, she knows; but the kids save her. She delights in them, struck by how much they've changed, Dominic thinner, his reading incredible, Ida's eczema finally starting to improve. It's as though they're not hers but the offspring of friends she hasn't seen for ages, and she realises that for weeks they haven't really been her children, just logistical problems, to be moved from one place to another, school or nursery, bath or bed. But now, their sun out again, they flower. She cooks them proper food, fish pies and lasagnes that Ida especially wolfs, as if spooning down pure love. It feels like the most valuable thing Alice has ever done, which spikes more guilt at the many times Loyd Grossman has done this for her. It's so simple: they just want me to see them. Want to know I made their food. They don't want me to be different people, just the one who made them. As their eyes leap up towards her she realises something that was obvious when they were babies: their lives feed on hers. She is almost everything they want in the entire world; but, however far her feelings respond and reach back to them, they don't go that far. How can they? Which means that in a fundamental way their love for her, like the love of all young children for their parents, is unrequited. All she can do is a better job of hiding this from them.

She tries this when they are out together, immersing herself into the day in a way that feels more socially inclusive than before, trying hard to demonstrate her happiness and contentment at simply being with them. She engages properly with other mothers in the playground, doesn't decline on instinct when, at playgroup, she's asked to join a group for coffee afterwards at a house on Devonshire Drive. It sends Alice back to James. Like the children, she wants him back too. Like them he eats her food, though not how she dreams of it. He's downstairs at midnight, the ping of their secret microwave sounding from the cupboard below the toaster. She watches him bolt it with the kids before rushing out, night after night, something she can't mind. She was off somewhere too and the fact that she happens to be back now doesn't give her the right to blame him. For she'll be off again. Another play? She's no idea, but the thrill of engagement with something long is a drug she's hooked on now. Just as James seems hooked. One night he comes home and tosses out the fact that he's been on television. She stares, horrified almost, guilty for the relief she feels when he says it was just for BBC Three. But how did he get this far? And why does she feel this way? She should be happy for him as he is for her, more psyched by the prize than she is, especially as the ceremony is getting closer. He'll be gutted if she doesn't win, much more so than her. If she does, it will be like being rewarded for something she did as a teenager.

Yet she should win. A furtive visit to the Piccadilly Waterstones where the shortlisted titles are together in a display tells her this. Under the aegis of a popular theatre director she has smashed her poems up and mangled the remains into a hybrid monster. It's almost a shock to see them here, just as they were before, unharmed. They are better than she remembered. She's hard inside, prematurely triumphant as she flicks through the rest of the titles and slays them, not even caring that the man behind the counter seems to recognise her as she stands there smirking. Only one collection is anywhere near the same league as her work, though she's never heard of the poet. Or has she? She shrugs and on her way out she checks her phone, despite the self-disgust flashing through her when she does so. She has not heard it ring.

And it has not rung.

College helps. Gives her something to really do, especially at this time of year. The admin mulch has flowered an event, an end-of-year reading and awards show for the students that she must organise and prepare for, a mirror of the real-world one she'll attend herself. She gets posters printed and a booklet made of all the work to be read. She organises a video to be shot and sends out invitations to local dignitaries, plus the various professional writers who have read at the university in the past, one or two of whom might attend. The show is held in the university theatre and she makes sure there is wine and crisps in the foyer, and students to serve them. She gets all the doors open in good time as she knows it gets hot in there and then ticks performing students off against her running order. She has mixed up poets with prose writers, putting students she suspects of flakiness into the second half so it won't matter if they're late. She is clear, organised, aware that it is the kind of work she won't have to do again, not when she's a Reader. For this reason she enjoys it, pleased to see the students and to feel the buzz of something different, an excitement born from culmination and the unfamiliar environment of hushed, darkened stage, of spotlight and microphone.

The only fly is the American girl. As the seats are filling Alice spots her with others from the MA and immediately winces, aware that she's failed her. Has broken her promise, forgotten to look at the poems she sent her. She swears beneath her breath but slips the girl's gaze, busying herself instead. When she thinks the girl is coming over she steps up on to the stage, a minute or so before she intended, and gets the proceedings moving.

— Hello, she says, and welcome to this showcase of the talent we have here at Wimbledon University.

Confidence. Is it her voice? The compère part is the element she usually shivers at, last year even bribing Linus to do it. She hates big lectures too, preferring intimate workshop groups, so how come her voice is unfurling itself so easily across these shuffling though attentive people? She even cracks a joke before gesturing towards the line of waiting readers.

— And to begin, please do all you can to welcome William Bryan.

A banker to begin. Billy is Alice's favourite kind of Wimbledon student. A bad lad from Enfield when he came, twisting in on himself with suspicion and unrecognised self-loathing. Talent though, loads of it, which he has, over three years, allowed himself to believe in, permitting his tutors to temper and direct it. But not too much, which gives his piece just the right amount of bite. It is, like nearly all 'performance poetry', nothing but self-assertion with little intrinsic value. It's great for her show, though, big and lively, and she laughs with all the rest, clapping madly when he finishes. He won't be a writer, William, but he'll be something. When he leaves the stage he punches the air, which sets the tone for the rest who, in their own more quiet ways, rise to the occasion.

A sheet of concentration is soon thrown across the room. Ranks of parents, siblings, grandparents and fellow students are struck by the quality of the material. For herself she is almost unreasonably proud of them, of the quality but more for the verve, few voices cracking, hardly a shake to any of the held papers. And the bravery. Nicky from the second year reads a story about an estate on which he clearly lived, supporting his family at fourteen with minor-scale dealing. Seeing his mother take his earnings to the off-licence while he cooked the tea. It is spare and without self-pity, which makes her want to hug him. Martha from the MA reads a raw and brilliant piece about being dumped by a shit-heel boyfriend. When Lucy from the third year details a visit to her dying friend, Alice realises something. She always thought that student writing wasn't real. Was *proto*. That people only became writers when they crossed the clanging junction into World. The published world. But this also is real writing, unconnected as it is to anything other than the writers' feelings and their desire to set them down. Would any of this sell? Exist out there? Maybe no, but they are not out there. The work is transient, will disappear, which is just what makes it so innocent, pure, and most of all truthful. She shakes her head, so pleased that her job is to help these people, then embarrassed for a second by love of them. When she wraps the show up she is misty, just about keeping it in as the room fairly thumps with ovation.

— Congratulations. Really great event, really well organised, Alice.

The Head of School gives her a thumbs-up from across the packed foyer. She edges over and Alice shrugs, trying to show a little annoyance actually as such employment really is beneath her now. Celia picks up on that and asks about her work.

— It's going well. Exciting.

— Great. I heard you on the radio.

— *Front Row* or *Open Book*? Or *Poetry Please*?

— Blimey, you have been busy. The latter. I'll check out the others on the iPlayer. You must feel, I don't know. Validated?

Is that it? Alice shrugs again and wonders about it as the Head of School is collared. The pleasure of having her work stamped 'Approved' by a higher power: is that what she feels? Maybe it's far simpler. Maybe, like Dom and Ida, she just feels noticed. Activated by focus. She looks again at the grinning students, still basking in the glow of this very public stroking, audience members still dolloping out their benedictions in the form of handshakes and hugs. We're all the same, she thinks, as she waves down the offer of wine. But you can only admit how much you need this when you have it.

— Alice, the American girl says, popping up by her side.

Apology. She gets it out before the girl can even say a word. Rubbish of me, though with this to organise... Jessica assures her it's okay, which makes her feel worse, for it isn't. She had time. She just forgot. She glances down at her watch and sighs inside. But she knows what she should do.

— Are you going to the pub?

Everyone is: an end-of-term party. The girl nods.

— We can talk there. An hour or so? I'll go back and read the work now. I was going to go running, but...

— Running? the girl says.

Forty minutes later the two of them are heading down the bus route into Wimbledon. Side by side they cut a right and run up towards the Common, scruffy-looking under a low, disinterested sky. Alice allows Jessica to set the pace, pleased that it's slower than she'd normally go. They chat. Alice is unused to this as she always runs alone, but she's been alone so much recently. She enjoys herself, chewing mouthfuls of hot air, thinking she could run forever like this, keep on going without getting any more tired. There is also something about the fact that while she has just read the girl's poems she hasn't commented on them yet, taking pleasure in having the power to do that when she likes.

— So, your work, she says, finally.

Jessica listens. She's serious and attentive, just nodding when Alice tells her that she was impressed, restraining the glee just to hear this. She concentrates instead on Alice's more specific remarks and doesn't demur or try to rebut any of the suggestions for improvement. A change here, one Alice has noticed since her nomination. Before it, students would try to explain themselves, justify things that didn't work. But now her words carry more weight, are not so easily deflected. Something about this disconcerts her for she'd have said the same thing three months ago, and been right. A wave of annoyance washes over her, a protective irritation at the way her more junior self was perceived.

Jessica left her bag in Alice's office, which means Alice has to get it for her. After collecting it they walk towards the gym. They undress quickly before going into separate, adjoining stalls, where they carry on a shouted conversation, not about poetry now but running routes. When Alice is finished she steps out, Jessica's shower continuing for a second before it stops too. They dry off. They are facing each other, Jessica doing nonchalance as she did when getting such good feedback, though again Alice can see right through it. For she is scarlet. Her face, neck and chest, almost comically red, which leaves Alice piqued. What is she, royalty? Why the hell can't this young woman act naturally with her, even in this unusual circumstance? An Anglo-Saxon thing? Would one of the Scandinavian students be like this? She sighs and then is given more pause for thought: by the tuft. As Jessica buries her face in her towel Alice blinks at it, sees that it is fading, being absorbed into the landscape like an ancient burial mound. She is oddly saddened by this, an alarm bell ringing somewhere, though not really loud enough for her to hear it until she thinks back to the girl's poems.

To another tutor it would have been obvious. But we think of our own style as natural, not as peculiarly our own. It's harder for us to tell we're being imitated which is, of course, to some degree at least, what Jessica has been doing. She's been copying her. Metre, line, enjambment.

And pube style, too?

Alice laughs at herself, though when they're dressed it doesn't seem so funny.

— Thanks, Jessica says.

They're standing outside the gym, students and staff flooding past on their way to the pub. Jessica's hair is wet, giving it a birdlike sheen, and Alice knows that her own must also look like this. Will anyone notice the two of them? She smiles and turns to go, a few things left on her desk. But Jessica stops her.

— I'll work on what you said.

— Excellent.

— I mean, it's so good to get an opinion. I've just been in the dark, not knowing which way to go.

— So now you do.

— Yes. Though. I mean. In the summer there won't be classes, will there?

An obvious point and Alice doesn't know what she means by it.

— So I won't get to see you.

— But you can send more if you like. I mean, not too many.

— If that's okay? Really? Excellent. And...

— Yes?

— Well, maybe we could meet up. Not to talk about my poems necessarily. For a drink. I mean, if you'd like to. Or something?

She lets it go right through her. Just brightens, purses her lips and does thinking. She says sure, maybe, though when? With the kids and everything and my own dissertation supervisees I'm just not sure if... The girl nods, says yes, of course, I understand. She's brave. She knows she's being knocked back and wants to leave, quickly, though Alice carries on explaining. She's lifted, she can't help it, though it isn't so shocking that a springy twenty-something of either sex should find her attractive, is it? It's happened before, though no one has ever plucked up the courage to ask her out so directly. What's especially flattering now though is that, while others may have daydreamed about the Alice beneath the clothes, this one has actually seen her: in the nud, no less. And her two-kid body hasn't put her off. This gives her real pleasure, so much so that for a millisecond she pictures herself actually meeting the girl, going back to some student flat. Doing it. Whatever *it* would be.

But then she looks at Jessica again and frowns at the expression on her face.

The girl doesn't just look rebuffed. Spurned. There is something deeper. In her rejection she looks hurt and a little lost, somehow even younger than she just looked, barely even a teenager. She's upset in a way that is familiar: yes, Ida, when she leaves her at nursery. Of course. For she's in a foreign country. She's far from home and something else is clearly missing too, something intrinsic, which Alice's presence has made her feel the absence of. Is it care? Touch, though not from someone like her, any of her peers who would happily engage with her should they share her inclination? But from someone older? Alice's brow tightens, the pleasure flowing out. She's left with nothing but irritation at the girl's desire, the silly fantasy crumpling that she is young herself, equal to this girl, less than equal actually for this subtle come-on suggests that Jessica surely must have some sexual experience with women, while Alice has none. But somehow she knows that it wouldn't be like that, not some *Desert Hearts* reversal of senior/junior roles. Instead she'd cling to me, she thinks. Pull. She'd bury her chubby face in my chest. She'd want me to stroke her hair and coo soft phrases in the dark.

Alice stiffens and stands up straight, angered now by their shared nudity, which makes her feel vulnerable. Old. For it wasn't an appreciation of a still-svelte figure that drew the girl to her. It was actually just the traces of advancement in her body that this girl was craving. Not a despite, she thinks, but a because of.

— I have to go now, she says.

In the pub it is the same. She wants to relax. Let go. She's exhausted and longs to sink into the tacky corporate ambience that is the best most pubs seem to have to offer these days. But scales have fallen from her eyes. Everyone is like Jessica. They all want to take from her. Her very presence changes the air surrounding the groups of students, both undergraduate and postgraduate alike. She approaches a table of second years who have just been reading, thinking she'll board the rowing boat of their conversation and grab an oar. But they stop talking, waiting nervously for her to speak to them. And when she does, a *hi there, mind if I join you*, they don't resume, don't pick up any of the previous strands, any of which she'd have been happy to talk about. She actually has an opinion on which of the current Apprentices is the most brain-dead but instead she is asked about next year's special study options. One starts to complain about his seminars in Poetry Today, how boring their tutor is. Another asks about the MA and she blinks, wants to wave a hand in front of his face and say *hello, there's a person inside here.* She says hell let's leave all that to school shall we and they shrug, but they still don't act the way they had been before she sat down. She leaves them, saying she has to circulate, hoping the MA students will be different. But they are the same. They're crowding around the bar with Linus and again when she enters their circle something changes. A glass of wine is pressed into her hand for which she is supremely grateful but the pay-off is painful. They are like small children, trying so very hard to wring signs of approval. They fight for her gaze, talking endlessly about poets she's never read, as if she really wants to talk about poets now, as if poets ever talk about poets and not *The Apprentice.* They then claw it all into themselves, what they are working on, seeking her approbation, not understanding that, out of the context of her engaged and dedicated teaching of them, she only gives a gnat's arse about their work if it's amazing. Like the second years they also bring up minor gripes about the programme they are otherwise supremely happy with and this is even worse. Whoa, she wants to say, I'm off the clock here. In case you didn't notice I'm in the *fucking pub.* It's Douglas, he's a moron; I wouldn't employ him to mow my bloody lawn.

Instead she wonders when it happened. This crossing over to the other side. Last year they weren't like this. Were they? No, for now she has the feeling that she could talk the most risible bollocks and they would nod and take it in. She's tempted, until it occurs to her that if she did it would all be repeated, that her words in this place won't dissolve into the air as they normally do. Everything she says will be remembered, and speech itself suddenly seems a dangerous and enervating enterprise.

— Linus, she says, I need you for a minute.

He follows her across the crowded room, the full tables like Pacific Islands populated by very different, genetically separate tribes. She might be imagining the gazes following her but she's certain that she is being talked about in some way now, though about what she has no idea. She shudders at the thought of finding out and sits at one suddenly vacated table, a group of economics tutors off to some seminar or other. Linus's pint hits the deck with a clunk and she lets out a breath, shattered, knowing that she can't answer another stupid question. She must just now speak as she wants and not as she feels she ought.

— Item for the next department meeting.

— Go on.

— We need to find a new place to drink.

Linus laughs. He looks sideways, back towards the bar. And laughs again. Alice takes the chance to study him, frowning a little to see that he's aged, his skin a fraction drier than it was, more tightly drawn into his face, a slight recession to the hairline he probably hasn't noticed yet. His ear stud doesn't sit quite right and neither does the Superdry T-shirt which, in a year or two, will look as if it must surely be a present from his children. Will he transition? Or – *dread thought* – cling? She's wondering this but sits up quickly because one of the economists has forgotten his bag and returns, fishing it out from beneath the table, and Linus chats with him, demonstrating again the ease with which he interacts with colleagues. The conversation is about nothing,

Linus asking if the guy ever managed to get the better of the photocopier he was fighting that morning. A joke is shared and Alice watches, confused as to why Linus would bother, why he wouldn't just hand the bag over and send the man on his way.

— I was passing the time.

— Did it need passing? Not like you're on a train or something and there's no *Standard*.

— Christ, Alice. I see the man. He's in some meeting I go to. I was just...

— Keeping him warm? On a bit of a simmer?

— You telling me you never have conversations like that?

— I probably take people too seriously. I listen to the words they say.

— And I don't?

— Not then. They weren't words really. You could just as easily have gone *blah blah blah* for a minute or two. You just had not to rush past each other.

Linus thinks, then nods to himself.

— Blah blah blah, he says, to Alice. Blah blah blah blah. Blah. He keeps saying this until Alice rolls her eyes, and then long past it when she's laughing and telling him to shut it.

When he does the two settle and, finally, she feels herself begin to sink a little, within herself. Relax. It's okay, isn't it? Linus looks back to the bar.

— New pub, then? Staff only?

— Absolutely. Go in one at a time in false beards.

— Wouldn't we miss this?

She thinks he's kidding. Would you?

He shrugs. Can't deny it.

— But why? Christ.

— I dunno. It's... it's like.

— What?

— The poet demands an image... Being under a sun-lamp?

— That's pathetic. Not the image. That it's true.

— I know. But it... it makes me feel warm.

— But it can't.

— It does. Probably...

— Yes?

— Because things aren't... He sighs. Lois.

— What about her?

— It's just not. I don't know. She's so clingy, rants on about settling down.

— The horror! The horror!

— Which might be okay, but...

— What?

— I'm not writing.

Alice blinks. Linus turns aside, the ear stud flashing in the light of the last sun, an oily block of burnt amber creeping across the table between them. He bites his lip as she stares at him.

— Since?

— Eight months. Nine.

— You're...

— Blocked? He shakes his head.

— Then...?

— I've words coming out. But all shit. Every single one. I may as well write the word *shit* over and over. I think that's just what I'll do tomorrow. So you may not need them, Mrs Carson Prize, but I do.

— But what do they do for you?

— Listen. Take my advice. Get better. I need that, seeing as I've nothing else to make me feel like I'm doing anything.

And they see me as a writer. Unlike my twat of an agent, might I add. Or myself come to that. You know what Martha just said to me?

— Fuck me, big boy?

— She told me she's just read *The Jupiter Seed*. She thinks it's better than *The Day of the Triffids*. She's pissed but even so.

— But don't you...? Alice shakes her head. She bucks her stool forward to accommodate more staff members piling in, driven by waves of end-of-term frivolity. Feel dirty? Walking home? Having lapped that up?

Linus doesn't answer, just looking to the side. Upset, something twisting in him. Alice stares as he bites his lip again and winces, cross with herself for not guessing this. The fear in him makes him look hollow, older still, and she frowns more deeply, knowing that at any time during the last six months she could have noticed this in him and that he's probably been waiting that long to unload this to her, embarrassed to do it with no reason. She wants to kick herself, the problem being that she couldn't have seen any signs of his distress because she's never had it. Block. She's always been able to get there, to that still, solemn place where she shivers naked before the full-length mirror. Where her poems are waiting. As Linus drags his pint to his face she imagines not being able to and then stares at her usually cheerful colleague, about to sympathise with him when someone else squeezes by the table and she's forced to turn again, her gaze drawn back to the students. And Martha, leaning against a pillar. Staring at them. At her, oddly. And, more oddly, she's sending knives across the crowded space from liquid eyes, which confuses Alice until she turns to Linus. Who has seen this, but is pretending not to. Alice spins back to Martha and the girl is still staring, determination and misery on her features. Alice realises that her own mouth is open. Her stomach has turned to steel.

— That 'fuck me' comment was a joke.

— I know. Why do you…?

— Her, Alice says. You. She can hardly say it. You have, haven't you?

— What?

She stares at him. He's edgy, nervous. Trying to act casual, then looking at her as if she's insane. Once again she turns to Martha and her face has changed again, a wash of scorn now sweeping over it before she shakes her head and turns to the bar. Alice shakes her own, Linus glaring at her now, doing outraged, like that Tory MP who called the press scumbags for accusing him. And she knows, *bang on*, that she is right. And then knows something worse. Looking at Linus, it's like seeing him for the first time, this man she's shared an office with for so long. He's slept with that girl. No doubt. But that's not all, because it isn't just a thing he did. It's a thing he does.

— Are you crazy? he says.

She doesn't answer, just pulls her bag from the floor and leaves him there.

Exactly an hour later she is standing outside her house. It looks sullen and squat, and she doesn't want to go inside. She stares at the bricks and mortar she shares the responsibility of paying for and it's as though she's still in the pub. Being pulled at. Eaten. All those jobs, all those things *to do*. Everywhere she looks there is something waiting for her attention, something impatient and demanding. Her exhaustion grows and she knows that she cannot deal with the children tonight. God, how she loves them. But not tonight. They should be in bed but if they're not she'll go for a walk. Do what she knows some men do, timing their arrival home. To find out, she moves to the window where solid, orangey light pushes out through the three-quartered blinds. She squints through it, at James.

He's in the living room. Standing, for some reason. Gazing into the mirror. Not doing anything. He's just standing there. Alice is about to move over to the door but she stops, studying his almost bearded, struck profile. And frowns. Is that terror on his face? Yes. Real terror. Alice is shocked, jolted from her own thoughts, unable to move as he walks right up to the mantelpiece and stares into the glass. *What is he doing?* She has no idea and is hit by the sudden urge to turn away. Instead she just watches as he screws his eyes shut, the lids like balled paper, and then another face comes towards him, another James, which he touches, very lightly, with his forehead.

17

— My poet.

She dumps her bag on the sofa, her question still lingering on her face. She throws her coat on the back of a chair and some old train tickets slide out of a pocket. He wants to pick them up but instead thinks about the answer he has given. It's true, something Alice accepts with no comment, which leaves him perversely disappointed. He should be happy she doesn't press him. So relieved. But for some reason he wants her to. If she did he'd say, my poet. And his hero, Frank O'Hara. The poems he wrote about walking around New York, his 'I do this, I do that' poems, the string of seemingly random actions from which he refused to extract meaning, or consequence. These poems have never struck James with such force before, have never felt so stark, chilling and profound.

I do this. I do that.

Alice walks through to the kitchen. He follows and asks how her show went.

— Shit. No, good. The show was good.

— So what's up?

Something is. She's tense, both sullen and on edge at the same time. And back early. She shakes her head and James braces himself, knowing he has the potential to handle these moments badly. Problems would sprout up in Alice's life, making her scream with rage in a way that used to startle him, not least because he was rarely the cause of them. Yet he would be the one trampled by her frustration. Why didn't she approach him, ask for succour? Why instead must she treat him as if he is on the other side, one more element in a world that has cussed her? He soon learned however to take it, be the wall she needed to bang against, though tonight is different. Scary. For she does not shout and neither does she hammer the kettle on to its base or throw down the lid of the tea caddy, its fetching dent the result of one such minor fury. Instead she just turns and stares at him. Almost as if she's wondering what the hell he's doing in her house.

— What is it? Come on, Alice.

— Why can't people just... be?

— Shit, is that John Lennon?

— Oh, fuck off. In spite of herself, she smiles. But not for long.

— Why is there always something behind everything? I don't behave like them. I don't want anything from anyone. I just want to live my life.

— So tell me about it.

— No. I mean I will, though not until I can find a way of doing it that doesn't make me sound pathetic. Work, people, that's all. How are the kids?

— Fine. Yeah.

— Of course they are. That's the fucking point.

— What is?

— We worry about them so much. But they don't need worrying about. Their lives are fucking perfect. It's not them that need worrying about, is it?

— No, he says, the truth of that so clear that something

sickly squeezes up from his stomach into the back of his throat in acknowledgment of it.

Alice trudges up the stairs to the bath. She looks so separate that it's his turn to wonder what she's doing there. Why live together, share so much that is both trivial and profound, if during the truly difficult moments you find yourself so alone? He can't help her. Not really, and she can't help him. Or is he being melodramatic? Is it just because she came home early that they bounced off each other, because they weren't meant to intersect yet, hadn't reorganised themselves for sociability like pulling down the seats in the people carrier? He nods to himself and resists the impulse to follow her. Instead he returns to the mirror, its antique patina like mild sunburn. How many people have stared into it over the years? Hundreds? Thousands? Were any of them as surprised to see what stared back at them as he?

The next day he's in the BL again. He manages to keep his thoughts just about on track, though it is slow work and dull, some background notes he needs to make. It's still a wrench to leave, though, which he must do early. As he slides his laptop into its sleeve he looks down across the desks, faces caught in the self-conscious rictus of public study. He has a sense of kinship with his fellow scholars until he realises how young they look. Trying to overtake him, though if he gets this book done they'll have a job. Two already, something these fresh-faced PhD students would give an eye for. Instead of making him feel old though it just makes him realise how young he is in academic terms, how much further he has to go.

And at St Saviour's it is the same. When his eyes meet Alice's within the throng of other parents outside the gates, she looks at him in comic dismay. Wordlessly – *oh fuck* – they share their disbelief at having arrived at this moment. Kids? Okay. Babies and whatnot.

But *Parents' Evening*?

James shuffles, the kiss Alice gives him feeling a little like an ice burn. He resists the urge to simply flee and then, actually, he gets interested. For in front of him, unusually, are couples: men and women he's noticed at drop-off or pick-up, but never seen together. Some fit, though there is always a second of disbelief that the two people he's looking at could be intimate with each other. Others most certainly do not fit and there are some – chic, suited, glowing – whom he has never once set eyes on. He's confused until he realises that a number of the playground women he's assumed to be parents are actually nannies. These are now at home; having done all the donkey work for the term, they've been dismissed from the showcase finale. Oddly enough these set-back parents look more as though they belong than anyone, while he can only shake his head. For wasn't it just last week that his own parents were coming home, reports in hand, his mother unable to hide the beam? His father more formal, refusing just to make a praisefest out of it. Fond memories these for he was good at school, crashing the top five in almost everything: or they should have been. The problem was Stephen. Top in half the subjects, vying with his best friend for the rest. All except English in which he 'struggled', as low as sixth one year. Was this why James took that path? He's thought about it often, though never connecting it to those Parents' Evenings, his father's congratulations fulsome though not as deeply felt as they were to Stephen, as if he was appreciating a second-growth Margaux after just having sampled a first. And none of his mother's compensatory ebullience ever quite made up for it.

There is a protocol to these things. They are funnelled into the playground like cattle into an abattoir. From here they proceed to the Reception classroom where, with Dom and Ida, they admire the work on display, calligraphy exercises and blurred self-portraits, egg-box dinosaurs hanging from the ceiling. This is of course a display of teaching skill rather than childish achievement and it works. It reassures James, as does Dom's work folder. He skims through it until Alice takes his wrist.

— It's time, she says. As if he's in some clinic in Zurich.

He follows his wife into the corridor outside the main hall. It's busy, fairly jolting with conversation. When it's time to go into the hall itself they leave Dom in the care of a teaching assistant, still too young to be nervous. James picks up Ida, knowing that if he lets her wander around on her own she's likely to get halfway up the wall bars before he notices her, and then sees Mrs Mason, waiting for them. A tall, thin woman in Eric Morecambe glasses, she smiles as they take the recently vacated chairs, which are tiny of course. In spite of her welcome James is suddenly nervous, incredibly so, half expecting Mrs Mason to talk about the fact that he hasn't shaved today. Is seen most mornings in the playground in a hirsute state. Instead she launches in on Dom, eschewing all pleasantries as they have exactly nine minutes to learn how his very first tranche of formal education has gone and not one second more.

Ding.

Will he always remember those minutes? Probably, though the words Mrs Mason speaks cannot be her own. It's a trick. Somehow she has entered his daydreams and seen the foolish fantasy he has concocted. For not only has Dom caught up with the other children who started earlier, but he has in all but two cases surpassed them, his reading well ahead of most of Year One in fact and his numeracy even better. He's also attentive, kind to the other children – James doesn't really care about that – and confident when speaking in front of others. Mrs Mason herself seems lit up with pride and James can hardly keep his seat. He wants to high-five his wife, take to the wall bars himself. Alice too is unable to hide her pleasure though she tries, blushing to her roots as she puts on an attentive nonchalance, listening to some details Mrs Mason is giving at the end, which to James are just fuzz. When they stand he – just – resists the urge to hug the teacher and then has to really control his joy as the next two parents are heading in. He doesn't want to seem like a smug cunt. They walk out and he sees Dom, being read to, made uncomfortable by the burst inside him for doesn't he just love this little boy? No matter what? Wouldn't he feel the same if Mrs Mason had spoken of solid, decent progress? The answer is no and he swallows at this fact: that his son's accomplishments have given him happiness he does not want to feel. He shudders with dislike of himself and that feeling only grows when the front door pushes open and another wodge of parents pushes in.

Not there for Parents' Evening. They are being shown round by two Year Six kids. The first through the door is a man James recognises, and behind him is the Queen of Royal Hill.

For a second he thought she was joking. James stared, mouth open: not at the offer but at the fact that she'd cracked this gag. Christ. He'd completely misjudged this woman. She wasn't what he'd pegged her as, she was wild, dangerous. A chameleon. She played the mum role with such aplomb but was obviously desperate now to find someone with whom to escape it. After the words had stunned him into temporary silence he jerked his head back. She turned to the side and matched his barking laughter, arms folded, about, he assumed, to break the moment by moving away. She should have done that. She should have turned into the kitchen and handed him his coffee, asked if he wanted a biscuit.

Instead she let the laughter tail off. She stood there, staring at the far wall when it was gone, eyes like the wheels of a fruit machine until they came to a halt. When they had, she turned back to him with poise that was exaggerated, and there was no trace of jocularity on her face. No trace of her at all in fact, the Thomasina he and Alice bitched about. Instead there was someone different in front of him, staring at him with sly, though very real determination.

They blinked at each other. He did not move. He said no, really. Thanks for the lift and all that but I've got to be… That's what he did. Except. Odd, for it didn't seem like that. It *seemed*, instead, as though he did move: towards her. Then it seemed that his tongue was inside her large, wide mouth, his right hand as far as he could get it down the back of her Levis.

I do this. I do that.

He pushed back from her. To stop? No. He just wanted to make sure that the person he was doing this with was not Alice. Just make sure of that because when doing this it had been with Alice, had been for many years now, for which he had become profoundly grateful. The further time had taken him into monogamy the more he'd found that, with her at least, it suited him. Sex had become a pure, unfettered thing, at once an immense throwing off of himself as well as a joining to a deeper, braver person who always seemed to be waiting for him on the other side of the tangled wood that was his life. He'd been a mess before Alice. Cast out from a long relationship that had become increasingly safe, and narrow, he'd found himself surrounded by healthy young women who, he was surprised to discover, liked well-practised sex just as much as he did. Or thought he did. For after a while he realised that all he ever did was make sure he acquitted himself well, knowing that, in a small town like Brighton, word spread. He was never in the process of doing it, it was always the before, or the projected after time. In contrast, from the first time he made love to Alice he felt that he had finally squeezed as much as he could out of the individual seconds he was living through.

Yumi, skin pale as the inside of a banana skin, screaming as if he was hurting her. Ending it when she asked him to.

Coral, saw him at a party and asked if he'd fuck her later. Just so we can have a great time and not worry, you know, about finding someone? So we'll leave together, okay gorgeous? James, right?

Nameless, from a comedy club. Six-two, black dress, not plain or unattractive but face-meltingly ugly. And with the body of a supermodel. He'd tried not to look at that but at her face, forced himself to do that while they jammed themselves together.

Becka, so paranoid about her bottom that she backed naked into the bathroom when they were done.

Janey, a standby, often knocking on the door at one, two, even three am to see if he fancied a jump. He'd wake in the morning with no recollection of letting her in.

The unknown one, any of the above who, left alone while he went out for milk one morning, scrawled the word 'Shit' beside every single poem in his notebook.

On and on, each leading to the next as if he were some kind of pyramid seller, getting recommendations. He couldn't believe it, thought how cool he was, David Hemmings though he only had a disposable Kodak. Until the time, so drunk, eyes shut, when he couldn't remember which of the two girls at the party he'd gone home with and, consequently, who was riding him so furiously. A pissed girl who wet his bed. On and on until he was saved by falling into a deep, endless lake of love he'd never for one moment wanted to climb out of.

— Shit, Thomasina said, stepping back on to a plastic number bus that played 'Twinkle Twinkle Little Star' as it skittered across the floor.

She pulled her blouse over her head. He yanked down her bra and took her left breast into his mouth. It was smaller than Alice's though the nipple was longer, something he was actually prepared for as these were nipples he was quite familiar with. He pulled her belt open, amazed by the leanness of her belly until he saw the ridged muscle, remembered seeing her getting screamed at by a personal trainer in the park. She pulled one leg out and hopped in a circle while she did the other, her twisted G-string like an abandoned cat's cradle. They fell to the floor and he went to kiss her again, his hand moving between her legs, though she wasn't having any of that. The time between the decision to do and the thing itself needed to be as short as possible or some wakened sanity might intervene. She lay back, hitched her legs up and dragged him to her by the scruff of his neck. Her free hand reached for his fly and then his cock and before he knew it he was inside her, something he could scarcely believe. The thing he'd sweated over for years before finally losing his virginity at seventeen. The thing that had crucified him with nerves that first time with Alice. And there it was, both done and being done, easy as opening crisps.

Chlorine, holding hands with the patchouli. He thrust, difference again presenting itself. He'd forgotten this: that the inside of a woman was unique. Degrees of firmness and moisture of course but he'd once known a girl who felt like a kind of stippled, rubber sandpaper. Others were tiny, or large, one girl somehow both, all warm and wet but with a grip like a tennis coach's handshake. With Thomasina he felt more resistance than he did with Alice, though that was surely understandable for they had not tuned into each other, hadn't developed the shortcuts to awakened desire. He tried to slow because of it but felt her legs grip harder so he carried on, thankful of the carpet beneath his knees though a little disconcerted to see Tigger, grinning beside Thomasina's head. He turned to the more patient expression of Kanga instead, who seemed to say never mind dear you just go ahead and play, though be careful not to hurt yourself now...

How sweet this is to do
We should do it more
Having a little fuck
On the playroom floor

She arched as though performing some yoga move in a class her husband had paid for. He reached beneath to her spine, surprised to feel each vertebra so distinctly, as if they were made out of stickle-bricks. They rolled and manoeuvred until she reached underneath for his balls, which began to make him come, so he pulled out, did so in spite of her protestations that all was fine. For there were degrees to this. Not doing it at all was obviously the best way to go but screwing around on your soulmate wasn't actually the worst you could do. If you didn't come you could claim a turn of thought, and he wanted to do that but Thomasina was on him in a flash, left hand still on his balls, the other directing his cock into her mouth. He frowned, never having understood the need women had to make a man come. He shifted, trying again to release himself, but then giving way, unable to resist the delicious confidence with which she proceeded to suck him off. He gasped. Then blinked into the face of his sleeping daughter.

So cute. So much prettier than that other one. Them being together like that, you could really see it. Then it began to happen and he thought it probably right to shut his eyes, which he did as about a week's worth of semen leaped and bucked and fought its way into Thomasina's mouth.

Eyes open again. Thomasina looked down at him, her slim fingers like scaffolding around his penis. A pearl on the top which, with a delicate little finger, she scooped off and popped into her mouth.

She left him. He stared at his now docile penis flopped, like one of his cousins, next to a very worried-looking Piglet. When she came back she was fully clothed. He stood, yanking his trousers up, after which she did in fact hand him his now lukewarm coffee. She got the beans from Borough Market, ground them herself in the mornings. He nodded, congratulated her on the flavour, but he'd best be getting on.

— Again?

— No. God. I meant leave, I've...

— I was joking. Of course. Right, then.

He did manage to transfer Ida without her waking and then let Thomasina help him get the buggy down the front steps. They said goodbye and she stood chatting to a neighbour, passers-by walking to and fro as he moved off. Did he dream it? Yes. But looking back he saw the redness above her collarbone. Disgusted by the way it thrilled him, he walked on faster, down to the cafe on Greenwich High

Road where he ordered a baked potato. The butter advertised turned out to be cheap margarine and he watched a slab of it melt, then slip into the sheer gullies he'd cut into the flesh, an oily yellow lake forming on the plate beneath. When Ida woke he mashed the potato up and they ate it together, his daughter holding on to his wrist as, with great care, she pulled the big fork towards her.

Alice and Thomasina chat in the busy corridor. James watches them. Hears Thomasina explain that they couldn't make the open day, asked if they could have a 'private view'. He knew this would come, this meeting. But not like this, not so soon, not without preparation. Passing on Burney Street perhaps? A wave from the other side of the road and then a quick glance at Alice to see if she'd picked up anything. This meeting here leaves him stunned and he watches his wife, certain that she must know. She can just tell, can't she, by being there? How can she not? He takes shallow breaths, amazed by how natural Thomasina is as they chat, knowing he himself would not be and so not trusting himself to speak. The husband is equally mute, the two of them like bodyguards until the tour must resume, though Alice touches Thomasina's arm to detain her a little more, tell her again how great St Saviour's is. She's actually speaking with more confidence than she normally would to her, gained he thinks by Dom's success or the fact that, while she and James have achieved this school, Thomasina is merely a supplicant. She lets her go though and they turn, only to be stopped again when Richard and Amelia Leigh burst in.

Both are big, overflowing with congratulations when they hear about Dominic. Alice, in contrast to her behaviour with Thomasina, seems to withdraw, leaving him to do the talking.

Outside he can let it all out. He takes a deep breath and then, hand in hand, with children in between, they walk towards the Heath. Again he looks at Alice, though he's safe here, isn't he? She won't question him now. He expects instead, once they are free from the school, that Alice will swoop down on her son, though she's a little subdued. He swallows and scoops Dom up himself, telling him how wonderful he is, his beautiful son beaming back with toothy pride.

— Right then, he says. Two words for you, young man.

— What are they, Daddy?

— Ice cream, he booms.

He has in mind the café by Blackheath station. Alice protests that it's actually getting late but he tells her hell, who cares, then let's have supper there. She agrees, which makes him feel good, manly and indulgent, like the guy at the end of *The Tiger Who Came to Tea*. Though he can't be like him, can he? Not unless he also has a hideous secret, his thoughts too being jagged by images of another woman, though maybe that explains his *distrait* smile. Did his wife suspect him? Was that why she threw off her duties that day? Was the tiger her husband's infidelity, which she was subsequently prepared for though it never actually returned, the lesson she taught him about consequences having been learned as she intended?

They crowd in on themselves at a small Formica table near the back of the thin, cosy space. Spaghetti is ordered, plus apple juice, both straws red to prevent a diplomatic incident between his children. He keeps his eyes away from Alice, smiling instead at Dom, still glowing. Ida, having refused a high-chair, is barely visible, though her presence as usual is strong. So strong, as are they all, which takes him back to what he did. There is such weight inside him, a sodden stew of guilt, and pure fear. But also its exact opposite. Such a light thing. Stupid. So *silly*. Like fluff compared to... this. Isn't it? To his amazement a small laugh escapes him and he is stunned: because he wants to tell Alice. Not confess. Beg forgiveness. He just wants to put it out there.

— Hey, you know what I did yesterday?

— What, love?

— Go on, guess.

— Right. Wait a minute. No, tell me.

— I fucked Thomasina Davis.

— You never. Wait, I thought there was something funny back there. That look on your face. And her, never been so nice to me. Where?

— Her place, right out the blue. On the playroom floor actually, which is fucking massive by the way. Whole place is and before you ask, it's not tacky at all. And we have to go to Monmouth, that coffee place. At Borough, you know, near the cheese shop. Apparently they do a decaf too and you can hardly even tell.

So easy. Natural. If he just tossed it out they could discuss it. She'd know what it meant, she always did, or at least have a take, something he hadn't seen. The words are on his lips and it would be so easy just to spit them out. But he keeps them there, which is when he gets a deeper and more tangible sense of what he has done. What he has lost. For the first time in more than ten years there is something he cannot tell Alice. He cannot tell his wife what he has done. He stares at a giggling Dom and the weight inside him grows, while at the same time he feels empty. Panicked. Dom is laughing at Ida, who has stuck breadsticks in both ears and is doing po-faced. It's hilarious, Alice unable to tell her off without laughing so much she can hardly breathe. He can't connect to it. He's cut off, because of what he did. So why did he? For what reason? He stares at Alice in disbelief and takes a breath for, actually, there's no way she could laugh like that if she knew. Or even suspected. So, then, in spite of the horror inside him, the leaking in his stomach, he did nothing. For they are the same. His family. They are just the same as they were yesterday and therefore what he did wasn't anything, was it? He changed the universe, no denying that. He threw poison on it, piped oil out from under the ice floes, but only in his universe. He can see it right in front of him: he has not hurt them. And there's something else. He stuck his dick in another woman. True and terrible: but aberration. A slip. He fell below the line, but he isn't below it now, is he? He pictures the Travelcards that slid out of Alice's pocket when she came home the night before. They were invisible to her. He picked them up. This is trivial of course, but unlike his actions her sloppiness is no mistake. It's ongoing, representing an inability to think about him, a small, hardwired selfishness. So even if it is in a very minor way, her shit infects his world. By contrast it is his firm intention that what he has done – now that he has done it – will do nothing to her at all.

— And what, really, have I done?

Alice, fork of pasta mid-air.

— Broken the sacred bond you made to me.

— Yes. But.

— What, you fucking bastard?

— I didn't mean to.

— Sorry?

— It rose from no need. No boredom, no marital problem.

— So why did you do it?

— She asked me.

— And you just had to say yes? Too polite, something your mother taught you: be nice to ladies, James?

— Maybe something in that, actually. She caught me off guard.

— Aren't you always on guard?

Normally. James pauses in his imaginary dialogue and nods. It was just this inability to see it coming that sunk him. With the students it's easy, the English roses from good homes clutching their battered copies of *Frankenstein*, holes in the wrists of their fleamarket cardigans. He can see their moony need a mile off, just as he sees the tentative suggestions of a couple of female colleagues for what they would be: muted, pointless affairs undertaken by people whose lives didn't match up to the books they pored over. He's never been tempted by either grouping but if he had he still would not have succumbed because he would have had time to evaluate, like seeing a pile-up far ahead on the motorway. Yesterday he'd come round a blind bend. Though didn't that make it worse? To throw away his perfect record for something trivial? He shakes his head, full of self-loathing now, his fists twisting into balls beneath the table.

But.

Funny. If put right. He could say it happened when he was single, some yummy mummy he met in the park. Back to hers, jizzed into one of Pooh's honey pots. Or on Eeyore. *Oh great that's right nobody cares about me all alone here every day with nothing to eat but thistles and now there's a big pile of semen on my head*. The shtick takes shape and by the time the mint choc chip is being demolished it really is like something that happened way back when. He insists on telling the waitress the reason for this outing, his clever son blushing as his mother did earlier, something that lets his love flow clear again, like the juices of a well-roasted bird.

Except. Was it seeing her at the school, or was she always going to return like this? For she's there. She has appeared at this feast, right in the centre of them. Alice once described their family as a wind chime, through which their lives blow. Each of them an element. He was stilled to read that and the image never left him. But it's twisted now. Thomasina Davis strokes his children's hair. She rips her blouse open and pulls her jeans down, laughing while she climbs on to the table. She opens her legs right in front of him while Dom and Ida giggle and Alice grabs her phone, a text coming through that it seems she's been expecting. It sets her on edge, though in a good or bad way he cannot tell. Something about her prize? He asks but she says it's nothing, though is still fraught later, at home, putting the kids to bed, making the mistake of showing them how much she wishes they were asleep, which always makes it impossible to get them to be so. He's angry with her for snapping at them, especially on this day, though he doesn't say so. It will be a long time before he gives her grief about anything.

When they finally settle she does casual badly.

— That text was from Amelia. There's something she wants to talk about. Okay? I mean if I go out for a bit?

He's disappointed. He wanted to lay down time with her to distance himself from what he did. He wants to focus on her, Alice, to make the mirage fade. But when she goes up for a bath it returns. Thomasina is in the kitchen this time. Naked again. He turns away, knowing it's just guilt, this, that if he lets it grow it will fester until only one balm will ever soothe it: forgiveness. To get that he'd have to tell Alice and he can't, no, he really can't: though didn't they agree to tell each other everything? They certainly did, Alice dissecting his sexual history with amused and steely determination that carried on to the present. Is that girl attractive? Would you sleep with her if you weren't married to me? Would you want to go out with her, have dinner, would you ever consider holding that girl's hand? On and on until, after initial fear, he turned his gaze on her in the same manner. What he'd found was a thousand people inside the mind and body of his wife, an inexhaustible supply of brilliant, attractive women he could never tire of, each one just a little out of reach.

So why not tell her this, given that it's the sort of thing she'd have laughed at if it had happened before her time? No. For telling is not honesty. Not telling would be closer to the truth because telling would give weight to events that – he is certain – have none. He'd smash her life up for something meaningless; it would be like a wrecking ball meant for a different building, taking out the house in one swing. Though won't she find out anyway? Maybe he got away with it at the school but he can't forever, can he? They're telepathic. She starts conversations milliseconds before he is about to, remembers things they have to do just as he is doing the same. How can she not see the pictures that are so close to the surface of his mind? She will if he's not careful so he must be strong. System-wipe, delete all. Like Gloucester if he has to, he'll put the pictures out.

He walks upstairs, ostensibly to piss but really just to see his wife. Look at her. And he does that. He pushes the bathroom door open just as she's lowering herself into the water. And she's done something. He gets the briefest flash of it and is shocked. She's never done anything like that before. Why did she do it? He's a little excited, though he pretends not to see, ignoring the waxing strips on the floor near the radiator. She'll show him, of course. He just smiles and goes downstairs again, holding his hand out later when she appears.

— Your phone, he says. Remembering last time.

18

THAT EVENING James has a choice. To be alone, but which self to be alone with? He is not going to think about what happened on Ashburnham Grove. He stands, listening again, and this time allows himself to hear the birdsong and light traffic in the background of the picture. The world, going on. Who does he think he is? Why, for one second, does he think that anything he does is important? He sneers at himself and Thomasina really does vanish. He waits for her to resurface but she doesn't, other things dropping away too. He has no gig tonight. His kids often wake at night but it's never before midnight. Whether it's because of what he did or just the fact that Alice is out he doesn't know but it feels almost as though he has no wife and children. It takes him back to Brighton, and Vernon Terrace.

He always wanted to live alone. It was one of the reasons he went back to university after four years living with the same girl. A lovely girl, true, but there was never a second when he felt he could, in any moment, do what the hell he wanted. In Vernon Terrace he had that, pulling on the exquisite loneliness that felt so much like the perfect coat for him. He wrote bad poems. He read and read, took long walks through the ramshackle, amateurish town. He could feel himself settling into himself, the comedian who had inhabited him beginning to leave him like an exorcised spirit. The sea helped. He stared at it for hours, dug in, throwing pebbles into the chop. One morning he found one that had been written on: 'Natasha' in blue biro. It was dated, and he realised with amazement that it was today's date. That very day someone had sat where he was sitting and expressed the fact that they were themselves and no one else, thinking of course that no one would ever realise. But he had. He looked around, hoping to see her, someone walking away whom he could run after. He was alone however and so he pocketed the stone and carried it with him for the next several months, trying to spot her, as if he could tell just to look at a girl – on her own in a café perhaps – that it was she. When he first met Alice his only disappointment was her name. He could really see her on the beach, writing the secret message of her identity on one of the millions of stones that churn and chafe in the back-and-forth but always remain intact.

More than a year later they sat in the same place and he pulled a pen from his pocket. He wrote his name and the date on one side of a flat stone and handed it to her. She took it but chose another instead, to write on. Then she walked towards the sea and threw the two stones in. Only now does it occur to him that the initial girl might have had a different motive. Not an expression of self but a desire to leave herself behind. And when Alice chose two stones instead of one and threw them into the sea, what did she really want to happen? How close did she think they would stay to each other as each day came and went, and came and went until, eventually, both names were eroded? How close did she want them to stay?

On another day he sat at the window of his flat, staring through the rain leaping off the eaves at people pushing umbrellas into the wind, the occasional dog walker looking sideways as his or her animal squatted on the crescent-shaped grass across the road. All day he sat there, letting thoughts wash in and out of him. It was perfect. As if, by stopping, doing nothing, all of the ragged bits of himself had joined back up. His motionless gravity had pulled in all the debris for a million miles. And even after meeting Alice he has managed to hang on to that feeling. Or believes he has. Maybe he's begun to meld too much, not into her perhaps but into *them*. The school. Blackheath. Greenwich. Would that explain what happened yesterday? No, for nothing did and he thinks instead of Stella, the girl before Alice, with whom he shared so much: a flat, a bed, friends, holidays, family members. How did he do it for so long when now it seems so hazy and insubstantial? So *before*. The answer is that he didn't, it was someone else, and when they disentangled themselves, he to Brighton, she to Paris, it was such a relief that he felt exhausted. She felt it too, he could tell, a great shrugging off of dead weight, for the relationship they had no longer contained either of them. He hopes now that she is happy, and does not blame him for taking up more of her life than was necessary.

He walks back down the narrow hall and into the kitchen. The house is quiet now. Creaking. It's been ages since he was Home Alone like this. No time pressure. Nothing expected of him by the children's diaries or his own. Earlier, while Alice wrestled with the kids, he tidied up, and it feels as though he can really live there for a few hours. He stands in the doorway of the kitchen and thinks that it's a good kitchen, professional-looking with its pan-hangers and magnetised knife rack, one of those chopping boards you can fold a little and tip the food off. The picture of himself there is one he likes, though having a glass of wine in his hand would improve it. He walks over to the rack where his first decision waits. He'd normally go for a cheapo on a night like this. He stays his hand though and not because of how the wine would taste. He simply wants to open something better, though not one of the Châteauneufs or Brunellos. Not without Alice. He stares instead at the middle range, spicy things from the Languedoc and Portugal costing between seven and ten quid. He'd normally save these for the weekend but picks one, the slight extravagance making him feel worldly. Taking his alone self seriously. He pours the wine into one of the big glasses and takes it to the living room, where the new telly waits on standby.

But is this really who he wants to watch himself being tonight? A man who, given this rare space, spends it in front of the box? The answer is no though it's hard to resist. Not the crap, people being given a shot at whichever short-lived dream has been invented for them. The latest one is waiters, something so surreal he thinks it must be a hoax. It'll be *plongeurs* next, sixteen hopefuls battling it out for the Golden Brillo Pad. These shows don't call to him and neither will he scour Netflix. Again, not without Alice, though she'd probably welcome that as she could then watch whatever he had when he was gigging. But putting on a film is a deliberate act, a marking out of the next two hours that he can't quite commit to. And it's still watching TV. He's more in danger of turning to and being hooked by one of the 'serious' programmes, Robert Peston on banking or another screen-struck scientist hitting the global warming ball back or forth. These leave him with the nastiest taste. For could he explain to a stranger tomorrow what a commodity derivative is? Or what sunspots do? If he were to read a newspaper article, perhaps, but these documentaries wash over, trick him into thinking that he's doing something worthwhile so that he doesn't have to concentrate. They're just an excuse for the middle class to veg, no better than *The X Factor*. So he turns instead to the collected works of his poet.

But not to work. He just picks up the bible he's been scrutinising all these months and flicks through, as he would on the TV, until these words strike him.

I sit at the reflecting window
watching you
leave until I can no
longer see myself

The wine has body. Is real in his mouth. He is someone who drinks good wine. Who shares that experience with himself. When the glass is empty he can still feel what it tastes like and he reflects that that's what good wine does: both deepens and extends the experience of time. This is something that would have horrified his poet, which, he realises, is why his poems only ever refer to white wine, gone almost before you drink it. He makes a note of this and pours himself another glass of Pic Saint-Loup, frowning to find that it is different now. The same in many ways but softer, longer, an extension of itself. Better, but missing something. He is instantly nostalgic for the way it was before, but as he drinks it the memory of the first glass fades until the two are indistinguishable.

Alice gets up early. Before the kids even. She sits on the side of the bed and wakes him, a cup of tea steaming on the bedside table. He props himself up, wondering if something is wrong. She was late last night; he went to bed before she came home.

But it's nothing. A favour? This play, she tells him, leaving the rest unsaid. Would he…? I mean, it's all inside my head right now. I'll make it up at the weekend, you can have Saturday at the library, Sunday too if you like. If you'll do today. She looks so quietly desperate that he agrees without even nailing down the deal. She doesn't know it but he owes her a thousand acts of kindness. He smiles and she tells him to go back to sleep, that she'll get Dom ready and take him to school, and wake him just before she has to leave. She kisses him with a tenderness that he can't quite accept and they are awkward with each other in the few moments before she leaves the room. After that he blinks up at the ceiling until he hears Dom putting his shoes on.

He won't look after Ida today. He decides that as he comes down the stairs, embarrassed when Alice opens the front door in case a passer-by glances in and sees him in his pyjamas. Instead he will spend time with Ida. He'll interact, be another human beside his daughter. If she behaves badly he won't chastise her, just enquire as to her reasons, what made her do what she did. And without telling her this he notices almost immediately the effect it has. Ida is relaxed, not at all clingy, and the atmosphere as they eat their bowls of cereal together is just as it is when he's with Alice. For the first time ever she toddles upstairs for a wee without asking him to come and he smiles, missing her until she is back in the doorway again.

— Flapjack? he asks.

They weigh the oats. Ida shouts out *Stop!* when the marker on the scales reaches eight. She settles her own hand on top of his as they cut a slab of butter, her fingers curled together like a shell. He explains that he knows that half a pat is four ounces but she's worried, wanting to weigh it to make sure, which he agrees to. They add brown sugar and he sets the pan on the hob, gets a chair and lets her stir, noting her seriousness, how aware she is of the steady blue flame. They know stuff, have no desire to hurt themselves. If we leave them alone they do perfectly well.

When they've mixed the oats and spread them into a roasting tin he asks what she'd like to put in. As well as jam, chocolate, raisins, nuts, and chocolate, she suggests peas. He gets some from the freezer and adds a few in the corner. When he takes the tray out of the oven twenty minutes later that patch is green and he breaks it off, offering it to Ida. She tells him no, that it's for Mummy. She licks her wooden spoon and he licks his and they do that for a while.

So where to take her? His first thought is a request she made at the weekend: a ride on an open-top bus. This would be great, though Dom would be scraped hollow with jealousy. Ida would gloat, as she has begun to lately, driving home the point that she gets more time with Mummy and Daddy than he does. Dom's response is to insist on utter parity in all things, even going so far as to ask what Ida had for lunch every day in case she got some pudding he didn't or the sweetie tin came down. So not the bus. It occurs to him to wonder what he'd do on his own if he wasn't allowed to work but had to entertain himself with one of the myriad cultural pleasures that drift past him every week. He decides on the Portrait Gallery and Ida's perfectly happy, her only alteration to the plan her desire to wear wellies instead of Crocs. He says sure, though we'll bring the Crocs in case, okay? No, she says, in case I don't want wellies I'll have my bare feet on and we're bringing those anyway.

James smiles, loving these word-mashes, as if a virus has infected her thoughts. At the airport she asked why they had to go through parsnip control. Home from nursery one day she told him that three wise men took Frankenstein to see Jesus. These things Alice and James write down in a book, knowing they will be far more valuable to them than photographs.

The Portrait Gallery is shut for a hang so they go to the National next door. Dom's mania for trains has to some degree rubbed off on Ida so he takes her to stand in front of *Rain, Steam and Speed*. She loves it, bellowing at the hare to GET OUT OF THE WAY. She asks for other train pictures and they look for some, pretty slim pickings but she doesn't mind. Entering each room he sets her tasks, to find such and such in the pictures, a hat or a vase or boobies that look like Mummy's. When she spots and correctly identifies another Turner he tells her yes, well done, pleased that a group of old ladies raise their eyebrows in appreciation. For himself he doesn't know whether this is spectacularly clever or just something most two-year-olds could do but it still delights him. He buys postcards of both pictures and a pencil case for Dominic.

On the train back his phone beeps. Carty usually gets in touch before lunch but it's not him. James doesn't recognise the number. He opens the message and then immediately shields it from his daughter, as if she could read what it says.

Can we talk?

He puts the phone back in his pocket without replying.

Half an hour later it beeps again. They're in Greenwich Park and the message is longer.

James, could you call me please?

Again he stares, but this time he deletes the message. And the first one. He takes a breath, fearful, eyes darting around the herb garden where Ida is throwing sticks into the fountain. What if she's there? It wouldn't be such a surprise on a nice day like this. He tells Ida they have to go up to Blackheath, even though they'll be way too early to pick up Dom. As he hurries her up the hill he looks around, relieved when he's out of the top gate.

— Can we see Amelia? Ida asks, but he says no, knowing it would be an imposition, taken as a sad attempt to get someone to help him with his childcare. Nevertheless he has an image of it, Ida rooting in some box while he sits with Amelia in the kitchen. And tells her. Lays it out. Asks what he should do.

— Christ, he thinks, livid with himself, slamming the lid down fast. He takes Ida to Jade even though Dom will moan; sets his phone on the table between them.

At school Ida charges round the playground as if she already attends the place. Dom explodes with unfettered happiness to see them, in a way that is becoming rarer. James chats with some of the mothers and the contrast with his actions yesterday is so vast he can scarcely believe the two things can fit into the same life. Was this it, then? To err. Transgress, after a year of being Daddy, bland and bankable, the silly Daddy whose only vice is his naughty stubble. Had the picture begun to appal him so much that he had to deface it, do a Duchamp on his own self-portrait? Yes. The secret he has gives him a flush of dirty, self-disgusted pleasure, and makes him feel alone again. And separate from Alice too, which increasingly is something he hasn't been able to feel. And this achieved in the most cowardly way there is, only made possible by the fact that Thomasina is married. For he never would have done it if she weren't, if she didn't have that house to lose, that sacred fridge to come crashing down on top of her. He feels shit now. Does she not? She must, to some degree, surely.

So why the fuck's she sending texts?

He's angry, not least because he'd managed to start moving past it. Be in his life again. And something else: he's never been unfaithful but even so he knows *there are rules*. When another comes, just question marks this time, he deletes it immediately and shouts to his children that they must leave. As they walk home he's on edge, as if the phone in his pocket is a bomb. And, the next time he hears it, it is ringing.

Alice comes home happy. Beaming. He recognises the feeling: of having really got something done. The kids mob her and she laughs as she tries to get her boots off, saying quick let's get them in the shoe cupboard BEFORE DADDY GETS MAD. Ida grabs one and won't let him take it. Dom, in rare mock revolt, hides the other behind the sofa. He roars with fake anger and tries to retrieve both boots and he's back again, a well-oiled cog in this wonderful, organic machine.

He doesn't hear the phone at first. It comes through eventually but not before Alice is moving towards the mantelpiece and grabbing it for him. She doesn't look at the number. She even pulls Ida off him and clings on to her so that he can take the call. He thanks her, hollowed out inside, near terrified, using the excuse of the noise to walk out. He shouts wait a sec as he unlocks the back door, only pressing the phone to his head when he's halfway down the garden.

— Hello?

Hurries past the bike shed, glancing across the fence to make sure Neil's not on his patio. Calm down. It's *okay*. It's not what he thinks. She's probably feeling what he is. She's mortified and wants to hurry past it too, only she can't until she knows that he's not going to do something stupid. She wants to tell him God, crazy shit huh, but can't we just forget it? Relief pops, though his pride fights it. At least if she's serious it would have meant something. But if she laughs, says shit, really sorry, don't know what came over me, apart from you that is, it'll be nothing. It might even tell him that she's done it before, that he's just one more in the line of Thomasina Davis's consolations. God, how pathetic. And this word makes him shudder because he has now, finally, arrived at the correct label for his actions which is, coincidentally, exactly how Alice would see them. If she ever found out what he did it would cause her pain. Real pain, but he could deal with that. How, though, could he ever live with the knowledge that Alice thought he was pathetic?

— James, finally. A hard man to reach. Janet Sanderson.

A friend? Calling to warn him off? He stares at the open back door.

— I'm sorry?

— Jay's assistant. He wanted me to say that he really enjoyed your chat the other week. And he loves your pedalo idea.

— My...?

— Though he thinks it should wait for Comic Relief.

— I see.

— And in the meantime we need to build your profile. So we're thinking *QI*. A few in the autumn. *Just a Minute* perhaps? Though first Jay wants you at the Apollo.

— The...?

— And soon, or with the schedule you'll have to wait until next year and by then, who knows?

— Who indeed?

— So I've a date for you. James? Are you still there?

He hurries back into the house. Hunting for a pen he pictures this man, this odd, benevolent stalker. He simply cannot understand it, sees no reason why he's doing this. He stands in front of the calendar, pinned to the door beneath the stairs, and flips the pages. And then he stops as Janet gives him the date, tells him when he'll be on primetime TV for a whole hour, just him, an event that could fire him towards places he can't even properly contemplate. He locates the square and moves his pen towards it, adrenaline storming through his veins. But the square is full. Completely. On it is a star. He drew it himself, going over and over it in gold pen. And then, with Ida, they got Pritt stick and sprinkled it with multicoloured glitter as Alice sat smiling, a little embarrassed, at the other end of the kitchen table.

19

As she approaches him the irony does not escape her. He turns his head and she feels the way they must: her students, beating paths to her door, the products of their various labours waiting to be withdrawn from personally customised folders. She's late. She strides across the road, shoving the phone James handed her into her jeans, wishing he would step back into the house and stop looking at her. It makes the fact that she'd lied to him worse: but she couldn't say she was meeting Richard. He'd want to know how it went. He'd ask to read it too. He would have opinions which she would have to triangulate with Richard's and her own, a tangle of thought strands that would leave her bamboozled. It occurs to her now that she was completely unprepared for the ways her new writing project would impact on her life. She'll have to sit James down, tell him how she needs to guard her work. They'll agree to an operational procedure when she's writing something long, work out how to manage the border between her writing and her life, what checks to put in place to prevent migration between those zones. In either direction. This temporary fence, *lie*, is way too flimsy.

The Café Rouge is fuller. Her own feelings are different too. In place of the derision is nostalgia. Ownership. She looks at the same walls, chairs, even waiter, and then the table where they sat. It's occupied by four hunched businessmen and she's disappointed, as if it really were her table, hers and Richard's and then that horrible, arrogant man. Having been so angry then, why she should feel warmth and recognition on her second visit she has no idea. She remembers how the guy hardly saw her, moving into the platform of their conversation like some vain soloist, relegating her to the second violins. Yet she is happy to be here, the images in front of her overlaying her memories of the first time like tracing paper.

Richard is at a small table to the left. That he's sat near the door makes her suspicious. She jokes to herself that he's done that to make a swift exit, so disappointed is he with the work she's sent him.

But it's not a joke. What happens then is dreamlike. And yet, too, it feels so much like being jolted awake. When he has gone, and she is alone at the table, she lets the feelings run through her and tries to recognise them, the only thing close that time in Sixth Form when Sam Williams dumped her at the beginning of their second date, left her standing at the bar in Scarfe's with too much make-up on. Everyone staring. Like then, she can barely move. Again she sees the last time she was there, how superior she and Richard had been, demanding a particular table to sit at, ignoring the waiter, waving away the menu. In truth it was Richard who had done that but she'd gone along, found it exhilarating, as suddenly and only now she knows she did. She and James are polite. They do not rip great holes in life. Now she just feels small and very stupid, brought down to earth with a bump that all but disables her. Nothing she's ever written has been treated like this. I'm on stage, she says to herself. The walls are board, the hubbub coming out of loudspeakers.

As if to underline the point the waitress chooses that moment to walk up and ask what she would like. Blinking back tears, she shakes her head, but then realises that she's hungry, not having been able to eat in Blackheath with the children, nerves having turned her stomach to feathers.

— Cassoulet, she says, making herself busy, not looking up. And a glass of red wine.

He said, Alice, you've really no idea, have you?

— About what?

— What happens to people when they read your writing. You think they're impressed, don't you?

— Sometimes. They have been. They've told me.

— Right. But who the fuck wants to be impressed by someone?

— I'm sorry, I don't understand.

— You just wanted to impress me with this. But it's only children we like being impressed by. Anyone else and it makes us feel shit. That how you want people to feel?

— You don't want me to impress them?

— You have to move them. And before you wet yourself, I don't mean get all teary. I mean shift them. Move them from where they are.

— And I don't?

— Because you're too clever. Christ, you're all squirrelled up. You make these little carvings. Totems, clues to yourself. But there's only so much running around after you the reader can take.

— So?

— You have to give. Be brave, let it out of yourself. In your poems you do that now and then because you think no one's watching. But here? How clever this is, people would say, before deciding not to come back after the interval.

What's here for them, Alice? What do you give out to anyone else?

Richard's comments filled her with rage. It was the words first but then the way he put them across, as if she was *taking up his time*. As if she hadn't given any thought to what she was doing. And yet, she said to herself, as he found yet another hole in her 'play': *he* badgered *me*. Just like Sam fucking Williams. Now it seems like the other way round: as though she'd demanded some audience which, when he got fed up with being hassled for it, he granted her, his savage treatment of her work meant to say *well you asked for it*. And it was all over in less than twenty cringe-making, patronising minutes.

Her notebook is lying on the table. An odious thing. She can't touch it. When she finishes her meal she has the impulse to leave it there, like a fourteen-year-old with a squirming bundle wrapped in newspaper. But she doesn't do that. She takes it outside and wanders home, only one goal now: to be there. She wants James. To lie in his arms. Cry, do that before explaining anything, let him fill her with his innocent, worried love. The mere thought makes her even more incensed that this man should have done this to her so instead she walks past her door and round to St Alfege's churchyard. She used to sit there sometimes. Just for a minute or two, on her way back home. Imagining what was waiting for her, just James and Dominic to start with and then Ida too, noticing how happy she was at the thought that she was about to plunge into it all.

She finds a bench. Under the street lamp the annotations he'd made looked ghostly. She hadn't expected them. They're clumsy, written in hard, thick pencil, subjugating her own tightly sewn script like iron bars. Hardly a page is untouched by them. Again she has the impulse to leave her book or dump it into one of the wastepaper bins. Instead she forces herself to read his comments, read them without making any sort of judgement, allow them access to the play that still sat inside her. When she's finished she stays where she is as the too-big church looms over her, staring at the puddles of ink in the shadows of the trees and the benches, and the gravestones.

Why can't James say no? Frown and spit fuck off, it's your turn. Why, next morning, when she asks him to look after Ida for the day, does he so easily capitulate? As she thanks him and leaves him to sleep, she wants to beg him. *Save me. Tell me no. Live my life for me.* Do I batter him? she wonders. The way that Malcolm battered me? Do I bully him into believing that my own needs are more important than his own? And then, when she's dropped Dominic at church for assembly, and has to face that notebook, she so envies him for being a parent for the day. And only that. How many people was she expected to be, at once? Why am I doing this? she asks as she edges out of the playground with the other parents, some rushing, some chatting, others a little bewildered, as if they don't quite know what to do with themselves. Because I won't just fade? I refuse to let him crush me? She's no idea, and there's something else she hasn't thought of.

Where?

She can't go to any of the pubs or cafés she's been working in lately. They are contaminated by her failure. Or is it the other way round: did the very bricks and mortar conspire against her somehow? Thinking of them, she is puzzled, frowning to recall the *feeling*. Until yesterday evening she'd been convinced that she was writing well, honestly, that the relationships she'd created were taut and dynamic, the whole lot shot through with a sharp, black humour. How could she have been so wrong? I wasn't, she says to herself, as she stands out on the road. So is it Richard who is? No. That would be the easy way out. But she found something. She *did.* So maybe all it takes is a translation of that to the stage, an acceptance of the external. She realises then the mistake she made. These people in her mind are real. They live in real places. She has to make them false, theatrical, lessen them; she has to see them as they'd be played by actors, recreate them not as people but characters. You haven't done enough, Richard told her. But perhaps she'd done too much, and of the wrong thing.

When she gets to Amelia's, Alice is nervous. Is it a stupid idea? It's not really a creative space, is it, that big sitcom house? But today she can't be in public. She needs to be alone, without having to wonder what anyone might be thinking of the small, intense woman scribbling away over the same cup of tea. And when Amelia greets her with enthusiasm, waving her into the kitchen, she's instantly reassured.

— I was always doing that, she laughs.

— What?

— His book bag, Amelia says, laughing again, pointing at her shoulder.

Alice makes her request and Amelia doesn't even think about it. Go ahead. She shows her the spare room and clears the desk of shoved washing, the sight of which reassures Alice. They chat, Amelia telling her where the tea and coffee is, some leftover fish pie for lunch if she wants it.

— And it's your play? she asks, standing at the door.

Alice wants to deny it but how can she? Almost like a shameful thing, she nods.

— Richard says it's really good.

Liar. But it's a nice thing to say. She thinks back to her own lie and forces a smile, staring at the back of the door when Amelia has gone.

Walking home that day, Alice fairly romps across the Heath. The wind feels cold for the time of year but maybe it isn't, maybe it's just that Alice has one less layer of skin now. She spent the day pulling off the old one. As she cut and slashed and tore pages out, she knew she was doing something irrevocable. She wasn't just changing her work. It made her feel sick but it was exhilarating. And exhausting. Would she ever write another poem? It didn't seem possible, though, if she did, it wouldn't be like before. It wouldn't feel like before. Today has made her feel older, more evolved, having discovered new capabilities, though this last also makes her feels so young. Young, and raw, and boundless.

After the fish pie she went back up to the spare room. She lay down on the bed, more expensive and comfortable than the one she and James sleep on every night. She listened to a tick somewhere that did not seem to come from a clock. But from Richard. Keeping his time. In his house. She curled into a ball and let it run through her, each tick knocking another from her until they were all gone and she was left with nothing, just a sense of being enveloped. Some time later she woke and the feeling stayed with her as she wrote, only dissolving when Amelia came home with Niamh. She snapped her notebook shut and hurried downstairs, just nodding when asked how her day had gone. She had a cup of tea and chatted with Niamh, who was bright, open, not at all like her mother. Amelia, Alice has begun to realise, is more secretive, a darker person than she initially thought. She felt a connection to her that she'd never have thought possible. She imagined unwinding all the things that had happened in both of their lives until two little girls were standing there, both quite similar. So which is the better route? To carry that secret self with you through life as she has done, prodding it awake with her poetry all the time, or to leave it, lost from sight behind all the jobs and the children, the husband and the *things*?

— Tomorrow? Amelia said. Alice nodded.

— Though…

— It's okay. Amelia held her hand out. I won't say anything. Any time after nine, okay?

Alice nodded again and accepted a glass of wine.

Richard walks home with her. That's how it feels. All day he has been inside her, watching, almost editing her work as she went along. She wonders if crossing the threshold of her own house will shake him off but he's still there as she plays with the kids, accepting their anarchy for a change instead of instinctively trying to resist it. He's there as she cooks their supper and bathes them, when she puts them to bed. Either the day spent at the Leighs' or his presence makes the house feel small again, as it did when he really was there, and she wonders something. From beside the basin in the bathroom she pulls out the plastic step stool that Ida has only recently begun to eschew, and stands on it. What she sees astonishes her. On the shelf above the changing table are bottles of nappy creams and massage oils that haven't been used for months, their necks collared by dust. There is more on the top of the windowsill, grown mildewed with moisture. She can also see the cleaning products that she keeps on top of the bathroom cabinet, unnoticed and out of the way, a balled sponge scourer knotted with gunk and hair. What a crack they have left open, a fissure into which taller people can gawp into their lives. She's horrified and spends an hour cleaning, then going from room to room with the step stool. She feels like a secret agent looking for bugs, the integrity of her home in some way compromised.

James is quiet.

— Who was that call from? she asks.

— No one.

— Not technically possible.

— Oh, a gig.

— You didn't write it down. How can I plan anything if you don't...?

— Some shit thing. I said no.

— Sorry. Right. How's your work coming?

— I don't know. Okay, I guess.

— I'm sorry about today. Catch up tomorrow and Saturday, yes?

— Sure. Though if you need the time...

— Thanks.

— So you? How is it? The play you're writing?

— I don't know, she tells him, shivering a little as though Neil from next door has touched her.

They discuss the impending summer holidays and what they'll do with Dom. They've never had to face this before. James lights up with the days out: how, when Ida's in nursery, they can be alone with Dom for a change. He's stoked but she brings him back to the fact that Dom will need looking after *every single day for six weeks*. Until the end of his sabbatical, in fact. It leaves him short of breath and she pictures the little boy asleep upstairs with no idea that his mere presence causes problems for them. This thing he's looking forward to so much is filling them both with dread. What would it be like to know that?

They make love that night. Alice holds James' slim body between her thighs and enjoys the sharp orgasm he gives her with his swift, darting movements.

The next day she carries on scything. Alice the camp guard, consigning all but the lucky chosen to oblivion. She has another sleep on the big spare bed and then stumbles out for a pee. She goes downstairs and makes herself a coffee, sets it down on the side next to some kind of script. A screenplay, the title page announces: by Malcolm Harvey. *That guy?* Feeling hard and derisive, she picks it up and flicks through the pages, surprised to see no dialogue in the long first scene. It's all stage direction, or whatever they call it in a film. Assuming it's some macho crap, she begins to read, surprised to see that the only character is a woman. She's in a ramshackle kitchen at dusk, scrubbing veg, trying to light an Aga that's gone out, loading an old washing machine, the door refusing to close, getting more and more harried until she gives up and stands, stares out of the window into a yard. Outside are two boys. Playing, though not particularly pleasantly until, as she watches, they begin to fight, with petulance at first but then with determined, furious violence. The scene ends with the woman reaching forward to open the window but stopping and just watching, tears beginning to roll down her cheeks. It's beautiful, spare, and she can see it opening a film, a really good film, which makes her shake her head. That Malcolm, so objectionable the very air seemed to want to get out of his way? It must have been someone else.

Back upstairs, she pauses on the landing and blinks at the doors. All closed. Deliberately? Because of her? Thinking of that sends her forward. She should leave them alone. Of course she should. Shown a kindness. Trusted.

The first door, as the carved wooden initials indicate, guards a child's room. Opening it doesn't feel like crossing any real threshold. It is a generic space filled with things she isn't surprised by, could have predicted would be there. The next is the same, though this one is a boy's room. She backs out, knowing that she was just experimenting with these first two forays. Summoning courage. But now she stands in front of the third door and her legs feel heavy. She turns the handle. She cracks the door, listening to the heavy silence in the house. Her gaze flips back towards the stairs. She turns back again and it's like her parents' room. Pregnant with warning, the air made from something thicker. She can't go in there, though even as she says this to herself she knows she will. Her stomach tightens. She blinks and moves the door forward, almost stumbling, then stares hard at the still-drawn curtains, light pressing against them as if up to a dam. This feels wrong and it's not the only thing for the bed, to her left, a big bed, is unmade. The duvet is twisted, the deep cups of a black bra tossed like a ship in a force nine. The rush of the morning is so clear she can almost see them, Richard and Amelia, shoving past each other, hopping into pants and trousers, swearing as they hunt down socks. And is there something else? Did they? Like she and James did? That too stands up, a lumbering, slower, more gravity-instructed event. Somehow more important than what they did.

The pictures fade and she is then overtaken by an impulse. She takes a deep breath and steps forward, fish pie instead of porridge and she's no interest in any baby's bed. She moves to the side, the mattress high and bulky, sits and lets it take her weight. Then she swings her stockinged feet up and scoots quickly into the middle, enveloped immediately by a smell that is deep and complex, so many strands intermingled that she can feel its history, the most enticing and yet repellent scent imaginable: another family.

She pulls the duvet up to her chin and lies back, breathing again as her whole life seems to retreat, each problem in it tiny and insignificant. She's very glad that she's already had her nap, for if she hadn't she'd have drifted, nothing but bear-like hands rough shaking her in surprise and outrage enough to wake her up again. She stares up at the silent ceiling.

A clattering. A bucking panic sends her out of the room but it's just a pizza menu. She hurries back to her desk and carries on until she can do no more. She gathers her things and leaves to collect Dom, stopping in the kitchen and hunting for a Post-it. On it she scribbles 'Richard' and then sticks it on to her notebook, leaving it in plain view by the coffee machine, glancing at it as she opens the back door.

That night she gets a phone call. Him? No. A woman, who asks if she is Alice and states her own name, after which she adds 'Peter's mum'. That still doesn't do it though and Alice has to ask, actually, sorry, who is this? The woman is miffed to have to explain that Peter is in Dominic's class.

— He talks about Dom all the time. He says he knows everything about space.

— Oh, yes, that Peter, Alice says, though she's fairly sure she's never heard the name. Is it a party?

— Well, sort of. It's just that some of us were thinking that we don't really know each other very well. So, we thought, why not have a mums' night out?

Oh. Fucking. Hell. The icy, creeping horror.

— Great idea. When?

— The Friday after next seems most popular. Just after the end of term. The twenty-second?

— Can't, Alice says.

But what to wear? It isn't often she has this thought. In clothing she has up to now had all bases covered, an Einstein-like pre-emptive strike on dysmorphic indecision. She's happy with her work clothes and weekend gear, perfectly satisfied with the two or three posh frocks she steps into on birthdays, the children silenced just to look at her. Tops and jeans from Oxfam, Uniqlo, Jigsaw, trainers from TK Maxx. She takes pride in this masculine Calvinism towards her appearance, but how should she present herself at an awards show? Her only previous experience is a big literary one she covered for the *Issue*, a former homeless guy up though he didn't win. Three old birds were on the shortlist, one in flowing lilac like something out of a Mike Leigh. The other two had been sprayed by their local Kwik-Fit by the look of it and, from appearance alone (the only way she could judge as she hadn't, of course, read any of the novels) she was glad one of the wrinkly men won. He looked natural. In a tux, but not some lunatic version of himself. She remembers now how foolish the woman in lilac seemed afterwards, nobody too keen to talk to her, how depressing it must have been later, to take it off.

The grey one she got in the sale last year? Yes, though why not actually get something new? She can probably afford to and even if she can't, James has offered a trip to Agnès B. She resisted, piqued that he'd offered to take her, not clothes shopping, but to a specific store. No you don't, Henry Higgins. What did it mean? And she just couldn't bring herself to let either of them spend that on a dress. Whoever made it law that when you had more money you had to spend it that way, had to like things you never noticed before? Or spend it at all? She thinks of Samuel Beckett, how, once a year, he gave everything he owned away. And then she laughs because, actually, Agnès B does men's stuff and he'd have looked pretty good in it.

At work next week the teaching is finished and it's all meetings, a picking over of the semester like the aftermath of a tsunami. There is tons of marking and it depresses her, the poor stuff for its laziness, the better work because she suspects that most of the students won't read her comments, will just look at the mark and move on. Or maybe it's just being there, for she's dismayed by the thought of seeing Linus, which somehow she manages to avoid bar the odd meeting, where she sits on the other side of the table from him. She reads his emails though, asking her if she fancies a pint, the same breezy tone he's always used. He wants to explain himself, reorganise her thoughts concerning him. Jessica emails too, wondering if there is any chance Alice can look over her reworked poems, saying that she's around if Alice can find the time to talk again. She replies with vague comments, ignoring the idea of meeting. To Linus she does not reply and she remembers Martha's look across the pub, and how she had misread it. She'd thought it was jealousy, the girl thinking she was taking Linus from her. But it wasn't. The girl thought that Alice was, in some way, complicit. She won't talk to Linus, though she does see him: heading to the pub with some different students for a farewell drink, making them laugh about something. His girlfriend wants him to get serious. She wants to see who he really is. Will he leave her? Shack up with one of these young women? A particularly cute one? If so he'll be able to sit under the sun lamp full time, or at least until the bulb goes.

When Chris Carty calls, Tuesday afternoon when she's at home, Alice is surprised. Doesn't he have James's mobile number? And James is working, a daytime gig at a big law firm, some leaving do. Doesn't he know this? She shushes Ida and then frowns to hear what Carty has to tell her.

— I don't want James. I wanted to talk to you, Alice.

— Sorry, Chris, I'm not that funny. My kids laugh when I tickle them, and that's it.

Ida jumps up and down, smacking a pack of felt tips against her leg. Open them now, Mummy.

— James has been offered a gig.

— Great. So call him. You're his agent, aren't you? In a minute, Ida.

— *Now*, Mummy.

— He already knows. He turned it down.

Some vague memory. She sighs and takes the pack, can't prise up the tab.

— Well, isn't that up to him?

— Yes. But I thought you should know about it. He's told me why he won't do it and I respect that. I do. But, as his wife, you wouldn't want him to miss out on this, I'm sure.

— What the hell are you talking about? Alice says.

20

WHEN SHE GETS to the top of the road she shuts her iPhone down. She can see the trucks parked, fat cables snaking into the house, the catering wagon in the driveway. She walks towards and then past them, blinking in the brightly lit doorway. There's always a moment when she walks on to a set that jars. A street not a street. A shop not a shop. A bedroom so natural she wants to nap in the rumpled bed even though the room only has two sides and beefy sparks and chippies are moving round it. Now she knows why it gets her, for how is her own house different?

Did she not buy the things she owns for the same reason the set-dresser bought these? Aren't they, too, product placement, intended to put over what she wanted to put over? Didn't she organise everything to create in the eyes of others the person she wanted to be? So, by looking at their response, she could see herself? She got it wrong, that's all. None of the things stands for her, refers back to the person she is. She thinks of the Mencap shop she snuck into again on her way to the British Library, all those clothes, not discarded because they were tatty or losing their shape but because the messages they used to send have been washed out. People growing out of them, or so they think, desperate for a more accurate way of telling other people who they are. And Alice in that mac, not for one second pretending it was new, Alice who wouldn't be seen dead in a new Jaeger mac because that was what people like Amelia wore. What a message to send, she thinks, in real admiration. I value you so little I'm happy to wear your cast-offs. I take pride in not being like you as I come to the places that you are.

The British Library. How outdated those two words sounded when they tumbled out of his mouth that first time he came over. How distant the place seemed from hers or any normal life. Alien, as even James admitted. The impression is not dispelled by being there, which she is, in the hours before the shoot. It's modern, sure, and certainly impressive, chastising her for the fact that she's never been before. But it's like being in some temple. At the Alhambra with Richard she felt the vast importance of the place in a different time. Here she has a solemn sense of what this institution must once have meant in its former incarnation but, as with the Alhambra, she's disappointed by its present function. All those people secreted within the rooms to which she is denied access: will anything filter out? It's a sop, she thinks, taking a seat in the café from which she can see the tills. Society's gift to a class that has lost its meaning. The sunny atrium is clean and clear but she still thinks she can taste dust in her throat.

She takes her phone out, sets it to silent. She removes a compact and does her face: a little lipstick, not much. He won't be here yet. It's only eleven-thirty and she imagines him deep in his poet until lunchtime. She didn't want to take the chance of missing him though and so sits, people-watching, a fairly attractive bunch around her though most of the men would blow off in a gale. The age range surprises her: quite a few kids, contrasting with the crumblies bent over cups of tea. The civilians – office workers, a family of French tourists – look out of place as she knows she must. Interlopers. It's like being in a hospital, never feeling as though you ever get truly inside.

Two young guys amble past carrying files but talking about football. A hunched Japanese man picks away at an iPad while on the table next to him sits the classic English academic, a going-to-seed Bill Nighy in crumpled linen. A girl stalks past. Tall. Dark. Intelligent as well as pretty, a paperclip of frown lines between her eyes that are older than the rest of her. Her clothes are functional in the way that Alice's are, though more expensive, a short suede jacket that could be Margaret Howell, skinny grey jeans that bag beneath her buttocks to emphasise their rigidity. Bangles beneath the cuff on her left wrist but beside that the only significant bling is the Reader's ticket on a loop around her neck, a challenge perhaps to anyone considering hitting on her. Something about the girl makes Amelia feel wary so she shakes her away, gradually becoming aware of something.

The concentration she sees around her on many of the public café tables is not of the sort she'd assumed. A severe-looking girl in a slim grey suit isn't writing about Kant, or Charles Dickens. She's tapping away at a spreadsheet. A northern couple two tables over are discussing Samuel Pepys, but not his historic significance. She listens as they address a problem: the fact that on a Sunday some of the pubs he mentions aren't open. She realises that they're planning walks, for tourists, smiling when they agree to make do with an All Bar One instead. The place has free wi-fi. These people have come here to work, e-vampires, drawn to an energy. She sees a flip-flop-clad posh-boy in shorts and a pink shirt, iPhone to his cheek. She tunes in and tries to work out what he's trying to do, getting it soon enough: hawk a new dating site to an investor. She's disappointed, wanting something more exotic, until she realises that the site is specific: for cancer sufferers. She listens in real amazement as the guy explains how perfect the demographic is, how unlikely someone with a tumour would be just to wait for Mr or Mrs Right. The seriousness with which he talks about whether the paid subscription period should be six months or twelve nearly makes her lose it. Is this your life? she thinks. Of all the things there are out there to do, can this really be your life you're living here?

— May I? the girl says.

Amelia looks up. Lost in her reveries she's let down her guard, the one that usually stops people from joining her in public places. She tries to erect it again but the girl has already pulled the chair opposite halfway out and is merely waiting for a cursory nod to finish the procedure. Beaten, Amelia gives it and the girl sits, the academic looking up and smiling at her as her Reader's ticket clunks down on the tabletop. It's a friendly smile but no mistaking its purpose as it lingers that millisecond too long. The girl punishes him for this. The return she gives as she unzips a Notebook is ruthless: was there something you wanted? He turns back to his coffee quickly, pretending not to be flustered, though he is, and Amelia nods in recognition. For she remembers this girl. Girls like her. At uni they cut through campus as if it were butter, already on the fast track to the glittering first jobs in media or publishing she never bothered applying for herself. She was middle grade. Decent but directionless. The careers officer she saw in her third year asked what she liked doing and the question confused her. She could only give vague, general answers, which frustrated him for he was trying to find her shape, so that he could plug her into the world. But every single day she woke up different, the only constant within her the envy she felt for people with answers, for whom life was right there, up ahead, lit bright and staring them in the face.

Like this girl. She starts her computer, pulling her hair back as Amelia feels wistful, filled with a sudden tenderness for the girl she was. And then she's angry, though not because she'd already been there ten minutes and the loser hadn't tried to hit on her. She's never had a problem with her age, the fact that there are younger, fresher women coming up behind her. Nor has she ever felt the envy that fat or plain women must feel, for those of a superior species. She really had it, the ability to make great changes in the stability of the men surrounding her. She was perved at, smiled at, glanced at, chairs scraping as she walked by. And she was certainly as hot as this creamy bitch, for did not once a famous actor deem her a suitable prop?

So what is it?

The girl lifts her coffee to her lips. And the answer comes. Her surprisingly coarse fingers – eczema perhaps – are ringless. Of course. It's her perspective. Her vantage point. For, while she too had the power this girl has, the power to make a whole dimension turn around her, she never used it. She never stopped. She never looked at the world clearly, and assessed it. Honed in. Then chose. She never did that, and the jealousy inside her is suddenly molten, facts and realisations crawling inside her, trying to coalesce, which she doesn't want to happen out here. She mumbles unnecessary excuses and stands, hurrying towards the nearest toilet, shoving her face into the mirror. A good-looking woman. No doubt. Decent cheekbones beneath the bub fat. She focuses on the bunch of gripped daffs beside each eye, the thread veins like tributaries spreading out across her skin. But they don't hurt. What does is something no plastic surgeon could fix. That girl is on a cliff-top. She's looking out while Amelia has passed by that place and there is nothing wrong with that as many have and that girl certainly will, but Amelia spent no time on the top. She was hurried past, chivvied along before she could realise where she was, what was open to her. She never got to look out and she made no choice, something she doesn't know inside so much as see in front of her. A physical negativity, buried beneath the skin.

She has another realisation. Those women you sometimes see, sixty-five or seventy, those truly beautiful women. Given the number of pretty girls in the world, there should be more. She's often wondered what happens in the years between but now she knows, for it's not their genes that make them shimmer like that. Time can beat down any genetic inheritance. It does. No, their rare beauty has been sustained and even enhanced by something far more powerful than ancestry, or collagen, a knowledge inside that screams I did it, I really did.

I chose my life.

Amelia feels queasy. She blinks and nearly gasps, for suddenly she is surrounded by people. An infinite number of versions of herself wait patiently in line in the dark mirror. The figures retreat, rush into the past. But they never get there. For they cannot change. They cannot revert. She blinks into the horror of that, searching for the very last, tiniest figure she can make out, knowing that of all those identical images it is that one that most closely resembles her.

A woman pushes the door open with a buggy. Amelia struggles past it, back out into the high space. And he is there.

He's bought a coffee and is bumbling through the cluttered café, in his own world, so stubbly he's almost bearded, one hand lifting his tattered jumper to scratch his back, a band of Gap undies above the waist of his Carhartts. She swallows because it isn't him. It is. But not the James she knows. A dad? You wouldn't necessarily know that. Cool. Thirty-six or -seven if you had to guess. Not her age. She bites her lip, hard, her face like cement: which is when it happens. He doesn't notice the girl at the table, doesn't notice anything, that fact alone enough to hook her. Instead it's she who glances up. And checks him out, subtly rearranging herself in case he does look her way, after which she turns to Amelia, aware that she's being stared at. She reddens at the fact that Amelia has caught her, after which she smiles and lifts her brow, throwing a glance at James and then bringing it back to Amelia with a shrug. She draws her laptop a little towards her in the assumption that Amelia will retake her seat, but she does not.

How *ridiculous*. What a stupid thing to do. She cuts a look back to James, terrified that he'll see her, and then snatches her bag from the table. She leaves, hardly even breathing until she's out on the King's Cross Road, desperate to get away from there. The people don't look real. They are generic, have been cast. They are loud and far too happy, with no sense that life is rigid and unforgiving, a tunnel in fact, which you don't realise until it's become so narrow you can no longer turn around, no matter how much you might want to. You can only go on, and on, chilled into speeding up by what is behind you.

She hurries down to Russell Square and stands outside the ApartHotel. Then, up in the room she booked the night before, she stands and thinks about James. In her desperation she was going to tell him. Just say it. She shakes her head and winces, and then takes long, deep breaths before sitting on the perfectly made bed, the rustle of her lined skirt loud in the empty room. When she crosses her legs a thread vein appears from beneath her hem, like a fork of lightning. Car horn. Bleep of a pelican crossing. Fuck off, wanker. She places a hand on top of a pillow and looks up. There is a vase in front of her, sitting on a Danish-style sideboard. In it are five red gerberas, so still that she is mesmerised by them.

He's being a bastard. A real cunt. Known for this of course, part of his USP, but never this bad before. He drives the crew with a cursory violence that even she can see is unreasonable, their reciprocal hatred intended to inspire them to bridge the gap between their own average talent and his brilliance. It works, normally, which is why Malcolm has maintained his place in such a youth-obsessed industry. There are many who won't work with him, though, and she knows that after today this number will rise.

First he is vile to the lighting crew. Then he rips into the sound girl, even though it was he who insisted on using a real house, which makes her work so much harder. The atmosphere is shot through with bristle, especially when the mothers bring their children in and Malcolm doesn't tone his language down. Amelia tries to tell him but he isn't having any.

— Greedy bitches. Fancy putting your kid through this, all for five hundred quid and the chance to point out little Rupert on the telly to their Steiner friends. Tell them to fuck off. There's an estate round the corner and we can snag some kids from there, no bother.

The filming starts in the nursery. Twin babies gurgle in a cot. In the garden they film twin toddlers pushing carts full of building blocks, and then twin four-year-olds on tricycles. The seven-year-olds follow, looking blissfully happy with a train set, after which a pair of twelve-year-olds build a Lego castle. A chess game between seventeen-year-olds and then it is the turn of the grown-up twins, which is the real point of the ad. After six three-second scenes of previous brotherly bliss they are to fight over the last portion of cereal left, one smacking the other over the head with the box. Amelia cannot take her eyes off them. She makes her muted suggestions to Malcolm and then watches as one twin hits the other over the head with the pack, the cereal flying out. The table is reset and the two of them relax, joke, and she can't help but think of her own twin. The woman she might have been instead of that small, lost figure. She wouldn't have stood for Malcolm's tantrums. She would have stormed out, though would she have been here at all were it not for Richard? Yes. She is efficient and capable, inspires respect in all around her. Just being there tells her that, makes her sure that other doors would have opened, a superior success perhaps unfolding if she'd had the courage to be alone. She imagines that other self – single, sarcastic, backed by her own achievements. She'd own her own company, have moved into agenting where the real money is. She could have done this, she knows it, and she might even have met Richard at some point, vaguely remembering him from that pub theatre as she would only just remember the person she'd been then. Eyeing him up. Fancying him for his big personality, the way he nodded and took it, poking his tongue into the inside of his cheek and grinning, when anyone took the piss. She imagines the reverse of what happened: her choosing him. Getting pregnant. For what if this baby inside her were her first? How wonderful would that feel, to be carrying a first child not as a broody and befogged twenty-something but as the product of her established self? She can almost believe that it's true until she sees that mirror again.

Shit. James. He would have stared at her. Terrified, beginning to stammer about how flattered he was, but... Not even the tall beauty who had saved Amelia from such intense embarrassment could put herself between him and his close-kept wife. She sees him in that café, knowing that he will have stared into his coffee until it was gone, after which he'd have ambled back to the Reading Room, completely unaware of the four eyes that watched him go.

Her own eyes fall on Malcolm. The last shot he got was perfect, the cereal flying out in a perfect arc as the box connected with the actor's forehead, better even than if they'd CGI'd it. Malcolm watches it back twice and she's sure he's going to call it, as is everyone else, the ice broken now. But it re-forms because he doesn't. He insists on yet another re-shoot – the sixteenth – and then another, going on until a weal appears on the hit twin's forehead, the wardrobe woman screeching as a bead of blood drips down towards his shirt. Malcolm booms Jesus and the crew bitch, hiss, barely hiding their contempt. A mutiny? It might well come to that and she decides to tell Malcolm, ram her foot down, though when she turns to him she stops. Something is happening. There is sweat on his forehead. His fists are clenched. He should be scrutinising the set for lighting angles but he's just staring, right at the twins, his mouth wide open. Is it age? Fury at the growing sense that the game will soon be up for him? But then Amelia feels her own lips parting and her head rolls back on her shoulders.

— Fuck, she whispers.

— What is it?

— Nothing, she answers, turning to the second AD. When she turns back, the spot where Malcolm was standing is empty.

Richard told her. Eight months after they met. He'd asked if she wanted to go to Andalucía. He was going with Malcolm and his then girlfriend. She said sure, which was when he told her, needing a way of excusing his best friend's behaviour, knowing that Amelia could rightly find a thousand things to object to in it. She took it, not wanting to refuse any information at that point, though she had no need of this sugar to coat Malcolm with. She liked him, or if not that then she liked the fact that things happened when he was around. She doesn't remember much about the Alhambra actually, but she does remember Malcolm being there.

— That's rage.

— At who?

— His brother, Richard explained.

He used to be beautiful. An odd thing for a man to say about his friend, not least because she wondered why it was relevant to the story. Richard was insistent on it, though. Malcolm was whippet-thin until his mid-twenties, his skin so fine and his hair so silver you'd have thought he was an angel.

— So what happened?

— He just… I dunno. Gave up on it.

— But how could he?

— Inside. The body followed. He ate too much. Drank too much. He hasn't broken into a run for twenty years.

— But why? He's not…

— What?

— Lazy.

— No. Richard shook his head. He was just fed up with being wanted. Girls threw themselves at him. I caught the spares and I was thankful, but it was a bit bloody galling. Especially when he'd brush them off.

— He always dates models, though. Actresses.

— But it's different now. He wants to win them. Not be won by them. He wants to bend the world to his will.

— But why?

— Because it took away the one thing he loved.

He came from Somerset. He grew up with his mother and younger brother, his father dying when he was small.

— You should have seen the place.

— You went there?

— A couple of times. We met at uni.

— Kent?

— Yep. Eighty-five.

— You had some Charles and Sebastian vibe going?

— Something like that. We just recognised each other. Sitting in a crowd in the union bar. We just knew we were friends and he invited me home the next week.

— Footmen? Nanny in the attic?

— The opposite. They lived in this old farmhouse. It barely had a roof. Chickens in the kitchen.

— His family?

— The mother was nuts. She was really stunning but the sort that turns into a bag lady, you know? Made us mashed potato on toast with an egg on top.

— Sounds great.

— But it was all she cooked us. Lunch, dinner, two days running. Malcolm and Giles didn't seem to notice.

— The brother.

— Younger. Seventeen when I met him.

— Like Malcolm?

— No. Richard shook his head. He was quiet. Determined. And disapproving, as though nothing quite tasted right. They didn't get on.

— Why?

— They were so different. Giles was responsible. Malcolm just got on with things, sure they'd be okay. One thing was money. He went through it like water and the brother hated that.

— Sounds like a little prig.

— He was seventeen. Anyway, the first time I was there Giles caught their mother giving Malcolm a bunch of notes. He went mental, screaming about the mortgage and some finance guy. I thought he'd explode. Probably because I was there, he didn't. Giles stayed out of the way after that and he did that the next time I went.

— Mash on toast again?

— Courgettes. They must have been in season. I think we just ate courgettes. They were delicious; I've never had courgettes like that. I remember thinking it was perfect. The thing there. There was something simple about the place. I pictured us going there all the time, it becoming like my second home. But it was the last time I ever went.

— Why?

— It was her birthday. Early February. Malcolm had some money from somewhere, told me he was going home. I wanted to go and he must have sensed that because he explained why he wasn't asking me.

— Which was?

— Her birthday. He wanted to treat her. It could have been a date, the amount he gabbed on about it. There was this place about ten miles from them, all tournedos Rossini and lobster Thermidor, I expect. Just talking about it lit him up.

— And?

— It was perfect. Malcolm said he felt like a man, treating his mother, pouring her champagne and laughing off the price. Even Giles couldn't ruin it. He just sat there.

— So what happened?

— Malcolm says he drank, though he wasn't pissed. And when it was time to go...

— Oh, shit.

— Wait. He did get behind the wheel. But the brother threw one, just stood there with his arms folded and refused to get in, almost dragged his mother out of the passenger seat when she did. He'd only passed his test a couple of weeks before but he insisted on driving. Malcolm started to argue but his mother just looked at him, appealed to him. For the peace of it. Her birthday.

— So he gave in? And...

— Giles hit some ice. Only going twenty but he panicked, tractor coming the other way. He swung too hard and took them off a ridge. Halfway down they hit an oak tree.

— God.

— Giles lost a leg. Their mother was decapitated. Malcolm was explicit about that. Decapitated.

— Malcolm?

— Was fine. He was in the back. He said he just bounced around, wasn't even scared, hung on to the front seat when they were rolling. Though he did nearly go to prison.

— What for? He wasn't even...

— He broke into the hospital in the middle of the night. They caught him in his brother's ward with his hands around his neck. It's the biggest regret of his life. Being caught. He'll tell you if you ask him. He'll make a joke of it. Ask him – say, Malc, what's the biggest regret of your entire life?

She did, later. They were in a small restaurant in the Albaicín, had drunk two bottles of fino. He pushed his girlfriend's hand away from his arm. He glared at her, before glancing across at Richard. Then he threw his head back and laughed. That Mia hasn't got your tits, was his answer, though the cloud that came into his eyes told her that Richard was probably right.

— And the brother?

— Still lives there.

— Does Malcolm see him?

— Once. Some shrink told him to confront what happened. Probably didn't mean it the way Malcolm took it. He bought a sawn-off shotgun in some pub in Mile End. He parked a few miles away so as not to leave tyre treads and hiked through the woods. It was going to look like a robbery.

— And?

— He thought the place had been sold. It looked the same but in the farmyard there was a balding madman, muttering to himself as he collected the eggs. It was his leg that made him realise who he was.

— He couldn't do it?

— What if there's a God? he told me, when he got back. And he gets to her before I do? How can I live knowing that she's smiling at him, running her fingers through what's left of his fucking hair?

Do I look like her? Amelia has often wondered this but never asked. Do I look like the mother who made him feel like a man for the first time?

He's in the garden. She sees him from the window. He's kneeling on the lawn, still littered with identical trikes, tennis rackets, footballs, all brought in for the occasion. A sound reaches her. A bucking sob that Malcolm tries his best to staunch by ramming his fists into his face.

— Fuck, she says again.

She shouts out *wrap*. The crew turn and the producer is confused but she insists.

— Malcolm's called it. He has everything. Thanks, everyone.

There is a surge of relief, much back-slapping and jocularity, a sense that it wasn't so bad after all. Amelia smiles and then slips out to the garden where Malcolm is still on his knees. He looks up at her approach, his huge face like a dog's. She helps him to his feet and out along the side of the house to where the car is waiting. It was going to take both them and the producer to dinner but once she's helped Malcolm in she pulls out her phone and tells him she needs to make a call. She doesn't. She only pretends to do that, and then steps into the back seat beside him.

— Russell Square, she tells the driver.

21

Back in the room the gerberas are still where she left them. As if they have been waiting for her. She and Malcolm have not spoken, though in the car Amelia has been holding his hand on her lap. She sits him on the bed. She crosses to the window and draws the curtains to an inch, light squeezing through into the space. When she returns to the bed he mistakes her intentions, but it does not take long to calm his half-hearted fumblings. He is compliant as she removes his jacket, and then his shoes, then he moves up to the top of the bed to help her draw back the tightened sheets. She steps out of her own shoes and lies, clothed, with her head on the pillow, before drawing the sheets back up, and over them. She shifts a little and opens her arms, Malcolm taking deep, deliberate breaths as he stares at her, doubt and wonder on his face before he slides forward. He buries his huge head into her bosom and his belly presses up against her own. With her right hand she holds both of his, tight against her chest, feeling the weight of him, aware that she is with him for the first time, that she has only ever spent time with the chimeras he offered up in place of himself. She presses her temple against his forehead and moves the fingers of her free hand through his grey, silky hair.

When Malcolm's breathing flattens she kisses his temple, a sound escaping him like incoherent final words. A little while later, when she is sure he is asleep, she levers herself out from underneath him and returns to the window, slipping behind the curtains to look out on to Woburn Place. The bright light startles her, as if a crowd of people have been waiting for her appearance, and she recalls how she was startled by James. That first time. In the playground. Seeing him had told her what to do: anything at all that stood outside of what she knew. That was beyond Richard, and the power he wields but cannot know the effect of. He thinks he makes people happy. The children. Her. And he does – so happy – but in a world stamped with his seal. Which is his, into which he invited her, presenting her with decisions here and there, but only so she would not see where she was living her life. In his world. A world of men.

There are people down in front of her. On the street and in the big, leafy square. Walking, riding bikes, driving. Which of them, she wonders, is, at this very moment, choosing their direction? Has pure free will in that? Which of them has decided where to go? Not that bus driver, that cabbie, not that cycle courier or that woman in the Tesco shirt. Have any of them? And can she? Decide which way to go when she walks out of this building? The answer makes her feel sick, and hot, then panicky, stuck in a lift with no one coming. She continues to stare out across the square into all that light, into the space between her and the other people she can see, until it happens. Just arrives. The product of her desperation? She doesn't know but it's there. The way out. The path she has to take. So clear. So easy to do. It just settles itself in front of her, so simple that she laughs in pure amazement, nodding to herself. Then turns back into the room, hurrying in case somehow the answer flies away. She picks up her bag and leaves Malcolm on the bed, sleeping.

At home she finds her husband in his study. The kids are somewhere else.

— I need to speak to you.

— Yes, course, love. You okay? He takes off his reading glasses though he holds on to the script he's looking at.

— Not really.

— Oh. Now he does put down the script, swivelling a little though not to face her, quite. Is it the heat? Look, I know you want to carry on working but...

— It's not that.

— Oh. What, then?

— This baby.

He smiles but the smile dies.

— What about it?

— I'm very sorry, Richard.

— For...? I don't understand.

— I can't have it. I. Can't.

— You...? What on earth do you mean?

— *We* can't have it.

— Why in God's name not? It's not ill, is it? It's not...

— Yours.

Now he does turn. All the way.

— I don't think. I mean, I don't know. I can't be... Look, Richard, I'm so sorry, I really am. But I don't know if this baby is going to be yours or not.

Alice keeps looking for signs.

In the days leading up to the ceremony she searches for cracks in James's resolve. She's expecting a diffidence perhaps or unexpressed frustration, unreasonable annoyance that would tell her something's wrong. That in turn would give her the excuse to ask what the matter is, whereupon he would say Alice love it's nothing but I was offered this thing, it's on your prize night… She'll release him of course, as if from a spell, and he'll run off to his gig, his big shot.

But there is nothing. He seems happy. It's as if what Carty told her isn't true, though she knows it is. It becomes clear that he is giving something up for her, doing so without complaint, with no idea that she knows. All so he can be there for her if she wins or, possibly more importantly in his mind, if she does not. It's love. Alice knows that and she also knows how much that knowledge should move her. But instead of being thrilled by it she is so desperately sad. For how to tell him it doesn't matter? That it would make no difference? It's not just that the event has been superseded, is a speck in her life. They have kids to look after, a mortgage to pay, so many other things, and then they have their own lives to drag up out of it all somehow. So what place is there for this love? Here, now, it is quite meaningless and she shakes her head, knowing that once their love was a savage animal leaping back and forth in the gap between them. It felt unique, out of time, as if the world surrounding them was on the other side of a high, gilded wall. But that was a lie. Love only seemed to cut them off like that. For how connected to the world are they now? How socially integrated has that spun-off love left them? It wasn't even about them, they just thought that; instead it was a mechanism to pluck them from their single selves and deposit them in the place they are now, this tapestry threaded through with their children's lives and those of their friends and their children, the birthdays to be remembered, the parties arrived at late, but got to. And now that they are where they are, something else must drive them forward, some bigger thing than a need to be caring of each other, and supportive. Something that says I don't need you like that. Or even want you. For what her prize really means, if it means anything now, is that it justifies her lone self. She digs out her notebooks from the time before James and finds poems that are raw, loose, like her students' work. But like the very best of the work she marks it is shot through with the desire to move forward. To the future. To better poems. The honesty shames her, for what does she do now other than, very skilfully, cover her tracks? What do all the poets she reads do?

Grief now. Grief for the loss of that need to rush forward into a more complete formation. Now she never wants time to speed up. All she ever wants is for it to pause so she can find a little space in it. Grief also for the loss of James in the way she had him. What a lovely man. To be alone with him, in his flat, in a nest of beach stones, up with the wind on Firle Beacon or that church in Arundel, stilled by the plaque that lists the dead brothers, his hand finding hers on the cold stone. How terrible to have lost that and how much worse to have lost any need for it among the forest of her responsibilities. For it's not him she yearns for primarily, but herself. And how can she admit this to him, which she would if she told him she knows about his gig?

She squints into this dilemma and wants to back out. But she must tell him. She will not let him scupper himself for her. Fear stops her at first, and there is also a nagging sense that she has not quite got to the bottom of why he hasn't said anything. The kindness element: does she really believe it? Perhaps it's more complicated. Is there reflected glory for him, a validation greater than that gained by his own performance on that night? No, he's braver than that. She moves the thought sideways from a validation to an excuse. Is it a way out of this odd career path that has opened up in front of him? Does he want to turn? Or is he terrified that he'll fail as he did last time? Is he manufacturing a reason not to take a risk? Will he glance up at the Apollo in ten years' time and say hey, I could have played there. Never told you. Oh, it was on the night you were up for the Carson. I didn't want to go…

Again she rebukes herself. Why tangle it? She's the one with the problem. She can't face the simple truth that he's being a true partner, the kindness making her shiver. She hates kindness. It makes her feel cheap, meagre, that it's such a waste on her. Her father was kind. Her predominant memories of him revolve around simple moments of gentleness that made her glow inside her chest so hard she can sometimes still feel it. Until he vanished. Walked out of her life forever.

And spurned kindness hurts. So she needs to be careful about how she tells James. How she pushes him away, even if it is towards something that he must want very much.

After dinner one night she sets her fork down very deliberately and shakes her head.

— We need the money.

He blinks, trying to unpick it.

— From your gig. On TV? I mean we don't need it need it but God it would be good to have. We haven't been abroad since Ida was born, you know that? So how much were they going to pay you?

Silence. The beginning of denial, then the slumped sense of how pointless that would be.

— How'd you find out?

— Your agent called.

— The fucker.

— I know. He's truly evil. That's why he's a good agent.

James sighs, imagining some murderous activity.

— Well, I don't know. I refused to let him tell me. A lot. But money, though. We stack the pile differently. Your thing's higher.

— I agree.

— So...

— Meet me after. We'll celebrate.

— That's not the point.

— So what is?

— This. You're a really good poet. But what if they don't realise it again? What if I only get this one chance to see you up for something like this?

She hasn't thought about that. That he's going with her just because it's something he really wants to do. Like tickets for the Centre Court won in some lottery, that he doesn't want to sell for a fortune.

— The food'll be crap.

— Like I care.

— And the wine...

— Alice! I saw you at that open mic. Your first time. You climbed the steps like you were going to the guillotine. I saw you read your work out in that class. I saw you read from proofs and then from your own book, your photo waving about on the back. It's part of our life, Alice.

But it isn't. It's her life. Like when he's at the BL, or work. That's his life and she wants no part of it, doesn't care about the people he works with, tries not to glaze over when he comes home with departmental gossip. But, once again, how can she admit this to him: that she doesn't care what he does when he's not with her?

— I won't win.

— I don't care. I just want us both to be there.

But she persuades him. It's difficult and she nearly gives up but she manages it eventually, talking about their responsibilities to each other, how she has to make sure he doesn't throw everything over for her. How, though he denies it, he'll blame her. She goes back to the money, the loft conversion that could actually happen, Dom getting his own room because they can't go on sharing forever. They can get it all: if they focus. She lays her siege and eventually the walls rock. And then fall. Alice is relieved, the weight of the last week falling off her, so glad she no longer knows something he doesn't, exhaustion creeping into the space occupied by the stress of that. But then a strange thing happens. The stones that come tumbling down from James begin to hit her. They bury her, until she can't move. He starts to say if you're really sure, I'll get there at some point as they record these things pretty early so they can do re-shoots... And she finds it hard to breathe. She's there, alone, just her and all those people, all of them and just her, their faces and voices swimming round while James is somewhere else. Where she made him go. And him alone too with all those other people as he has been so often recently, all those people seeing him, loving what he's giving. But not her. Not once. How could she have let that happen? When did they forgo the joint experience of the external world? How did they allow their relationship to become confined to the four walls surrounding them?

Loneliness. Petrifying, like she can only just remember. She washes up while he dries and she can barely even talk. They're nervous, not really a couple. On *Wife Swap* perhaps. Tell me to fuck off. That you'll do what the fuck you like. She bites her lip and turns to him, about to say no, I'm sorry, I need you to be there. But he's turned away to his phone, is already pecking out a text to Carty.

Stop it. Don't do that. Daddy! A cry. Just Ida, talking in her sleep. They freeze and James' mouth opens, his face so cut with worry it's as though the nightmare's his.

22

Summer. It finally arrives like unwanted guests, loud and initially disruptive because there seemed to be no spring. The only indication of the advancing year is the increasing number of leaflets coming home in Dom's school bag. Adverts, fliers for holiday courses in football or tennis, art or music. James reads them intently, sees they all stress the instructive nature of whatever they're pushing. But it's just childcare they're hawking really. A safe containment until school starts up again and offers the same thing, with phonics.

Answerphone messages from other parents ask in varying degrees of desperation whether Dom will be going to this one or that. It's good that other kids want to be with him but how do they decide? He's shown no interest in football. He loves drawing but to James the idea of his boy inside all day is wrong. This never happened to him. During his summers he stalled, squirming in the sticky pap of boredom and heat, melting ice-cream and the various collective cruelties of unsupervised neighbourhood kids, marauding along the local canal bank and in the abandoned warehouses as if there'd been an apocalypse. He wasn't parcelled off. Summer was a break from that, a big stretch during which nothing ever really began, or ended. Summer was a pure experience of time, freed as he was from his constant term-time desire for it to either rush forward or slow down. The world was languid and vast, something he could really feel inside his body, along with his own sweet insignificance.

Did his mother work? She did later but not, he thinks, when he was Dom's age. They spent time together while Stephen was off at genius camp or somewhere. Being in the car. Shopping, gardening. Visiting her friends. Once popping in on Grandpa and finding him motionless, in his chair. His mother, walking forward, the little gasp she gave. Then touching his shoulder as if testing the firmness of a cake.

They'll look after him, that's what. Take turns. Don't they have the jobs that can deal with that? He'll just have to work around it. Next year perhaps he'll come home demanding to be signed up to something but for now they'll just present him with nothing. Steal him back for a bit. A male, modern-day Persephone. For even now Dom is going. Wants less of them. He reads books on his own, just sitting on the sofa, gets cross if Ida's making a noise. And other people are bringing him up now. On the last day of school James goes to collect him and spots him in the corner of the playground with his friends. They're making fart noises under their armpits. James is almost unable to recognise him, a stranger's glee on his son's face. The boy who uses playground phrases with covert meanings, brings home in-jokes they can't decipher, but which kill him. James shakes his head, knowing the boy didn't actually come out of him. Yet it feels as if he is constantly giving birth to Dominic, little by little, bit by bit.

School is not quite over, though. There is one last event to hurdle. Not sports day, for that has been. James could meld into that day but this other must be faced head on.

He turned it down at first, said he was busy. But he wasn't busy until the evening and, on impulse, he emailed back to agree. For what better preparation for his big show, the zenith of his new incarnation, than to run a stall at the St Saviour's summer fête? The idea was perfect, another new experience to throw into the mix. And, anyway, why change his *modus operandi* just because he's stepping up a gear? Jay Farrell asked for a script. James set to it but then thought no. That first gig, back at the Store. Ages ago now it seems but it's still the way to go. He'll get there late as he always does. Rush on stage. Eight hundred people and five TV cameras will stare at him and then, only then, will he decide what he's going to talk about.

He's on the Heath before ten. It's the spill-out space right by St Saviour's, where after-school tag and picnics take place. A lot of the volunteer parents are there already: experts, they know the drill. Stalls are being erected, bunting tied. The women demonstrate a clear, decisive efficiency while the men are more easygoing. He feels more affinity with the women, thinking that, having decided to come, you might as well get on with it. The barbecue holds some appeal though, charcoal being stacked by meaty arms, sausages skewered to the backdrop of wholesome, deep-throated banter. He almost wishes he were part of that but there is always the moment when, in the exclusive company of men, one of them makes a point about his spouse, cusses her discreetly for some slight pulling back of him, a curtailment of his self-defined, roguish masculine energy. The rest yuk yuk but he hates that kind of disloyalty, can't join in with the Masonic sympathy. He won't admit that he is, even in a tiny way, more like them than the person he's married to. Men and women are not different, not if you find the right one. It is people who are.

It's warm already, the sky clear but for a few small clouds stuck to the blue like twisted scraps of Sellotape. He announces himself and is shown to a pile of square metal poles, which he puts together with Dom and Ida. He has them as Alice is giving a reading and some interviews before the ceremony. They have fun, getting the stall up in no time thanks mainly to Dom, who has managed to translate his train track and Lego mania into something real. Once it's done they stare at it for a second, proud and a little disbelieving, and then hunt for Rachel Green to tell them what they'll be doing on it.

— Wotsits, is her reply.

It isn't long before the space is ready. And it's impressive, sure to attract locals as well as the school community. Fifteen different stalls are corralled together with a tombola, raffle, a duck dip and sponge-throwing among them. Quoits. Lawn darts. A small trebuchet built by Year Six, the aim being to demolish a wooden castle, the pieces of which were made by Year Five. It could be a fête from his own youth were it not dominated by two bouncy castles which James is immediately jealous of, as he is of all public-stroke-municipal children's structures. Why aren't there swings for adults? Giant slides? And why is it only kids who get to fling themselves around an air-filled structure with rarely any physical consequence? He imagines a grown-up version as 'Irreplaceable' kicks out of the PA. Yes, a Beyoncé Castle. He can almost see it, recumbent and huge on the stretching green, tubby dads bouncing in glee over undulating buttocks and wobbling rubber breasts. He smiles and then unpacks his case of shaving foam.

The game is genius. James realises this immediately. Children come with a parent and for fifty pence buy a small pack of cheesy Wotsits (profit to school, thirty pence). The parent is seated in a chair and James covers their face with foam. Then, from a distance of twenty feet, the child must throw the Wotsits one by one with the aim of getting them to stick on. James will count the result, a prize later for the most Wotsits sticking to the parent's face. It is the perfect mixture of skill and mild humiliation, a bonding experience too. He soon has a queue lined up and a crowd of observers cheering the contestants on.

And he, too, gets into it. The perfect ringmaster, roll up roll up. Ida volunteers to be dad for Dom in his stead and she squeals with delight, running up afterwards to give him a foamy kiss. The two of them disappear on to the smaller bouncy castle and James does his best to keep a corner of his eye on them. He's soon taken, though, swept along by the number of people vying for a go. His concession is clearly the hit of the day and he's proud of that, of its low-tech simplicity. He eggs the kids on, helping the smaller ones, blowing an air horn when someone matches or beats the current record. Time flies and he's lost in a whirl of laughter, whooping and dropped burgers. Is this really so bad? This unabashed wholesomeness? He used to dread it but the answer is no and he feels good, where he should be, like someone in a river, being baptised. Cleansed of his past life, most particularly of what he did on Ashburnham Grove, that thing perhaps necessary for him to be able to be here like this. As if, somehow, it showed him, not who he really is, but that the world outside him knows who he is. And has been waiting for him to know it. He feels himself opening up, becoming louder, thumbs-ups coming from passing parents and teachers. Would he have been like that with Alice there? He doesn't know but there's something about being included that he loves. Can't help loving. He glances around again and knows that yes, he is one of these people. The idea is comforting: he is real now. All those years single, or with Alice but a cool young couple, getting excited by the latest restaurant opening near their flat. All those years thinking his life was going somewhere, that he was on a unique trajectory. But he was just a shadow then, moving towards himself. He was on his way here, to this physical place and to these people, most of whom he and Alice might never have run into before. Or perhaps deliberately avoided. And they all had their own paths too, careers that dipped and surged, lovers lost, travels taken on distant continents. And now they are all of them together, like soldiers in a trench, sometimes talking about what they did 'before'. How interesting but also how irrelevant. This is where they are and it's where they were always going to be. And, for people like them, it's inescapable. He thinks back to that Parents' Evening and an odd thought strikes him. Does it really matter who any of the men and women there are married to?

Another thought makes him feel light inside. Younger, though older at the same time. The year has ended. Their very first as parents of a school-age child. And it has changed them, for good, for next year new parents will come with new little ones, his boy almost a veteran then in Year One. Other parents will stare out across the raw Heath and feel the strangeness of it all and some will be men who look at James and shy from him, fearful of what they assume he represents. And now, perhaps, he does.

Someone hands him a beer. That's something he really can't do, so he sets it down by the chair he hasn't used.

Where's Ida?

Momentary glimpses of her are all James has had for an hour. And he hasn't had one for a while. He looks around, trying to catch sight of her as another dad takes a seat. A stickiness begins to form in his stomach, and throat. He's mildly annoyed that no one seems to have thought about giving him a break but he can't disappoint the boy waiting with his pack open. He lines him up and shouts *fire* to start him off. He can't get out of the next one either but his whoops and hollers are hollow. He's growing concerned, so much so that he tells the rest of the queue that he's sorry, he needs a time out. The disappointment is huge but he doesn't give in, instead looking around quickly for someone to stand in for him. He grabs a bloke he vaguely recognises who can't think of an excuse fast enough. There's mild panic in his voice when he asks when James will be back. James pretends not to hear, hurrying instead into the throng of milling people.

It's brilliant. Near perfect. That's what Richard tells her, a distant horn sounding, as if in celebration of his words. He knew it would be. He thought it excellent before, when they met in the Rouge that second time. He didn't say. It needed to go up a level, become a real thing. Encouraging her wouldn't work. Somehow he knew that. He had to challenge her, throw down the gauntlet by dissing it completely. So she'd stretch herself. He knew she'd come back again with a better version but he didn't know she'd take it this far. That she would pull it off like this, with control and rigour to match the pure brilliance of her writing.

— I love it, he insists, though his voice is oddly flat. He picks up a glass of bright orange juice at his elbow and takes a sip, without offering her any. He sets it down on the breakfast bar next to one of those snow globe things. Broken. The plastic cracked and the woman out, her face down on the work surface. Some cheering sounds, another horn blowing out on the Heath.

— The only problem, he adds, is that I just don't care.

He searches the stalls. He stands on tiptoes, visoring his eyes as he turns a full circle. He takes a breath and looks out from the fete area, down towards the church. But she's not there. She doesn't seem to be anywhere and panic grips him, the sort he saw once on the Southbank, a woman screaming for her child with tears rushing down her ravaged face. He doesn't scream. Even though the stickiness is glue now and his ribcage seems to be expanding until he thinks it'll crack. He just looks around, efficiently, swiftly, eyes like a torch beam. Still nothing, no sign of her, and he's on the verge of calling out when he spots Amelia Leigh. He takes a breath, trying hard to compose himself before asking if she happens to have seen his children.

Which is when he sees them. Sweat prickles on his forehead and under his arms, a shiver running through him. He blinks, to be sure it's them, and it is them. They're at the coconut shy, which he'd previously checked out twice without seeing them. Dom is just finishing his go, giving unwanted instructions to Ida as the tape is moved forward for her. James lets a long breath out, kicked with the relief, both at having found them and that no one witnessed his terror. He's relieved too that no one saw how pitifully he was supervising his children. Least of all them. They are blithely unconcerned, though there is one problem. Ida has a hand between her legs, and as she throws her ball with the other she hops up and down frenetically.

He waits until she's finished and then asks if she needs a wee. She denies it on reflex, but then nods. Hard. The acknowledgement intensifies the desire so he tells Dom he'll be back in five and scoops her up. He crosses the road and hurries down the Vale, the school opened up for the toilets. He implores her to wait, knowing he has no spare pants for her, or shirt for himself for that matter, and is intensely relieved when she does. He sets her down outside the Reception cubicles and she scampers into one; he holds the door open and watches her. Smiling. For he loves taking Ida to the loo. He loves the focus she brings to it, pulling her jeans and pants down, then climbing up on the seat. The concentration on her face as she fires her stream into the bowl and then as she reaches for the loo roll, crumpling up a square. She insists on wiping her own fanny and then climbs down, throwing it hard into the bowl before pulling up her pants again.

They are spotty ones. He notices that. White on green. And for some reason he never, ever forgets that she was wearing spotty pants that day.

— What? You don't...?

— Care, he repeats, shifting in his seat. Staring at her. He offers no further explanation and she swallows, staring back at him, the words they have been saying seeming to move to the sides of the room like dancers clearing a space. Leaving the two of them there. In the silence. She swallows, her stomach churning, the fact that they are alone in that big house striking through her like a gong. Shit. *Shit*. So is this it, then? Is he going to...? She shakes her head, trying to stretch back in time to catch the signs she's clearly missed, until she wonders, actually, if she did miss them. Has she been lying to herself? She flushes as one simple truth burns into her for the first time: she didn't want to write a good play. She wanted to write a good play for him. And in that second a flash of wanting strikes, a desire for him to come around towards her. And take her hand. Pick her up maybe. Carry her up to that big, adult bed. For he did pick her up: he did it with that first phone call. He picked her up and carried her away and it was *such a relief*. Being told. Not having to decide. Anything. Will she let him do it again, now? Take her upstairs and undress her, push himself inside her? She tells herself no, that she will not, no way, and she steels herself as he lifts his chin and then steps down from his stool.

Walking back up the Vale. Hand in hand, Ida telling him what she's going to learn when she goes to St Saviour's. Sums. Flying a helicopter. Punching. He doesn't see Mrs Mason until he's right next to her, though Ida does, slipping his grasp and grabbing Dom's teacher round the legs. She smiles and starts to tickle her, until something takes her, some commotion on the Heath. She looks up in alarm, just as James hears Dom's voice calling out to him.

— *Daddee.*

He turns. And is confused. Dominic is on the edge of the grass, across the road. Crying. Really crying. And covered in something. James squints and sees that it's ketchup. What? And bits of bread. A slew of onions down his neck, and front. It's hard to compute but he soon realises: someone has thrown a hotdog at him. He can't see how this can be true and almost refuses to accept it until he spots Milo, Dom's best friend. Or former best friend because Dom has spread his wings, insisting on playing with other kids too, opening out their former double act. Milo has refused to accept this, has taken it badly in various different ways and this is clearly one of them.

— That was a very naughty thing to do, young man.

That's Amelia Leigh. James is grateful she's intervening, bending to wag her finger, but she hasn't realised how serious it is. Hasn't seen that Dom is scrabbling at his neck as though he's being eaten, which means that the onions are hot. It's probably shock more than pain but still James leaps across the road towards him.

— *Daddy*, Dom screams again, as if it's his fault.

Why does he look at the text? In that moment? Hours asking this. Demanding of himself. Some latent part of his brain, tuned into the gig, worried that it's Farrell? Or is he still terrified of Thomasina? He doesn't know. Will never know, but the beep beep gets the response it demands for he only uses one hand to pull the polo shirt over Dom's head. With the other he reaches for his phone. And sees. A text. Not Farrell or Thomasina. Not even Carty. But Alice. No worries there until he reads it. What? He squints at it through the sunlight.

— *Daddy!*

Shakes his head again. Cannot compute. *Richard Leigh says you're a cunt*. Him? Richard Leigh says he's a…? What?

Then: *What the fuck did you do with Amelia?*

What?

Dom calls out again. Yanking at his arm. But he doesn't respond, stays glued to the impossible words, speechless. What on earth… And why now? Alice is giving interviews. She's up in town. Isn't she? So why is he sending this now…? Unless. Stunned, he turns across the Heath towards the house. The Leighs' house. Which is why he doesn't see it.

He hears it. He hears it clearly but he doesn't see it, what Dom sees.

What happens.

Alice stands too and stares at him as he plucks her notebook from the counter. She realises for the first time that he looks ill. Liverish. He doesn't say anything, shaking his head instead as heat runs up her neck on to her face. She is about to speak but what he does stops her: he flings the notebook at her, the naked leaves exposed until she grabs and pulls them shut.

— Keep it.

— What? I've worked, I've worked like shit. You said...

— God you're so naïve. Don't know, then?

— What? She glares at him.

— Almost as bad as me. He's not told you? 'Fessed up?

— Who?

— That cunt of a husband of yours.

— That... Told me what?

— She won't tell me. My pregnant wife. Not who it is at least. Not fucking hard to guess though, is it, Alice?

— *What* isn't?

But again he doesn't answer, walking over to the door instead and pulling it open, just as another air horn calls out from across the Heath.

No screech. Not that. Or cry. Just the small thump. He barely registers it, one more channel amid all the other sounds, the PA, people talking, laughing, Dom crying. And Ida's voice. Calling. But not to him. To Amelia? Just the tiniest hint of the sound of it, perhaps real, or maybe supplied by his imagination in the hours and days that followed. It precedes the thump, of course. Then the only sound he hears is a rushing, the blood in his own brain, like water in a tunnel. He is in a tunnel as he turns, swivels towards the sound, ripping his eyes away from that house. He rushes forward after Dom who has already broken his grip. Is sprinting towards his sister.

As other people are. A crowd. A moving tableau. Towards the shape beneath the back of Rachel Green's Range Rover, the limp pale shape, the shape that stays still, quite still, until the yelling and screaming force the car to pull forward again.

Amelia didn't move. The only one who didn't. She stood there, transfixed. The boy jumped up and down. He tried to get to the little girl but his father beat him to it. Then he stood by his father with his fingers in his mouth, jumping up and down and screaming. A lot of screaming though she didn't move. She was motionless, as she had been seconds before. She took her mind back to that even then, did a brief rewind. The girl, across the street, seeing her. *Melia, Melia.* Rachel Green's car. Can any blame be attached to herself? To see two objects, to see the future and be stilled by it. Paralysed. Unable to break in. Can any blame be attached to herself for seeing that? Even then she wondered, as James began his wailing. Some people stepped back. One guy had the presence of mind to dial 999. A teacher ran over and grabbed the boy, which was when she did move. He'd dropped his phone. James. Amelia lowered the arm that only then did she realise was raised, in a wave. She bent down into the road and picked it up for him.

23

ALICE IS SITTING in her garden waiting for the man she hired. Man and Van, number in the newsagents. It's too cold to sit out really but she does it, not wanting to go inside while Dom is next door. He's with Neil, helping him build knee-high walls to surround his flower beds. Neil has been incredible since it happened. Offers of help made while retaining distance. This bricklaying project is the first thing Dom has been properly interested in since then and she couldn't deny him, when Neil asked, pretending he really needed help. He's been over there four or five times, twice with Neil's family there, his sister's family, loud chubby girls a few years older than Dom. Dom loved it, just being around them. Now she looks over the fence and sees him paying complete attention to Neil, who is letting him flatten a line of mortar with a trowel. Alice lowers her head, remembering the thoughts she used to have about this man. She has already taken down the note above the door. She's asked him in a couple of times too, though he's declined. She'll persuade him next time, for Dom needs the company of normal people, needs as much of it as he can get. She too, just to chat about things. The weather, anything. No one but Dominic has been with her in the house for longer than she can remember.

The van pulls up outside, the top visible over the garden wall. It's come to pick up the pedalo that she only realised was still there a couple of weeks ago. As the guy strolls in through the garden door to inspect it she can't help but think of James. She barely sees him, just ten minutes or so when they change over at Great Ormond Street, Dom between them, making no secret of the fact that he does not want to be handed over to his father. He has no choice however and Alice knows that he blames him, is furious about what happened to his sister. One day, will she tell him her part? And there was a part. A splinter of one. She'd told James she had interviews. Why did she tell him that? She can't think about it now. All she can do is stare down at the suddenly tiny creature in the huge bed, or lie next to her, sometimes sleeping through the long, beeping night, but mostly not, just staring at her lost face, wondering where she is and if she will ever come back. And, without wanting to, thinking about what James told her, confessing through the sobs and tears and snot in those first hours. Not what she accused him of but something else, something so random it was far worse, like a stranger turning around and stabbing her in the stomach. A stranger, yes. Immediately that, as soon as the words left his mouth. Because he did what she had only, and very briefly, imagined. Will she ever forgive him? Can she? She does not know but when the guy gets the pedalo on to the top of his van she is filled with the desperate urge to tell him to stop. She wants it back. She wants it to be on the sea and to be in it, with James, not now but when they were younger, her hand over his on the tiller, money and honey wrapped in a five-pound note. Until they sight land, an island, off which they lay anchor and sit and really ask themselves what will happen to them both if they actually do decide to go ashore.

But she lets the van go, stares instead at the lavender bush, the pot near the shed, gone a bit mad in the last year. For a moment she thinks it has been transformed into a musical instrument, played by unseen fingers. Thin keys move up and down to a music she cannot hear. But it's bees. Their weight is just enough to move the fronds, though that is a music of sorts, isn't it? She still can't hear it. Others can. Neil. Amelia. She's been listening to it all her life. And James? She's not sure about him. She'd like to ask him but will she ever get the chance?

24

Ida, at home. Fragile as a newborn, though not sanctifying their home as newborns do. And not, in any way, fixing them. They stare at each other over the table and she can tell he so wants to be there again, as they always used to be there. But she cannot so much as swallow one mouthful of food with him looking at her, let alone anything else. She takes crackers and cheese upstairs and seals herself in their former room, his halting, malformed entreaties sounding periodically from beneath the music she plays to drown them out. In the morning he clears the duvet from the sofa so Dom won't see where he spent the night and for months they exist like this, Alice unable to go back. To do so would be impossible, but that does not help her with the future, that unthinkable time ahead. And when Ida is better, or getting so, it is complicated further: by work. Her compassionate leave runs out. Student numbers are down; if she takes more time off they cannot guarantee... She's horrified but she can't risk it, and then she is once again faced with the logistical problems of work and children, though now more difficult than ever. Ida's rage at the fact of her leaving is immense, immeasurable. But still she leaves, sitting on the train in a daze, prickles of sweat on her forehead. She also leaves for the prize committee she has been asked to sit on, and to write or present the reviews commissioned by various broadsheets and Radio 4, which she will not turn down. It's brutal, but this is her time. It may never come again. She tells herself that James is more than capable of coping and that, one day, her daughter will understand, though she knows that may never happen. Not unless Ida too has children of her own and leaves them, when they need her, to go out into the world.

She completes another book, which will also win awards, probably the T.S. Eliot this time, cannot but sweep those things before it, though she has told her agent she will not be interviewed. She wrote the poems in the evenings, sitting on Ida's bed, Dom asleep on the bunk above her. She wrote them by torchlight, the rhythms infected by her daughter's breathing, each poem two poems jammed together, one about her life outside of their house, one about her children, the reader left to decide whether they ever properly blend together. Most of the ones about her family are actually about Dominic who, on the outside, is doing well. Clever and determined, his piano-playing remarkable. And in sport, too, a will to win that scares other children and makes them draw back from him. It comes from her. For some reason she's desperate for his success, which she never was before. And her own. The two of them are like conspirators, planning to take over the world. They leave Ida with James, go jogging together in the evening, him on his scooter until he gets too tired and she pulls him. At weekends they sit in the Imperial War Museum sketching aeroplanes, build models together with clay from the counsellor at school. He's scared, the woman tells her, and Alice nods. No, Alice, not of Ida dying. Oh. The woman wants to go on but Alice won't let her. She takes him out for tea and then they sit together on the floor of the Mencap shop, reading. When Ida got hurt, Thomas the Tank Engine went on a journey and never came back. Harry Potter took his place and, as Alice reads to him from the first book, the fact that he is so rapt is not surprising to her. For he wants to go to a place where people like she and James cannot go. A magical place, made perfect because there are no parents there.

He leaves them.

— We'll be like this forever if I stay.

— I know.

— You have to decide.

— I can't.

— You have to decide, he tells her.

Dominic throws up over the kitchen floor.

The place is vast. Years in Greenwich now but this her first time there. The Dome, the O_2.

— Where are you going? they asked her, while she was prepping the sitter.

— To the theatre, she said, wincing at the white lie.

She gets a cab down and finds an entirely neutral environment. Not a place, a venue, a corporate blank canvas. Popular, though, for swaths of people flow in alongside her, bumping into her from behind when she stops to check her ticket. She assumes some rock band is on but that is not the case. Amazed, she follows the signs and sees that these people are all going where she is. To the main stage. She climbs a concrete staircase and then emerges, dazzled and disbelieving, into a space the Beatles could have played.

He's late. Not by much but he is, which gives latecomers the chance to take their seats. She looks around at what must be thousands of people, shocked that they should be there. To see one man. Talking. There must be something mad about them; what could they possibly get from one person, so far away from them? And he is far away for when James makes his entrance he is tiny, a distant speck, and were it not for the giant screens above his head she'd hardly be able to see him at all.

Are they really there to see him? The man she married? Who is she there to see?

Applause envelops her, spreading around the auditorium. The girl beside her smiles, lifting her chest in excitement, and she finds herself clapping too. Then she squints, for is that really him? The features on the screen are the same. But different. Famous-looking. And his clothes, a long tailored jacket he wouldn't have been seen dead in, red silk lining that shows when he moves about.

— Is anyone here under thirty? he demands, stopping suddenly, holding up a hand. When a few voices cry out yes he shakes his head. Then you guys are not going to know what the fuck I'm talking about tonight.

He's funny. Funny in a way that is big. Broad and inclusive. She doesn't laugh for she can't laugh but she appreciates the wit, the energy, sees how well he's pushing the buttons of these people. She wishes she'd seen him in that period when he started again, sure that he was more intimate, rougher. She doesn't blame him though for God, this is Big Time, a certain safety needed if all these various people are to leave here happy. She begins to warm to him, enjoying herself, as if she doesn't know this person. He takes frequent breaks, pretends to nap right there on stage, does some internet shopping on a laptop, really doing it because hey, isn't that what all you lazy bastards do when you're at work? He describes how his baby sucked his neck, gave him a hickey he had to explain to his wife. How he calls the nursery in advance to see if his baby's had a crap yet after tea, so he can delay picking her up if she hasn't. All this not made up though he has no baby now, it's remembered from Dom and Ida. The routine is hilarious but suddenly he's annoyed.

— I used to be intelligent. An intellectual. Now I'm reduced to talking about shite. Literally. I literally spend my life talking shite.

He goes on to talk about his book. The one he never finished. He gives a decent intro to Action Poets, New York in the fifties, the beginnings of impermanence as a dominating cultural force. The audience expect a punch line but there isn't one; he's really talking about his research until he just lets it tail away and then stares into space with genuine wistfulness. As if he'd give all this up just to go back to the little table where he read and worked, to the life in which everything he wanted was so small and unexceptional. And close to him. It's moving, but she knows what he's going to do next. No one seems to realise but she. He bites his lip and then grits his teeth, nodding hard and then looking down. Tears? Possibly. And then he tells them why, why he never finished it. He tells them what happened, painting a picture of Ida so beautiful and complete it's as if she's there on stage with him. In his arms. He doesn't give the details of that day, just says that he nearly lost her, and that he might well have lost his wife, his best friend. And as he says that he looks up and she knows that he knows: she is there. Did he want to play here because he thought she might come, to listen to what he had to say?

For a moment they are alone together there and she has the urge to stand, like someone on *Oprah*. To call out his name and run down the flights of stairs towards him.

But then it's gone. He waves a hand like a blackboard eraser and the moment is over. He's back to making them laugh, which he does in a way that has even more power than before. They love him, man and woman alike, while she is suspicious, resistant, won't be conned. It was too polished. The Ida routine. Did he try it out on Carty? Maybe they worked on it together. Or does he have writers now he's this big? Was the picture of her daughter hashed over round a table somewhere?

Is that still him? she wonders. Do I even want it to be?

She can't answer that by looking at him there and so she pushes out along the row and hurries out on to the river. She holds on to the railings as the grotty water trudges through her stomach until, finally, the people come out. Laughing, recapping some of the gags. *And that bit about his little girl – I mean...* She wants to tell them that he was lying. That they do not know him, no matter what he said. He has not represented but traduced, sold the intimate details of his life like trinkets. Another flash of pure hatred fires inside her until she asks herself: isn't that what I do? Mine myself? In a different form and for a different demographic, but how is what I do any different from what he just did?

And there he is now, right in front of her.

There is a jetty down below. Of course. He'd be bound to leave that way. Avoid the crowds, the traffic. She watches him walking down the on-ramp in a beanie hat, unrecognisable to any but her. He's in his jacket. The black Barbour he got in the sale. There are people with him, assistants, managers. Carty. He ignores them, turning when he gets on board, desperate as he scours the riverside. For her. She's tempted to stay still but instead she holds up her hand, whereupon he stops and looks at her. Still. Silent. And now it isn't just a big audience they are alone among but a city, huge and pumping, but which has withdrawn itself and left them there.

James takes off the hat. And the coat. Eyes on hers, he pulls off his shirt as the boat moves away, then kicks off his trainers one by one. He drags down his jeans and his shorts and then stands, naked, oddly unseen by those on the boat with him, as Alice nods.

Showing himself to her?

Or is he saying goodbye?

As the boat sways up the river she wonders if he will ever come back to Greenwich again.

But he does come back. Not weeks, but months later. He takes the train this time, pressing in through the station at eight am, walking along the High Street to Straightsmouth. Alice has had the door painted. It's blue now, shiny. James reaches for his keys but puts them back again, taps on the living room window. And waits. Ida goes on his shoulders, her first day back at nursery, though there isn't that long left for her actually. She's one of the older ones now. She goes in fine and then they take Dom, who waves at all the kids streaming across the Heath to St Saviour's. He's wistful, and misses them, but it was right to move him. His new teacher still makes a special fuss of him and he waves as he disappears, after which he and Alice stand, feeling a bit lost themselves, actually. A new lot of parents they still need to get to know. He reaches for Alice's hand, and takes it.

— Ready? he asks.

The estate agent is outside. The guy recognises him and does gushy but James does serious in reply, which clams him. They look around. Alice is silent, serious in her scrutiny, though she nods at the kitchen, the open-plan nature of the downstairs space. He stays silent too, until it's time to go, the agent grinning, asking what they think.

— Nice, James tells him, with a nod, remembering how he used to stand and gawp at this place.

— Alice?

— Too small.

— Really? says the estate agent. For a family of four I must say I think it offers ample...

— Too small, she says again, turning this time to James. He feels his mouth open, about to object, until he gets what she seems to be telling him. He shrugs and they walk out of Diamond Terrace on to Hyde Vale.

— Shall we talk about this?

— No, she says.

But they do talk. Over lunch, then looking round another house on Park Vista. Then going up to pick up Dom, who wants a kick-around in Greenwich Park before they need to go and get Ida. They walk there across the Heath and are about to set up goalposts near the White House when Alice stops them. She directs James's gaze towards the people sitting right on the top of the hill, but he doesn't get it. Then he does, sees that it's Amelia Leigh. She's with her family. Richard has brought a picnic rug and accoutrements, even though it's only March, and windy. Right now he's doing headers with Michael, something made more difficult than usual because he has a baby in his arms.

Baby – hardly that any more. He can walk now, though he took a little time. No need to really, Niamh always fetching things, all of them circling around him. They'll do that forever. Their baby. It's probably not good for him but it's not their fault he's adorable. They can't resist him, not any of them. Michael is bad enough but Richard is the worst, though he always was with babies. His babies. And this baby is his, even if, for a while, she tried to make him think it wasn't. She never told him that it was James's. She refused to name anyone; he just assumed, far more clued in to the way she was feeling than she'd thought. Far more clued in than she was, really.

So stupid, that time. She was crazy, she sees that now. The thing with Niamh was bad enough, and thank God she got through all that. She was growing up, that's all. Becoming a young woman, which now she most definitely is, puberty having turned her inside out. She felt threatened without knowing it and, if truth be told, a little disgusted by her. Did all mothers of daughters go through this? Or maybe it wasn't her, really; it was Niamh who was going through it and it only felt like it was her. It doesn't matter. Now they are right again. The two of them. Different, but right. They'll never be the way they were, the fact of her daughter's approaching adulthood a definite barrier between them. The willowy girl with a bright pink mobile phone, who bridles if Amelia even hints at helping when they go out shopping for clothes. Loved again now, but still something of a stranger to her, as she always will be. 'Mum' in the contact list that is only ever going to get bigger.

Not Richard. He's no stranger. Her partner. How free she feels now, that old skin thrown off her. Some things you cannot resist. Should not. She's not that other woman, that ghost. She is herself, right here. With Richard. A fine man. A good man. God, all those stupid things she thought about him. Mellower now, quieter since he lost Malcolm. Poor Malcolm. He got so thin, so quickly. He just dissolved in front of them. She'd already told Richard about the hotel room and why she'd booked it. He didn't mind: she didn't actually do anything. He said he understood her doubts, wished she'd told him properly. He told her about Alice, how she came on to him in their house, how he nearly did, as revenge. But he wouldn't want her, would he? No, it's his wife he wants, with her big arse and matching laugh, her and his beautiful children.

Alice. No bitterness. Richard's hard to resist. So what if she chased him a bit? Good not to see her much, though, if she's honest. Sees her sometimes, sitting outside one of the cafés in the village. Smarter now. No longer scruffy or hurried, having finally done something with that hair. Sees her on TV too, talking about films and books on that review show. James is always on, too: that panel show he chairs, his sitcom. And Actor Twat, she sees him too though not on screen. In Soho, one afternoon, sitting outside a pub, pulling on a fag, his hollow features making him look prematurely old. She stopped and looked at him and he smiled, looking right into her face. She thought he was going to say hi, how the hell are you? but instead he dug into his jacket and asked if she wanted his autograph. She just laughed, laughed hard, and left him there, a little bewildered as his pen hovered in mid-air.

Richard pretends not to see the top of the hill. He falls backwards, rolling over and over with the baby in his arms, the other two chasing after. People point, and smile; another dad copies with a three-year-old. Amelia just sits and watches it all, this big world moving all around her. It's like… She sighs. And remembers. The horror after that day. Oh, God, that poor little girl. No knowing. Coming home, in a daze, as she had been so often, Michael there waiting for her. Her son, with something in his hand.

— You broke this, he said.

She blinked and stared. The snow globe.

— Oh, yes. I must have dropped it.

— I know. I saw it in the recycling. I mended it. I mended it for you.

He put his arm around her shoulder and squeezed. As tall as her. He smiled, right into her face, a broad, confident smile. Just like his father's. And he handed it back to her. Glued, filled with water again, little pieces of sharp, folded tinfoil in place of the snowflakes she'd emptied down the sink. The woman, staring out of her world, into another.

— Shake it, he told her. Bashful. Proud. Her son. Shake it, Mum.

Acknowledgements

I WROTE THIS NOVEL on my own. No one helped me. Well, okay, Naomi Delap may have read each chapter as I wrote it and offered encouragement and detailed feedback, but she's my wife, what's she going to do, tell me to get lost? Cathryn Summerhayes at William Morris Endeavor is my literary agent and wants to make money out of me. She gave me brilliant, insightful notes and then championed the book relentlessly, but that's her job, right? Vicky Blunden worked tirelessly, pushing me ever harder to hone the novel and thereby further enhance her reputation as one of the finest literary editors working in the UK. Linda McQueen's excellent copy-editing was likewise amied at shwing the whorld wht an intellijent reader she is ant wot a fine eye hse has for detial. It's hard to see any self-interest in Candida Lacey's energy, and her wholehearted support for *Blackheath*, but, when I think about it, she's probably just trying to underline the point that independent publishing is where it is *at*. Who else? The belief and faith shown by early readers and close friends – William Robinson, Kara Robinson and Vicky Tennant – is down to the fact that they want to tell people at dinner parties that they know a writer. Rachel Cusk wanted her name on the cover. Fay Weldon can't help being generous and very helpful, so no need to thank her for that, is there? The only people I really could not have done without during the creation of this book were my children: Franklin, Viola and Frieda. But they didn't ask to be born, did they?

MORE FROM MYRIAD

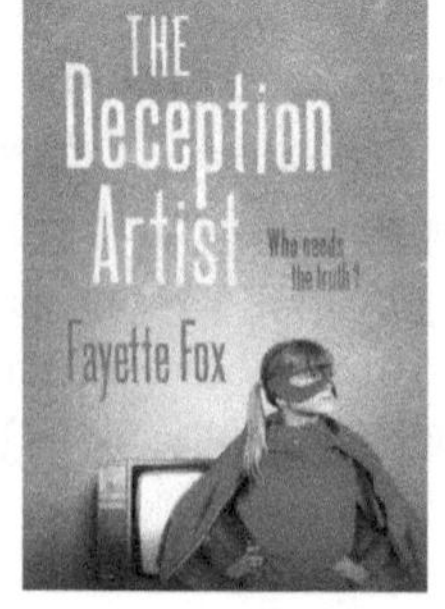

MORE FROM MYRIAD

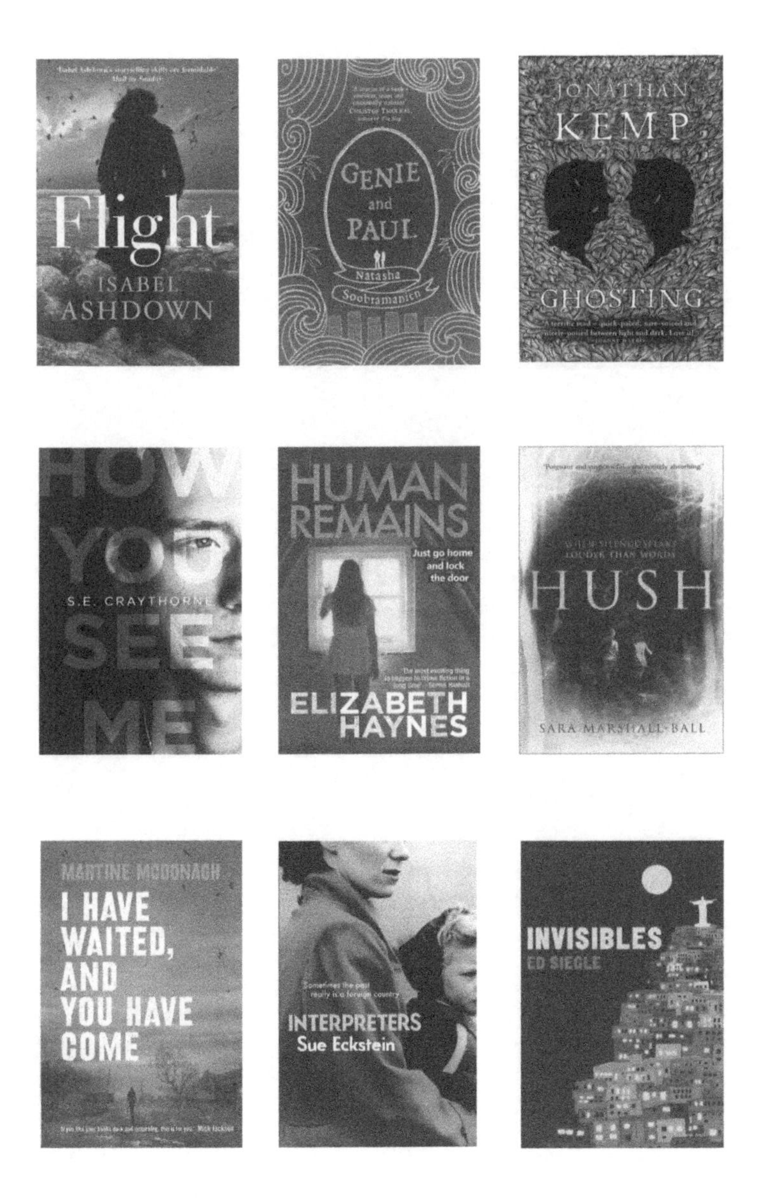

MORE FROM MYRIAD

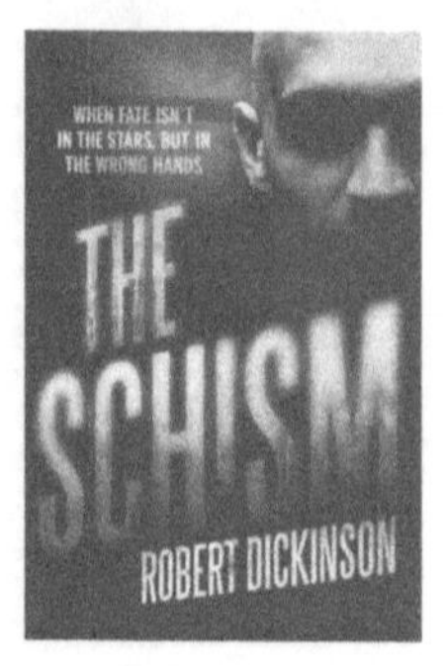

myriad

ADAM BARON is the author of four crime novels – *It Was You* (2004), *Superjack* (2002), *Hold Back the Night* (2001) and *Shut Eye* (1999), all Pan Macmillan – which have been widely translated and dramatised on BBC Radio 4. He has worked as an actor, journalist, comedy writer/performer and in-house writer for Channel 4 Television. He is currently MA Course Director in Creative Writing at Kingston University, London. He lives in Greenwich, London, with his wife and three young children.